FURIOUS

JILL WOLFSON

IOUS

HENRY HOLT AND COMPANY

NEW YORK

Henry Holt and Company, LLC
Publishers since 1866
175 Fifth Avenue
New York, New York 10010
macteenbooks.com

Library of Congress Cataloging-in-Publication Data
Wolfson, Jill.
Furious / Jill Wolfson.—First edition.
pages   cm
Summary: After becoming the Furies of Greek mythology, three angry high school
girls take revenge on everyone who deserves it.
ISBN 978-0-8050-8283-8 (hardcover) — ISBN 978-0-8050-9756-6 (e-book)
1. Erinyes (Greek mythology)—Juvenile fiction. [1. Erinyes (Greek mythology)—
Fiction. 2. Mythology, Greek—Fiction. 3. Revenge—Fiction. 4. High schools—
Fiction. 5. Schools—Fiction.] I. Title.
PZ7.W8332Fu 2013   [Fic]—dc23   2012027653

First Edition—2013 / Designed by April Ward

Printed in the United States of America

1   3   5   7   9   10   8   6   4   2

In memory of Nancy Redwine
Furious and forgiving in all the right ways

"I tell you, ladies . . . you don't know how good it feels
till you begin to smash, smash, smash!"

—CARRIE NATION

PROLOGUE

In times past, *all dramas started with a prologue, the* before *before the beginning.*

Enter the character to tell you what you need to know.

Enter me, Ambrosia.

Here is what you see. Someone tall and straight, dressed always in black, unruffled in every way down to the clean, classic lines of my designer clothing. I am not perfect by contemporary standards. My almond-shaped eyes—a legacy from my ancestors—sit a little too close together, giving me a penetrating gaze. My nose is too pointed and prominent to be considered an iconic profile in this culture of perky and pug-nosed Anglo-Saxons.

Yet mine is the face that all other female faces at Hunter High are unfavorably compared to. Beauty is not merely in the eye of the beholder. It exists beyond fashion and trend, and everyone feels drawn to it, to what's deep and unshakable.

From this description, you think you know me, right? I'm the girl who has it all—the looks, the grades, the boobs, the family connections. But my face, this mask of self-assurance, covers a seething anger.

Because in truth, I have nothing worth having. When someone has wronged you and gotten away with it, when the guilty walk free, that miscarriage of justice makes your very soul writhe in agony.

Let bygones be bygones?

Come to peace with the past?

What rot!

Animals may forgive and forget, but not a human. I will never find relief, not until a certain someone pays for the crime and suffers as deeply as I have.

I've been waiting ages, and finally all the elements are coming together. What a rare alignment of sun and stars and flesh it is. It's been up to me to find the talent, coax it, feed it, and slowly cultivate it into its full dangerous bloom.

I have two-thirds of what I need. I wait for the missing piece to reveal itself.

I can already taste the iron tinge in my mouth, blood calling out for blood.

It's time for me to close the book on the prologue. But there's one more crucial thing you must understand:

This story started long ago, when the wrong that haunts me was committed and left unpunished. When a spoiled and selfish young prince picked up a knife and decided that it was his gods-given right to plunge the blade deep into someone's back.

That someone was me.

PROLOGUE, THE BOOK OF FURIOUS

When you've got an overbite and only one real friend and you're what grown-ups euphemistically call "a late bloomer" (meaning I'm short and skinny where I shouldn't be skinny and I *just* got my period), you pretty much accept that every day is bound to be a series of humiliations, large and small.

So given the sucky reality of being me, of being Meg, it's really something to say that in my almost sixteen years of living, despite my many episodes of blowing it big-time, this particular day turns out to be the most humiliating one of my life.

More humiliating than when I was five and going to scary kindergarten for the first time and had to be pried loose from my foster mom. I was screaming and got a bloody nose from freaking out, and all the other kids were just sitting there—cross-legged and staring.

More humiliating than finding out too late that an eighth-grade girl should never stand at the school entrance and hand out valentines to all 167 members of her class. Especially when the cards are personally signed and individually addressed.

Even more humiliating than last week, when I must have had a brain drain that erased everything I ever learned from my previous humiliations. That's the only explanation for how I could walk right up to this guy Brendon—this popular guy with adorable eye crinkles when he smiles—and blurt out that I had a two-for-one mini-golf coupon and maybe he might want to go with me sometime. I love mini-golf—I mean, who doesn't? But Eye Crinkles only stared at me blankly, like he'd never seen me before, even though we've been in a ton of classes together for the past three years.

And now his friends make pretend golf swings whenever I walk by.

So probably you're thinking, what could be more humiliating than that?

Hold on. It gets far worse.

A brief setting of the scene. Third period. 10th grade Western Civ, my favorite class this year, even though Ms. Pallas makes you work your butt off just for a B. All the usual characters are there. Our teacher is standing to the side of the room, arms crossed, listening to our first oral presentations of the semester. I am in my usual seat—not too close to the front, not way in the back either—right in the middle where it's easy to get lost in the pack. Next to me, my best friend, Raymond, is totally engrossed in whatever genius thing he's writing in his notebook.

In front of the class, one of the Double D twins, Dawn or DeeDee, is giving her presentation. Not to be mean or anything, but her report on ancient Sumerian civilization is crap. I'm just being truthful. I can't imagine that she put in any more than twenty minutes to plagiarize from Wikipedia. Doesn't she have any pride? Ms. Pallas won't let her get away with it.

Anyway, the thing I remember next is getting distracted by what's going on outside the window. This is taking place in a coastal town, a slice of surfer paradise wedged between the Pacific Ocean and a redwood forest. The geography here makes the weather unpredictable: sunny one minute, and then warm air hits cold ocean, which makes the fog roll in, and that's what happens right then. It's like the whole classroom gets whisked to a different place and a different day without anyone leaving their seat. Poof. It's gray, dreary, and Jane Eyre–ish, which is fine with me. I'm not exactly embracing life these days.

And I'm not going to lie. As I watch the weather change, I am trying very hard not to think about that guy with the eye crinkles who happens to be sitting a mere few seats to my right. Only, of course, my mind-control technique is backfiring. All I can do *is* think about him.

What's the matter with me? Wasn't living through that embarrassment once enough? Why do I keep replaying it? For about the two-millionth time, I put myself through every mortifying detail. The pounding heart. The sweaty palms. My own voice confessing my love of mini-golf. The condescending look on his face. The heat rising to my cheeks. My stuttering apology for bothering him.

How could I have been so stupid?

Could I have made a more pathetic cry for love?

Why did I pick such a popular guy?

What was I thinking?

Why do these embarrassing things always happen to me?

Why me? Why not to other people? Why not to *him*?

Just once, I say to myself. *Why can't he feel what it's like? He should try being me for once. He should feel every aching throb of longing for me that I feel for him, and then get shot down.*

I let that idea sink in very deep, and—I'm not going to lie about this either—it gives me a real charge, a jolt of pleasure, to think about getting back at him in some way. I decide to stay with my fantasy, go with it. I let myself get really worked up at him, then even angrier. Why not? Who am I hurting?

So while Dawn or DeeDee drones on, and outside the fog turns to rain—not drizzle rain, but *rain* rain that slaps the windows in sheets—I let myself hate that boy with all my might. I savor every sweet detail of revenge that my mind conjures up. I let it become real.

First he will come begging to me for a date. He'll be all shy and scared, and I'll listen as he fumbles his words.

Then . . . and then . . . I won't answer. I'll just wrap both of my hands around his neck and pull him close and kiss him. I'll kiss him so hard that he won't know what hit him.

This fantasy is so much fun. It feels so good that I have to stop myself from cackling out loud like a crazed chicken. I actually put my hand over my mouth. It's kind of scary how good it makes me feel, but scary in a very satisfying way.

And when he looks at me, dazed with love, I'll ask, "So, change your mind about mini-golf?"

He'll nod eagerly, hopefully, practically in pain with love for me, and I'll shoot him down. Bam! I'll yawn and say, "That was the most boring kiss ever. For you, Brendon, the mini-golf coupon has expired. Permanently."

In public. So everyone hears.

And after that . . .

And after that?

I don't know what happens after that. I really don't. Something. I don't remember much, not a whole lot that makes sense, anyway. A light flashes and the air moves in a swirling distortion, like the whole world has suddenly tilted on its side.

And there's music. Definitely music. Who is playing music? Why is music playing? My mind latches on to the individual notes, a series of them that rise and fall in an eerie, whistling way. I don't know this song.

But then, I do know it. I do! I don't want it to ever go away.

Under the music, someone is laughing. And then someone else is shouting the word *hate*.

Hate! Hate! Hate!

A hand cups my shoulder, but I push it aside. There's so much power surging through me. Someone is pulling on the hem of my shirt. I slap at it.

"Meg!" Pause. "Meg!"

I hear a bell then, loud and sharp, and I tremble with a jolt, as if waking suddenly out of a dream when you have a 103-degree fever. The music is gone. An empty silence has taken over. Reluctantly, I blink open my eyes.

I'm standing.

Not standing on the ground like your average, normal person, but standing on my chair.

In the middle of class. With my neck muscles straining and a layer of sweat on my forehead. And my throat dry and raw. And my fists clenched in tight balls at my side.

Ms. Pallas, directly in front of me, slams her ruler on my desk, and I feel the vibration ripple up through the bottom of my feet to my head. My brain feels like it's been punched in the gut.

It all becomes clear then, too clear, and the word *humiliation* doesn't begin to cover it.

It had been Raymond tugging on my shirt, calling my name. The bell was the end of class. And I was the one standing on my chair shouting, "Hate! Hate! Hate! I hate all of you."

"Meg-o-mania, what the hell was that about?"

That's what Raymond wants to know, and I can't blame him for pouncing on me as soon as I leave the classroom. While I was getting a stern talking-to from Ms. Pallas and promising her that an outburst like that will never happen again, and that I completely understand how Hunter High is a hate-free zone, and that words have consequences, and that shouting in class is definitely on the school's list of no-nos, and that in her class *especially* she won't tolerate that kind of ugly talk, Raymond waited patiently for me in the hallway. His long, thin body is slouched against a locker. I'm so happy and relieved to see him. I give him a sheepish smile and a weak shrug.

"Just a warning," I say.

He lets out a low whistle of relief. "Lucky. Pallas doesn't usually suffer from Pushover Teacher Syndrome. I figured you'd pull detention for that spontaneous outburst of misanthropy."

Classic Raymond vocabulary. According to Hunter High

mythology, my best friend started talking in complete sentences when he was six months old and hasn't shut up since. That's not his only achievement. He's a whiz in math. He skipped fourth grade. He plays first violin in the school orchestra and composes his own music. Plus, he can speak pig Latin in Latin. He's by far the youngest, smartest, most accomplished person in our class, but also kind of an idiot.

His most recent form of self-amusement is saying things like "What I lack in maturity, I make up for in infantile behavior," followed by his enormous high-pitched laugh.

The truth is—and I'm not talking behind his back because Raymond would admit it himself—he drives most people up a wall. It's not polite to say this, and maybe my thinking it makes me an awful person, but I'm actually grateful that Raymond is so irritating. Otherwise he might not have been so desperate to have me as a friend when I met him three years ago. On the surface, I know that our friendship doesn't make much sense—the ethnically ambiguous, awkward girl who loves BLT sandwiches and happy romantic comedies who is inseparable from the big-brain gay kid who's a vegetarian and obsessed with horror films—the older the better, especially the campy black-and-white ones from the 1960s.

But it comes down to this: he and I click in a way that we've never clicked with anyone else before. We can tell each other anything. To Raymond, I'm not some shy dork who, when she does speak, always manages to say the wrong thing. I'm—get this!—smart, tolerant, funny, a deep thinker, a survivor, and a closet optimist.

And I think that he's the most unique person on the planet.

"Let's get out of here," I say. I glance around nervously to see who might have heard about my Western Civ breakdown. There's only a couple of freshmen hurrying to their next class, and none of them are staring or smirking. Raymond and I have study hall next period and can easily ditch that. With a quick pivot, I start walking down the corridor and he follows, not bothering to lower his voice. "Not so fast, Meg. You were dauntingly intimidating. Terrifying! You hate everyone? Speak!"

And say what?

I push through a set of double doors into a stairwell, and I'm so befuddled that I can't decide what to do next. Where was I going? Up? Down? My hands claw through my hair in frustration.

"Sit!" he orders, pressing on my shoulder.

I do. He joins me on the bottom step. "Deep breath in and out. Explain."

I swallow hard, shiver a little. How do I start? I can't explain it to myself. I just want to rub out the whole incident, make the collective memory of thirty-two students disappear. I don't want to think about every pair of eyes trained on me, some kids laughing so hard they had to put their heads on their desks, others dropping their eyes in embarrassment, like I just confessed in public that I masturbate every night. I don't want to think about how angry Ms. Pallas is at me and how Brendon—that boy with the crinkle eyes—turned so pale, like he somehow sensed that my hate was focused on him.

"Well?" Raymond asks again, and the question echoes in the empty stairwell.

I let my body cave in on itself, dropping my eyes to the floor, my voice a mumble, as if making myself smaller will make the whole subject disappear. "It was nothing. A blood sugar drop or something."

"Blood sugar?" His voice is loud and cracking.

I cobble together a few coherent sentences that I hope will satisfy him for at least right now. "I don't know what happened. I was thinking. It was . . . slippage."

"Slippage?"

"From my brain."

His face lights up. "Oh! You mean brain slippage! Good old brain slippage. That explains everything."

"It does?"

Raymond sighs, not buying it for a second. "I'm not talking about the content of your impromptu confession—we'll come back to Meg's astounding moment of existential crisis in a minute. It was how you said it." He cups his hand into a megaphone. "Cue the zombie."

I shush him. His eyes search my face. I look away—at my feet, at my nails, at the square tiles of acoustical ceiling, at a big wad of bubble gum fossilized on the wall. But it's no use. Raymond has infinite patience for my avoidance techniques. He will wait in annoying silence until I spill every detail.

"Talking it through might help," I finally admit. Who else can I talk to about it, anyway? My understanding foster mom? My *other* friend? "Okay. But Raymond, don't you dare laugh."

"Why would I laugh?"

"'Cause you laugh at everything."

He makes a big drama of swiping a hand magician-style across his face, pretending to wipe away any trace of humor. "Totally serious." Pause. "Devoid of levity. You may proceed."

I force a calmness into my voice that I don't actually feel. "I know it was strange . . ."

So much for calmness: I blurt everything, at least as much as I can remember, because it's all beginning to fade. "That's the best I can do, my explanation for being, you know, not like myself."

"Not yourself? You were positively Demon Girl—with a strong hint of Possessed Person." Raymond turns his body rigid, arms glued to his thighs. "I hhhhhhhate everyone."

"Well, I do!"

"Do what?"

"Hate!"

Only when I say the word *hate* right now, it's nothing like what I was feeling before. This hate is ordinary hate, like when you hate Brussels sprouts or PE. That *other* hate had weight and texture; it took up space and vibrated in my chest like a gong being struck. I try to explain.

"I don't hate *you*, Raymond! And not everyone all the time. But some people some of the time. Like Brendon— you know I hate him, but when I say that now, it's different than when I said it in class. That was *hate* hate. I don't . . . I can't . . ."

Raymond puts an open hand completely over my face,

fingers spread, palm on my lips—"Interrupting starfish"—then removes it. He studies me. "This is serious. You're mega upset."

"It was horrible, Raymond. Humiliating! Everyone laughing at me. But before it was horrible, it was . . ."

I stop short because I realize that I'm about to say something I'm not sure I want to say aloud. Because saying it aloud will make it real, and I'm not sure I want it to be real and I'm not sure that anyone should know this about me, not even my best friend who knows just about everything else.

"The truth? It's kind of ugly."

He puts his fingertips on his wrist, mock checks his pulse. "I took my vitamins today. I can handle it."

"Before. When I shouted 'I hate everyone.' It was fun—the best feeling I ever had in my life."

He looks puzzled. "You mean, letting it all out and saying what you felt? I get it. That can feel good."

"Yes! No! It was more than that. A power! The way it took over and took me away. I wanted to stay there."

He's still confused. "What took you over? Stay where?"

"There!"

I realize how whacked that must sound. I don't have a clue about where *there* is or what I'm really trying to say, so I give a nervous giggle and pretend to make light of it. "So what do you think? Am I a complete raging psycho?"

Instead of answering with one of his wisecracks, Raymond lets his eyes go vacant and his jaw drop open. I hear him breathing through his mouth. The first time I saw him get this look, it freaked me out. I worried that he was having a seizure that knocked out fifty IQ points. But with

Raymond, the more stupid he looks, the harder you know he's thinking. Right now he looks really dumb, so I assume his synapses are working overtime. He murmurs a few random words and half phrases. I know to keep my mouth shut until he's ready.

He drapes his arm around my shoulder again. He's a toucher, another thing that annoys most people. I scoot closer to him on the step. I like feeling Raymond's weight on my shoulder, knowing that he's on my side.

When I wake the next morning, the sunlight is streaming in the window. It's so toasty in bed I don't want to move. I study the dust particles in the slant of light, watch them twirl. My eyes move around my small bedroom and admire how I've perked it up with some of the personal things I cart from foster home to foster home. On the dresser there's a ceramic frog planter that I named Francine. My comforter has a bright sunflower pattern. I stretch and yawn, feel myself crackle to life, then spring out of bed feeling light and optimistic. I even think I smell fresh-squeezed orange juice.

That's the truly messed-up thing about sunshine. All that bright, glittery yellowness blinds you. It takes about two more seconds to register: I am screwed. This day is going to totally suck. No amount of sunshine can undo that.

By now, word of my freaky outburst is sure to have made the rounds of all the Hunter High cabals—especially the merciless group of smug, too-tanned surfer royalty that rules my bus ride every morning. Those *dudes* will be my first hurdle of the day. I am going to be bombarded—zombie

imitations on the bus, zombie imitations in first-period physics, in second-period English, in Western Civ of course, and
on and on. And each and every one of my pop-eyed, twisted-
mouthed tormentors will think his particular imitation is
the funniest, most original thing ever.

I hate everyone, I say to myself. *I really do.*

I brush my teeth, spit a big gob of white foam into the
sink. How will I get through this day? I have no idea how
I'm going to survive. Where will I look? What will I do with
my hands?

I try to conjure up some of the power I felt yesterday,
but thinking about it only makes my stomach hurt.

I dab on a little face powder, smear rouge on my cheeks.
I clip and then unclip my hair, feeling it spring into its usual
uncontrollable state. If every teenage girl in the world of
every ethnicity started complaining about the problems with
her hair—*too frizzy, too limp, too wiry, too big, too kinky, too
flyaway, too flat on top, not brown or blond or red enough, just a
blah, watered-down nothing color*—I could join in the conversation at any point. I run my fingers through the maze of
knots, tuck what I can behind my ears, and feel the rest of
it frizzing out.

My stomach still hurts. What if I have the flu? That would
be a good thing. I could stay home all week, and by that time
I would be old, tired news.

I pray for food poisoning.

I open my closet. How *does* one dress for one of the
worst days of her life?

I settle on my usual black pullover and jeans. Safe.

I take a deep breath and remind myself of three things

that Raymond says I should love about me: I'm smart. I'm strong. I'm a survivor.

But before this dream of a day gets off the ground, it's time to go into the kitchen and get my usual send-off to school from Lottie Leach, my foster mother, and He-Cat, her butt-ugly pet whose most prominent physical characteristic is the goopy stuff that hardens white in the corners of his eyes. They both hate me.

I've been living in this foster home for about six months, but I'm still not immune to the cringeability of what greets me each morning. He-Cat, as usual, is plopped over the floor heater vent soaking up the warmth, his big belly splayed out like an oozing dark puddle. Even on a fairly warm morning, Mrs. Leach—cheapskate that she is about everything else—keeps the heat blasting just for him.

I open a cabinet to get a cereal bowl, and a half-dozen plastic containers tumble out. I straighten them up fast and pour cereal into one. As always, those Leachy eyes are on me, measuring every corn flake to make sure that I don't eat more than my allotted share. She's sitting at the kitchen table, her right foot unsocked and propped on a ripped vinyl chair. Her veiny bunion is enough to put me off my breakfast.

Still, I keep a good-girl smile glued in place. I know that putting on this phony act would be living hell to most of the teenage world, but it's survival tactic number one for me. Imagine that anytime you talk back to your father or roll your eyes at your mother, they threaten to kick you out of their house—and mean it. I am so polite that my jeans would have to catch on fire before I'd complain to a foster parent.

Well, the jeans on fire only happened once, which is a whole other story.

Unfortunately, though, as I carry my cereal to the table I accidentally kick the kitty litter box, which sits practically in the middle of the floor like a decorative centerpiece.

Mistake number one: my foot sends a hard, twisted Tootsie Roll of cat crap onto the cracked linoleum and a galaxy of toxoplasma spores into the air. We studied parasites in bio last year, and now I can't *not* imagine the invisible creatures that live in cat crap flying up my nostrils and landing in my cereal bowl, where they will proceed to invade my cells and live out their whole life cycle—going into parasite puberty, having promiscuous parasite sex, producing a slew of parasite babies, and then dying messy parasite deaths, all in my major organs.

Mistake number two: I say, "Damn it!"

"You'll clean that up right now," Mrs. Leach orders. "And watch that language."

My face prunes, only not the face she can see but the hidden twin beneath, the face I've learned not to show to foster parents. I say, "Of course, Mrs. Leach."

Satisfied with my groveling, she nods. I sweep. I do everything but whistle while I work. I pretend that I don't notice how the Leach—the perfect name for her—is shifting in her chair and moaning about the arthritis in her feet. If she tells me to rub her tootsies again, I'll say hell no! That's my limit. That's my breaking point. I won't do it!

"Rub granny's poor tootsies, would you?"

A collapse inside of me. I have exactly two choices: rub those tootsies or risk getting on her bad side. And if I piss her off, she might decide that she doesn't want me living here any more. And that means putting all my stuff into a suitcase again, and living in some awful shelter before they find another foster parent—maybe someone even worse. It could mean a new school and not seeing Raymond every day. It might mean being sent to a group home and sharing a bedroom and dealing with the craziness of ten other foster kids with lives just as sucky as mine. I don't want any part of that scene anymore.

So I get down on one knee and wrap my hands around a foot that has the texture of a cold, dead fish. I massage. I imagine twisting so hard that her foot comes off like a screw top of a jar. She groans—not with pain, though, with pleasure.

"It's so nice to have a young person in the house." The Leech smiles a smile that pulls her lips back over her gums, displaying a rainbow of food particles stuck between the teeth. "Just like having a granddaughter."

A granddaughter to order around like a servant.

"I have to go now," I say. "I'll be late for school."

Irritated, she shoos me away.

I slam the front door behind me. At least I can do that. That feels good! But only for a second, because now I have a whole day of zombie imitations ahead of me, and even though it's only 7:30 a.m., I'm exhausted.

It's not the easiest thing to be one of the world's best foster kids—the cooperative one, the one who doesn't talk back, doesn't run away, doesn't steal, doesn't get pregnant, doesn't drink or do drugs, doesn't even get mad, doesn't cause anyone any trouble.

Hunter High kids are all majoring in meanness, and they get big, fat As because it comes so naturally to them. First period, I take the long walk of shame into physics class, where Kai "Pox" Small, Hunter High's very own shaved-head, six-foot-two-inch brick wall big-time surfer, continues the same brutal imitation of me that so amused and delighted the entire busload of kids only minutes before.

Word of my spastic meltdown also obviously made it into the inner sanctum of the faculty lounge, where things must be unbearably boring if I'm a big event. I notice our teacher, Mr. H, studying me, like I'm bubbling or changing colors, a science problem that he's determined to puzzle out.

Question: Why did the human doormat suddenly turn into an exploding doormat?

Mr. H shuts down Pox by sliding a finger across his throat, and for that I want to kiss him. Not *kiss him* kiss him, because he's married and old and shaped like the first letter of his name, short and boxy. But I do feel grateful when he deflects attention from me by putting himself into the line of fire. He launches into his science teacher comedy routine.

"Why did the chicken cross the road?" he asks. "Because chickens at rest tend to stay at rest. Chickens in motion tend to cross roads."

Right after that class, with Raymond as my combination cheerleader and bodyguard, I take another walk of shame down the interminably long corridor of lockers toward the classroom of dark, intense Mrs. H for English. Yes, she's been married to Mr. H forever, and I guess it works for them even though I don't get their attraction to each other. He's so jokey, and she starts each of her classes with a poem about death or suffering or the struggle to find meaning in the meaningless nature of human existence.

When I slide into my seat, one of the Double Ds slips in a dig. "What exploded your tampon?" She asks this loud enough for everyone to hear. And to visualize. In every detail.

As degrading as the morning has been so far, I know it's probably a breeze compared to what's next. A return to the scene of my crime. Normally I look forward to Western Civ. It makes sense that someone like me who's not too thrilled about the present enjoys looking backward. I can't get enough of learning about all the ancient superstitions and what people ate, wore, and cared about. I keep thinking that in the past things must have been better than they are now, despite the lack of indoor plumbing and frozen pizza. Maybe people stuck by their friends and families and they protected and sacrificed for the kids. Maybe there was more tolerance of people who were a little different, and life was more fair. I want to believe that there used to be a time like that, because if such a time existed once, it could exist again.

Ms. Pallas keeps pointing out our similarities with the ancient world, rather than our differences. As she said in class the other day: "People eat and work, they fall in love and go to war. There's the same day-to-day struggle for existence and night-to-night struggle with fear and uncertainty. Always has been, always will be."

At the present moment I have my own personal struggle, which is getting through this class and then the rest of the day, and then I can go home and take a nap. I try what Raymond suggests and envision myself wearing a noise-blocking air controller headset to block out any more snotty comments from the surf crew. I imagine the headset huge and hand-knitted in pink yarn, more like earmuffs. I take my seat. Ms. Pallas shoots me a warning look and I do something squishy with my features that I hope translates into the nonverbal-communication form of—No problemo. I have everything under control. You can definitely count on me.

I think that satisfies Ms. Pallas. I sure hope so. She's very strict. Even the way she wears her hair—an old-fashioned wheat-colored braid that crisscrosses her head like a rope—is tight and intimidating. She has this way of demanding everyone's complete attention. Even the usual class goof-offs keep it under control. I don't want to get on her bad side any more than I already have. She writes something in a notebook, and when she pivots around to face the class, the blue scarf draped around her collar makes her deep-set eyes pop with color.

"Continuing with oral presentations," she says. "Is there a volunteer?"

To my left, there's already a hand waving in the air. I watch a short girl with dreadlocks named Stephanie take large, confident steps to the front of the room. I settle in. This should be good. Despite how lots of people make fun of a white girl with dreads, I respect Stephanie. She puts a lot of passion into her work. I'm a big fan of her editorials in the school paper, and she even has her own blog, *Green from Tenth Grade to Death—One Student's Commitment to Save Mother Earth*.

From her hemp shoulder bag she removes a binder with her presentation, and begins reading in a voice that sounds like she's presenting a proclamation to the United Nations. "Topic: Is contemporary society more—quote—civilized—unquote—and less violent than the ancient cultures that we have been studying? To those who argue that modern mankind has evolved in any meaningful way, I offer indisputable evidence to the contrary: Number one . . ."

Behind me, Pox Small clears his throat. Danger ahead. I immediately go into emotional duck-and-cover response because I figure he has just come up with another so-called hilarious comment aimed at me. But when he whispers, "If it's yellow, it's mellow," I'm relieved. This is mean of me, but I'm happy that the bull's-eye has shifted to Stephanie. He's latched onto her reference to *number one*. Stephanie recently posted *IF IT'S YELLOW, IT'S MELLOW* hand-made signs in all the student bathrooms, her one-person campaign to cut back on flushing and trim the school's water consumption by half.

If that were me in front of the class, I'd be praying for an earthquake to hit, but not Stephanie. She folds her arms across her chest and stares down Pox without blinking. I admire how she stands up for herself and what she believes in. I also admire her blouse, which is gauzy and embroidered white on white; I saw it on sale at Global Mama, the fair-trade import store downtown.

"Number one," she repeats with extra-hard emphasis. "At this very moment, innocent animals are suffering barbaric torture under the guise of improving civilization. In corporate labs across this so-called enlightened land, you'll find poor, helpless monkeys being injected with chemicals so toxic that these innocent creatures—who possess nerve endings the same as yours and mine—develop humungous cancerous tumors."

Stephanie's voice quivers at the word *tumors*. She reopens her binder, and with a dramatic flourish she whips out a picture of a big-eyed, helpless monkey tied down on a gurney.

Pox now starts making sarcastic little monkey *eeking* sounds. He's got the rectangular jaw and underbite for it. I can't believe he's pulling this stunt in Ms. Pallas's class, and neither can she. She gives him the look she's known for, a flash of her cold blue eyes that usually makes anyone shut up. But Pox is on too much of a roll. He keeps eeking, and the laughter builds up around him. Stephanie keeps going on with her rant. The worse he gets, the louder and more outraged she gets. I swear that they are fueling each other.

"What is the justification for abusing this animal?" She pounds a fist on a nearby desk. "I'll tell you! Money!" A stamp of her foot. "So that greedy corporations can sell their overpriced products to consumers who have been brain-washed from birth to believe that they can't possibly live without softer hair, redder lips, and armpits that don't smell like armpits were designed to smell!"

As much as I admire Stephanie, she is asking for it with that last line. She practically handed Pox a script to start sniffing his own pits, and most of his obnoxious surf crew joins right in.

Knock it off, Pox. I think. *Someone should tie you down and experiment on you.*

"Knock it off, Pox! Someone should experiment on you."

I start at hearing my own thoughts expressed aloud. The voice is coming from the back of the room, and I'm not a ventriloquist. "Let her finish, asshole."

All heads now turn to Alix Wolfe, serious surfer and the toughest girl with the worst temper at Hunter High. I get a gag reflex just thinking about getting in her way. It's not like she's Stephanie's best friend or anything like that. I doubt that she has any particular love for monkeys or the environment or Stephanie. It's that Alix can't stand Pox and the feeling is mutual. Everyone knows that. Nobody knows exactly what started the feud, but I think that maybe it's because Pox can't stand that a girl is as aggressive and competitive, in and out of the water, as he is. Other girls who surf, even the really good ones, also flirt shamelessly. Around guys, they pretend to be weaker and less skilled than they are. Not Alix. She shows off at every opportunity. She torments Pox and vice versa. Raymond says it's been this way forever, both of them always ready to get into it with each other.

Their hostility charges the room. Pox, pumped up, swings around in his seat. "Who you calling an asshole, asshole?"

"Shut up, Pox," Alix comes back.

"No, you shut up!"

"Wrong! You!"

Ms. Pallas tries to intervene. She really tries. Her eyes flash with a threat. In a tone low and intimidating, she orders Alix and Pox to stop it now. But things are moving too fast.

That's when the air in the classroom does something strange. Strange as in the same strange as yesterday. I hear a rush, like all the air is being sucked out of the room, and into the void comes static, and in the static I hear that music again. Faint notes repeating themselves, vibrating not in my ear but in some place deeper. I try to hum along. I let the notes pull me in their direction.

From the back of the room, a mass streaks past me. I see an arm lunging and pulling its body behind it. It's Alix, like a deadly Pox-seeking missile. She's on him, her right fist connecting with his left ear. The room explodes into total chaos. Ms. Pallas waving her ruler, pounding her hand on a desk. The Double Ds shrieking with excitement. Books fall to the floor. Ms. Pallas rushes across the room. Chair legs squeal. Stephanie is taking large, loud gulps like she's hyperventilating. There's a rumble and then a clap of thunder from outside. Real thunder. But the sky is totally clear. The overhead light flickers on and off a dozen times. Ms. Pallas, arms stretched high, ruler held high, orders in a voice that can't be ignored this time: "Stop! I demand it!"

It takes two of Pox's surfing buddies—short, wiry Gnat

and *him*, Brendon—to pull Alix off of him. They have her between them, one on each arm, her feet off the ground, her short, powerful legs pedaling hard like a cartoon road-runner.

"Put her down!" Ms. Pallas orders. "Immediately!"

Alix's feet hit the ground, her knees buckling slightly. She spins to Ms. Pallas and holds up her palms in surrender. "Yeah, yeah, I know. Your classroom is a hate-free zone. No-tolerance policy. Principal's office. Suspended."

But when she's halfway to the door, she freezes, seems to have a second thought, and whips back around. Pox holds up his fists in defense. Ms. Pallas positions her ruler against her chest like a ninja warrior. Alix stabs her finger in my direction. "Hey you."

I actually do that lame thing where I look behind me and turn back around when I realize she's talking to me. I point to my own chest, mouth the word *Me?*

"Yeah, you. I hate everyone, too."

The room shakes as she slams the door behind her.

No one moves. Not Ms. Pallas, whose jaw is clenched, or Pox, who is holding his ear in either real or fake pain, or Stephanie slumped against the chalkboard, or Gnat or Brendon, or the Danish foreign exchange student, who looks like he might cry, or the Double Ds, or Raymond. And not me. I definitely stay put, even when the bell rings for the end of class.

The only one to rise is Ambrosia. I can't believe I haven't mentioned her yet, because it's a rare Hunter High student who can get this far into a day without Ambrosia's name coming up. As always, she looks completely serene, the *After* from a commercial about taking a sun-drenched, massages-around-the-clock vacation in some paradise.

She takes her time putting her books into her backpack, and I swear that she's savoring the moment, lolling around in the sheer pleasure of everything that just happened.

What did just happen?

She straightens the creases in her skirt, sways her back, and tucks some loose strands of long, dark hair behind her ears. Big hoop earrings, her trademark, catch the light and glitter real gold, not the filled kind.

This next part, I'm sure of it. I'm not imagining it. Ms. Pallas glares at Ambrosia, who holds up three of her fingers with their long, red-painted nails. It's like she's flashing the teacher some kind of gang symbol. The letter *W*? The number three? It happens fast and then it's over.

Ambrosia then peers over her shoulder.

At me.

Her eyes narrow like a cat catching a glimpse of a mouse. Her lips press together and I can tell she's humming. I can't hear the melody, but . . .

Ambrosia winks.

The hairs on my arms stand up like bristles on a brush.

For the next few days, there's a break in the school weirdness. Things quiet down. I notice a lack of heart in the zombie imitations of me, and then they totally taper off. There's no more strange weather and no more winks from Ambrosia. Ms. Pallas has gotten her classroom back under control. Pox is just Pox. Alix does her suspension time and comes back to school, a little less pumped up with anger and adrenaline than usual, it seems to me.

As far as my own venture into the world of shifting reality, it's like the whole intense, swirling, humming, hating event only happened in a dream. I could almost believe that. The only tangible change I notice is Ms. Pallas, and maybe that's not connected to any of this other business. Talk about intensity. She's fine-tuning her reputation for toughness, piling on extra homework and deducting major points if we slough off in any way. Twice in the past two days there have been pop quizzes, and when Pox complains, she lashes out: "Those who cannot remember the past are condemned to repeat it!" She seems to be on a mission to make us as passionate about ancient *everywhere* and ancient *everything* as she is.

She's also on a democracy kick, quoting Thucydides, a Greek historian whose famous quote is "The secret of happiness is freedom."

For me, that raises a lot of interesting questions. Such as, what is freedom anyway? Can things ever truly be free or fair? What happens when one person's right to do something bumps into another person's right to have them *not* do it? Everything gets tricky as soon as real, live human beings are involved.

So I give Ms. Pallas a lot of credit for trying to make democracy work in high school. It's definitely a major time suck. For instance, today half the class is eaten up with voting. Do we want weekend homework, or to have her pile it on during the week? By an 80 percent majority, We the People of Hunter High approve a resolution to limit oral reports to fifteen minutes. For our next major assignment, Ms. Pallas lets us work in groups with the freedom to pick our own partners.

She's wearing a silvery, almost metallic tuniclike top over flowing black pants, and the shiny material swishes when she turns to read aloud the list of possible topics that are written on the board: "The influence of ancient architecture on our buildings today. The role of women in the visual arts of the ancient world. The great lovers of the myths. These are just suggestions. Use your creativity."

"Ms. Pallas, does this mean we can report on anything we want?" someone asks.

"As long as there's a sharp focus. Nothing like 'A Huge Mishmash of Plagiarized Info about Greek Life.'"

"No fair! That was my topic," one of the wiseasses whines.

She writes the due date on the board and underlines it twice. "No late papers accepted. Five to six references, but only two can come from the Internet."

The Double Ds, who consider books to be dust collectors that cause their mascara to run, raise their hands, but Ms. Pallas covers her eyes. "No, no, no. I don't see you. This is where democracy ends and teacher rule begins. We're not getting into another discussion about why actual books with pages are necessary for research. They are." Her attention returns to the rest of us. "Other questions?"

It's the usual. Footnotes? Bibliography? Cover page? The Danish foreign exchange student asks, "Ms. Pallas, this project counts for exactly what percentage of the final grade?"

Another arm shoots into the air, and I find myself staring at it, the way the short sleeve of the tight black T-shirt shows off the mound of the bicep and the little tufts of dark hair on the knuckles.

"Question, Brendon?" Ms. Pallas addresses the arm.

This immediately raises a question I have for myself: What did I ever see in him?

Brendon might not have a nickname like his friends, but he's still part of that surf crowd—Pox, Gnat, Rat Boy, Bubonic, collectively known as the Plagues. I order my mind to make a comprehensive outline of all the things I can't stand about Brendon. For example, number one: He's *too* cute.

Yes, a guy can be too cute. It makes him stuck-up. Number two: He actually dated one of the Double Ds. Ick. His girlfriends are so predictable and his taste is so bad. Plus you know that he knows that he's got those eye crinkles and the effect they have on girls. I don't like the way he hardly ever smiles. He thinks he's too cool to smile. He's moody. I don't like moody. And I don't like the way his friends make fun of Raymond and anyone else who's different. I don't like the way the girls in his crowd lie on the beach sunbathing and pretend to be too scared to try surfing. Who you hang out with says everything about you.

Brendon's arm shoots into the air again.

I don't want to look at that arm. But I do.

I don't want to feel my stomach flip. It flips. That arm is not sexy. I repeat to myself: *not sexy.*

I don't want to think about how, whenever Brendon passes me in the hall, I'm hit with the smell of pine and ocean. I don't want to think about his curly dark hair that corkscrews over his eyes. I don't care that his back is broad and his waist is narrow. I don't want to wonder if, just maybe, his coolness is really shyness. I don't want to think about how his face sometimes takes on a whole different expression. I've seen flashes of it when he doesn't think anyone is looking. His usual cool surfer-dude aloofness gets replaced by something else, a quiet intensity that makes me wonder if there's an entire other Brendon locked away inside of him.

Stop thinking about him. Weren't you embarrassed enough? I shake myself out of the reverie.

Inside the classroom, there's a lot of noise as project teams start coming together. Chairs squeak. A group of girls laugh. The echo of high fives. Given free choice, we're all totally predictable. Team Meg and Raymond, of course. We only need to move our chairs a little closer together. The Double Ds team up with their redheaded mutual best friend. The earnest Danish foreign exchange student sits with the president of the Future Leaders of America club. There's Pox with the usual Plagues, Brendon in the middle of them. He and Rat Boy share a fist bump. I force myself to look away.

Across the room, I notice that Ambrosia's followers have formed a semicircle around her. No surprise there, either. They are making a big fuss about her hair, which today is pulled back tight ballerina-style, the bun circled by a garland that has the shine and luminescence of real pearls. Then Ambrosia says something that puts them into a state of hysterical cackling. Only her expression remains flat, the sole sign of life a slow lifting of her left eyebrow that's been plucked into a high, perfect arch. She shakes her head in a way that clearly means: *I wasn't joking. I'm serious.*

The laughing stops like someone pulled the plug on them. One girl lets her jaw drop and it hangs open in a fly-catching pose. I can see right into her mouth, even her retainer. The others turn in the same direction, toward me, and all those eyes make my stomach jump. Their expressions are exaggerated, like they're mimicking the Greek theater masks in our textbook. A mouth in a perfect *O* of shock. The wide-eyed look of surprise. The tense, squeezed brow of tragedy.

But it's not me they're looking at. Thank goodness. Their focus passes through me and lands way at the back of the room, last row, corner seat. Alix.

I don't think there's anyone who isn't waiting to see what happens next. Ambrosia does that to people. I'm not sure how. She's not even pretty in the usual way. But if she's in a room, it's impossible not to be aware of her—the high cheekbones; her close-set eyes that look right into you; the expensive, clinging black clothing; the perfectly manicured nails. You know that she knows things, grown-up and so-phisticated things that you want to know about. Next to her, even the Double Ds, who can pass for at least nineteen, resemble sad, wilted flowers. As Ambrosia weaves through the rows of desks and chairs, I study the way she moves, like if I could pick it apart, figure out the formula, the relation-ship between the swing of her arms and the length of her step, the exact angle of the tilt of her head, I could under-stand the power behind everything she does. Maybe then I could get a little bit of that power myself. As she gets closer to me, I feel her, like an air conditioner on high, and then the temperature returns to its normal state as she slides past.

"You," she commands, pointing a red dagger of a nail. "Wake up. What good are you asleep?"

Alix has her head on her desk. She stirs. She moans. She digs her fingers into her scalp, scratches, and sends a flurry of sand from morning surfing onto her arm. "Go away."

"Wake up!"

Ambrosia spins, a startling 180-degree turn, and now I'm looking into the point of the same red-nailed finger. "You, too, wake up."

What does she mean? My eyes are open. I am awake. But then she claps her hands, and in that instant, just for that instant, I swear: my hearing does seem sharper and colors more vibrant than usual. Every part of me, even my toenails, pulses. The space in my head expands and I have the strangest thought: I wasn't awake before. That wasn't awake. I've never been awake. But now? This is awake. Super awake!

The feeling, that amazing feeling, disappears as suddenly as it came over me.

How did she do that? What did she do?

I inhale sharply, the edges of my nostrils flaring. How do I become awake like that again?

So that's how it happens, the formation of the least likely project group ever concocted under free will at Hunter High. Members include perpetually pissed-off Alix, aloof and worshipped Ambrosia, Meg the socially lame, and Raymond the brain. I insist on him, even though Ambrosia tries to ignore my suggestion. I find the courage to say, "No Raymond, no me," and she relents.

One more member: Stephanie is sitting alone until Ambrosia leads her over by the hand. I make a space for her on the other side of me, and the five of us close into a tight circle.

"Meg will be our secretary and take notes," Ambrosia announces. "She's got elegant handwriting."

I didn't even think she knew my name, so I don't know how she knows about my handwriting, and it makes me self-conscious, but secretly thrilled that she's noticed *anything* about me. Plus, my handwriting is one of the things that I'm most proud of, not that I've ever told anyone that, not even Raymond, since it's such a lame and pathetic thing for someone my age to feel superior about.

Ambrosia crosses her legs, slides the black pearl on her

necklace back and forth on its thin gold chain. "Our topic should be theater."

She is not someone you argue with, or question. On the top of a notebook page I write: *Topic: theater.* The letters roll out of the pen evenly, with style, elegant.

"But what exactly about theater?" she continues. "Let's brainstorm. When I say ancient theater, the first thing that comes to your mind is . . ."

Alix stretches, makes a loud yawn. "Action. Write it down."

Me: "Masks. Comedy and tragedy, happy, sad."

Stephanie takes a sip from her stainless-steel water bottle. "Ancient plays are political. People stood up for what they believed back then."

From Raymond: "Deus ex machina." He watches me write it down, correcting the spelling. "It literally means *god from the machine*. There was an actual crane on stage. Some-times the plot got so convoluted that an actor playing a god appeared out of the blue and helped a character get out of a jam."

"Cool," Alix says. "Everyone could use a god machine once in a while."

"Definitely," Raymond agrees. "It comes right down from the sky, a god who takes care of the problem. Stops a flood, drowns an army, rescues a baby—"

Ambrosia interrupts. "Kills off who needs to be killed off." She pops the pearl into her mouth, runs it around her gums and cheeks, lets it fall back out like the dark pit of a fruit. "The best plays—those by Aeschylus, for example— are about revenge."

Raymond nods. "True. What the ancients lacked in a fair and impartial justice system, they made up for in blood-thirsty feuds that decimated entire families for generations."

"Huh?" Alix asks.

I translate: "Revenge is a big theme in the plays."

Ambrosia presses her hands together by her chin, like she's praying, and starts tapping the fingers in an increasingly fast rhythm. "Retribution. Payback. Getting even. Tit for tat. Eye for an eye. Tooth for a tooth. Settling a score."

"A major theme!" I jolt at the voice from behind me. I hadn't heard Ms. Pallas come up. She has this way of sneaking up on you that unnerves me. I twist around. She puts one hand on her hip; the other makes a fast sweep across the arc of her braided crown. "However, the plays also grapple with mankind's glorious struggle for a moral and just civilization in the face of its darker, revengeful instincts."

This interpretation immediately appeals to Stephanie. She nods enthusiastically, her head reminding me of a bell. Her long, dangling earrings make a clanging sound. "We must fight for justice. That topic is still important today. Look what the forces of darkness are doing to our planet."

"Exactly!" Ms. Pallas says. There's triumph in her voice.

"And I, too, agree." Ambrosia directs this next statement to our teacher. "The past is definitely not old, dead business."

This gives me an idea. I know it's a good one, but my throat goes dry like it always does when I have to give my opinion in a group. "I have an . . ."

"Go on," Ambrosia encourages.

"I have an idea. How about this as our topic: 'Bad Blood in Great Theater.' "

Alix is chewing on her lower lip. "Topic after my own heart."

Ambrosia rises. She passes in front of Ms. Pallas, a little too closely, close enough to bump her a little with her shoulder, close enough for me to know that it wasn't an accident, even though she does offer the teacher a smile. Only it's not a smile that's an apology, but more of a sneer with challenge etched into it. I see that clearly. There *is* something going on between them. Does everyone else notice?

I try to catch Raymond's eye, but Ambrosia positions herself in front of me, blocking the view, offering her full radiance. She takes both of my hands in hers and I feel myself sinking into the texture of her skin. It's soft, but not like a baby's, more soft and strong like well-worn leather. Her eyes lock onto mine and hold them there. No one has ever looked at me so deeply. I feel her presence in my knees, up my legs, my chest, my throat, at the point between my eyes. Her perfume isn't a brand I recognize. I pick up hints of roses, mint, and damp, rich soil. It makes my head spin.

"You, Meg," she says, "are a treasure. You are exactly what we need."

After school it's raining again, a sudden storm that wasn't in the forecast. I tell Raymond that I want to skip the bus despite the weather and walk home. That's one of the ways we definitely aren't alike. He doesn't get why I like the rain and fog so much, how bad weather makes me feel in tune with the world as I know it. Raymond's more of a sunshine and clear skies person, but he's willing to humor me. We zip our jackets. His face peers out of his hood. He's stuck on the same subject that's obsessed him from third period on. Can't blame him. I'm right there with him.

"You *have* to go there," he says again.

"As if I wouldn't."

"I don't know anyone who's been inside. Sneak photos with your cell phone, okay? Take notes with your *elegant* handwriting. Promise? You can't say no. Tell me exactly how Ambrosia invited you."

"Again?"

"Every detail. Let me relive the thrilling moment with you."

"Like I said before, she was holding my hands. You saw that. Weird, night? Then she leaned in and whispered, 'You'll come to my house. Tomorrow after school.'"

"That's so Ambrosia. She didn't ask. She ordered. Nobody ever says no to her. I wonder what she wants from you."

"Why do you think she wants something?"

"Of course, she wants something! Meg, under Ambrosia's flawless patina of impeccable mystery beats a core of pure emotional manipulation. Surely you've noticed that."

"Maybe she . . ." I pause a second, remind myself of the pull of her perfume, the tickle of her breath whispering in my ear. I take a leap over Raymond's logic. "I don't know, maybe she wants to hang out with me. Maybe we"—I struggle to find the right word for what happened between us—"clicked."

I immediately catch myself. Saying this might hurt his feelings because of the special Meg-Raymond bond that we're both so protective and proud of. "Not click like you and I click. You know I don't mean that."

He extends his pinkie and I hook it to mine, and at the same time we say "Pinkie Pull of Trust."

I go on. "But maybe she, you know, likes me."

He lifts an eyebrow suggestively.

"Not that way! Maybe she thinks I'm cool."

"Ambrosia? Don't be ridiculous!"

Ouch. That hurts. The word *ridiculous* seems to echo in the damp air. At the corner we wait for a car to turn and then cross the street. At the curb there's a big puddle that Raymond leaps over and easily clears with his long legs. I jump, too, and wind up soaking the cuffs of my jeans. *Ridiculous*. He talks on, either ignoring or not noticing the impact of that word on me.

"Earth to Meg. You spy with your sharp little eye the type Ambrosia surrounds herself with. Those girls date college guys. Not community college, four-year college. Sophomores. I've taken the time to look beneath your surface to discover and appreciate your core of pure wondrousness. But Ambrosia? Don't be ridiculous. You're not in her league."

A knot in my throat tightens, twists. Things get quiet after that, and it's not the comfortable silence between two close friends who agree on everything. With each step down the street, I flip between two feelings that shouldn't even exist at the same time in the same mind together: I'm pathetic. (*Of course he's right about me not being in Ambrosia's league. Nobody is really in her league. How stupid can I be?*) I'm pissed off! (*But Raymond didn't feel what I felt. It happened! Ambrosia felt it, too. Raymond must be jealous of her. I bet that's it! She didn't call* him *a treasure.*)

The next block is where we split off in different directions, and I'm more than ready to go. But Raymond holds me back by wrapping his arm around my shoulder. I start to push it off, but instead stand rigid to show him that I am not returning the hug.

"Meg-o-mania, don't be mad at me. You know how my mouth works. I can't help myself sometimes. When I said that you're not in Ambrosia's league, I meant it as a compliment. Take it that way. There's something so cold and calculating about her, and you're . . . you're so warm and *not* calculating."

I shrug, won't meet his eye.

"Come on! Don't be stubborn."

I shrug again. I'm sure I'll get over the sting of his insult eventually. That's me. I always get over anything. Forgive and forget. Turn the other cheek. But right now, I don't want to. I don't feel like it. I'm glad that we live on opposite sides of town. He gives me his pleading puppy-dog look, and in return I lift my hand in a quick half-wave, show him my back, and walk away. I hope that motion says to him: *I get to be mad sometimes, too.*

I'm definitely in no rush to get back to the Land of the Leech, so I take the long way. I have a lot to think about besides Raymond. Something is going on. Ambrosia. Ms. Pallas. How do they fit together? Alix is part of this something, too. I feel it. And what is Stephanie's place? Is she part of it? I weave west through some neighborhoods and eventually wind up on the single-lane walkway that borders the cliff along the coast. Being here clears my head a little. I can never get enough of the kelpy, salty smell and the cold fog on my face and in my hair.

I head north, my left hand tingling cold from the wind off the ocean. Ahead of me, I spot the town's famous surfer statue that stands on a pedestal on a spit of land that protrudes above the water. The statue's a little corny—a thick-haired stereotypical surfer dude, his chest broad and expansive as he grips his board behind his back, his chiseled profile contemplating the ocean for the next wave to catch. I get a kick out of how people decorate it according to the season: in December there's usually a Santa hat on that head of metallic hair, and in the summer a baseball cap.

As I get closer, I make out a carved jack-o'-lantern with

a broad, leering grin sitting at the statue's bare feet, near the plaque: *Prince of the Waves*. The statue was dedicated to the community a long time ago, and there's something familiar about the shape of the surfer's head and the set of his mouth. Up close, you see a tension in the surfer's jaw, and this makes me certain that he's more than a fantasy archetype. He's human with human feelings. My guess is that the sculptor based him on a real person.

I wrap my hands around the metal railing that separates me from the steep twenty-foot cliff and the ocean below. I bend back my head to follow a V-shaped flock of pelicans that are struggling against strong headwinds.

Who was this Prince of the Waves?

I bet that just like me, in weather just like this, he stood on this spot, the edge of an entire continent, the point where land ends and there's nothing left, nowhere to go that's solid. I wonder if he, too, imagined how these waves started far away. Something big and dangerous—an earthquake or hurricane—set them in motion, and they traveled through space and time, gathering strength and eventually meeting their end here.

A crash on the rocks below my feet.

I'm sure a science teacher like Mr. H could explain exactly how the shape of the cliff, the direction and pull of the current, and the force of the wind all come together to make this one of the most famous surfing spots in California. On most days, the waves roll in steadily and evenly shaped, musical like a poem. But right now they remind me of an argument, yelling and screaming, starting in one direction and suddenly veering into another, breaking apart, colliding and unpredictable.

I squint through the fog and light rain, and I can't believe what I'm seeing. There's actually someone, a surfer, in the water. A wave slams hard, burying the figure and tossing around the board like it's nothing but a toothpick. There's so much churned-up water, it looks like angry milk. Not even the Plagues would be out there today. You have to be crazy. Or you have to be someone who doesn't care about getting hurt. Or you have to be obsessed. Or part fish. Or someone who's a match for these waves, as fierce as the ocean itself.

I loosen the string of my jacket hood, let it drop back, then remove the clip from my hair. I shake my head. Each strand swells with moisture, turning my hair even wilder than it usually is, as coarse and tangled as a steel-wool pad.

What would it be like to be that surfer? To kick my legs and pound my arms, to punch my whole body through thick walls of water. To yell and scream and charge. To have nothing to lose. To have that much anger and not be afraid of using it.

All along the cliff, there are signs—DANGEROUS. UNPREDICTABLE SURF. STAY BACK—but right now instead of warning me, they tempt me. I lean forward on the rail and bend way over, far enough to see the cliff from a whole different angle, the way the surfer sees it.

Smash. The waves crash again on the rocks below. I breathe in, feel the power of each wave unleashing its force on the ground beneath me.

My eyes follow the surfer, who is now paddling toward the cliff, following some invisible diagonal line to where I'm standing. I begin making out individual features that confirm what I already know. I don't know how I know, but I do.

Alix hoists herself out of the surf at the base of the cliff, like she's been coughed up by the sea. Her hands tear away at the brown mass of kelp, skinny strands like mermaid's hair, or witch's hair, that's wrapped itself around her ankles and the board. She shakes water from each ear. She turns to squint at me.

I want her to wave. I want her to recognize me as the girl who hates everyone, too.

But no, she glares at me and spits on the ground. With her board under her arm, she walks in the opposite direction.

"You're late!" the Leech yells.

What I don't say: I hate you!

"You forgot the cat food! What's He-Cat supposed to eat?"

What I don't say: Poison!

"Look at the mud you tracked onto the floor! Scrub that now!"

What I don't say: You scrub it!

On my hands and knees, I wipe the floor clean of scuff marks.

What I do say: "Clean enough?"

"Enough of your sass."

I see her arm swing back and then forward. If I have the time to see it, why don't I move away? Why don't I block it? Why don't I defend myself? I feel her palm hard across my face. What she just did, hitting me, that's against the law. She's not allowed to do that. But it doesn't matter. The law is meaningless. Who will enforce it for me? Who will take my side against hers?

In my room I cry, but it's the kind of crying that is silent and only a little wet.

I cry because I'm so alone. Because of the way Raymond hurt my feelings today. Because of the way Alix ignored me. Because a boy like Brendon will never notice me. Because I'll never have a real family. Because of all the times I held my tongue and this is what it got me. I cry because of so many hurts and insults that I can't begin to name them all. I still feel the Leech's slap across my face.

Enough. Enough!

I don't want any more of this. I want things to be different. My whole life to be different. Especially for me to be different.

It can happen. It has to happen.

I feel something brewing.

I'm ready.

But ready for what?

What?

The rest of the night I spend on research for our Western Civ project. I dive into it. Here's one of the things I learn:

The ancient world didn't have much in the way of official laws and punishments. It was eye for an eye. If you hurt me, I hurt you. In ancient Greece the practice of personal vengeance against wrongdoers was considered natural and necessary.

I don't need a map to get to Ambrosia's. You can't miss the place, a three-story, red Victorian on a hill overlooking the ocean. It sits all alone up there. Before Ambrosia's family moved in a few years ago and fixed up the peeling paint and broken window frames, everyone knew it as the old Hamilton place, and it was haunted. Kids dared each other to creep into the overgrown gardens and through the creaking front door. I personally never set foot inside, but I know somebody who knew someone who did, and she ran out screaming about how the invisible hand of eccentric, long-dead Edith Hamilton had tapped her on the shoulder.

I get off the bus and start walking up the road, which quickly narrows and twists. In only a few blocks, our usual crowded surf-town atmosphere turns more isolated and rural. Trees thicken into a canopy over the road, and then there's a sign with the address. The metal gate creaks and swings open with a light push. Despite all the money that Ambrosia's family supposedly poured into fixing things up, I'm still getting the creeps. I try to shake off the feeling that eyes are watching me from deep in the trees. I follow a wide gravel driveway as it leads through a stand of redwoods, and beyond that the path curves for a while before opening into a clearing.

I gasp. It's the landscaping, the intensity of it. It reminds me of the old movie Raymond made me watch four times, Dorothy from the world of black and white landing smack in color-saturated Oz. There's a rumor that Ambrosia's family imports flowers and plants from all over the world and somehow manages to get them to grow like crazy in our foggy climate. I can report for a fact that the rumor is absolutely true.

Pinks and blues and chartreuse. Plants climbing up and hanging down. Thousands of flowers in the shape of tiny silvery fairy bells and others like huge upside-down mixing bowls. There's a line of cactuses as big as men that are draped in shrouds of white cobwebby stuff. There's one section of the garden in particular that draws me closer. I didn't know so many different kinds of pure-white flowers existed. White tulips and white roses and heads of what look like albino cabbage and a semicircle of silvery plants with huge fluffy, fringy petal wings. But it's the plant in the middle of the garden that makes me walk right up to it.

It's like from another world, a world where plants mimic human body parts, and these are the lips, parted, cracked, and red. From the center shoots a stalk, a sharp, silvery spear of a tongue—it must be twenty feet high—composed of all-white flowers, hundreds of them, thousands of them, and I know that I'm seeing a bloom that doesn't happen very often. Maybe once every ten years, maybe every hundred.

The wind shifts and I'm overcome suddenly with the smell of rotting meat oozing from that plant. No bird or butterfly would have anything to do with it. This is a lure for maggots and beetles. Who planted it? Why put something so amazing and yet so disgusting at the center of so much sweet-smelling beauty?

I hold my nose and back away. I start to jog, glad to leave behind that stink. A few more twists on the driveway and the sprawling red house comes into view. I also see that I'm not the only guest. Alix is standing beside her battered brown Volvo with the surf racks on the roof. It's parked next to Ambrosia's gleaming convertible, and I doubt that any car with a cardboard back window and bungee cords holding down the trunk has ever parked in this driveway before. Stephanie is kicking at some gravel. Her bike is propped against a fence, and she's red-faced with sweat from the trek up the hill.

None of us is thrilled to see the others. That's obvious. Alix glares as I approach, her upper lip curled. Well, I'm disappointed, too. Not that I have anything personal against them. But—I know what Raymond said and I can't help it—I thought Ambrosia invited only me. The way she whispered the invitation and didn't let go of my hands, I figured it would be just us. Her and me. What are these other two doing here?

At the front door, Ambrosia, dressed in her usual black— pants, silky blouse with a sweater, cashmere of course, that drapes like a cape—observes the scene. She's standing in the redbrick doorway, which must be fifteen feet high. Her dark, almost purple, hair hangs loose. With both hands she lifts the huge mass and twists it into a pile on the top of her head, which shows off her long, slender neck. The hair drops, settling instantly into glamorous waves. She beckons us over. "Come on in. This is home."

We enter. We stop. We stand. We gawk.

"My family, we're collectors." Ambrosia clearly expects our stunned reaction. "My people despise anything modern or contemporary. Loathe it."

As she gives us a quick house tour, her voice strikes a tone that somehow manages to combine bored and bragging. "Drapes, red velvet with silk lining imported from Turkey. Carpet, eighteenth-century Afghanistan."

There's so much red in the living room, it's like walking through a sore throat. My brain spins with the dates and origins of rugs, fabrics, and vases. I'm not the only one who's awed. From what I've seen of Stephanie, she's not normally a person who cares about things like wealth, power, and precious heirlooms, but her head snaps from side to side, trying to take it all in. In intimidated silence, we follow Ambrosia upstairs. Alix walks practically on tiptoe since our path is lined with about two million dollars' worth of breakable stuff. At the landing, I catch a glimpse of myself in a huge hallway mirror. Framed by gold leaf and filigree, even I look like someone important and powerful. I like it. I give myself an approving last look and follow the others down the hallway.

"My room."

Ambrosia opens a door into a space that is less like a museum than the rest of the house, but still not like any teenager's room I've ever seen. It is very much Ambrosia, whose style is what fashion magazines would call classic. Only instead of her usual all black, the bedroom is glaring white—white walls, white bedding, everything understated and reeking of money. My eyes lock onto interesting treasures. These aren't the usual clutter of knickknacks and memorabilia from childhood visits to Disneyland. On a table there's an ornate jack-in-the-box inlaid with scenes of mountains made out of what look like real jewels. Only Jack, this pitiful Jack, lies toppled, his head half ripped off.

Ambrosia takes note of what I'm noticing. "Meg, there's something special that might interest you." I follow the line of her pointing finger to a snow globe on her bookshelf. It's the size of a grapefruit and not the cheapo souvenir kind you buy at the boardwalk.

"Pick it up. It won't bite you."

From the heft I know it's real glass, not plastic, and my first reaction when I look at the scene inside is: *Something's seriously messed up, something's not right about this*. I hold the globe at an angle to study it better.

No, it's not messed up accidentally; it's meant to be this way. Suspended in the liquid there's a slanted cliff, and all along the jagged rock are tiny figures in various actions and positions. One figure, a man, is caught in the moment of jumping off the cliff, his arms spread in panic, his features painted to show fear and dread. On a rocky outcrop another figure sits huddled, head in arms, the posture of despair. Another figure is frozen in the act of pushing someone off the ledge.

I shake the globe, and instead of snow, black ash falls on these miserable, tortured figures.

I know it's only an inanimate object, but I can't wait to get it out of my hands, and I feel a peculiar relief when the globe is back on the shelf. I push it as far from me as possible without sending it over the edge. Behind me I hear a faint tinkle of a laugh from Ambrosia: "It's a work of art, but it takes a little getting used to. Give it some time. You'll appreciate it eventually."

Across the room Alix is pacing like a caged animal trying to make herself comfortable in all the finery. Out of water she's so awkward. She flops on the bed, quickly stands, and with a look of apology to Ambrosia slaps her pant legs to remove some dried mud and sits back down. So, I think, she does have manners after all.

In the meantime Stephanie, dressed in her usual layers—long hemp blouse and thrift-store sweater over a flowing paisley skirt—has curled up in the window seat. She's taking everything in, less impressed and more judgmental now, probably disgusted by all the wealth. I imagine her calculating how many monkey lives could be saved by the price of Ambrosia's brocade drapery alone.

Behind her, with those drapes pulled open, I have a perfect view of the all-white garden, and behind that I can see a broad sweep of the ocean. I'd give anything to have a room of my own with a view like this. The weather report said that the last freak storm was over, but it sure looks to me like another is brewing. It was clear this morning, but now a cloud bank, thick and gray, collects on the horizon.

I choose to sit in a white wicker rocker, and Ambrosia offers me first dibs on the snack she's prepared. Crackers are fanned out like a deck of cards on fancy white china, accompanied by a bowl of purple-colored dip. I dig in. It's garlicky, salty, and sweet, but not sweet like sugar, more perfume sweet, the very essence of sweet. Delicious. Unlike anything I have ever tasted before. I have to stop myself from licking it off my fingers. My mind concocts recipes. I want to smear it onto bread, coat spaghetti with it, slurp it through a straw.

"I am totally pigging out on this," Stephanie agrees. "I never want to eat anything else ever again."

"All organic, of course. Olive and fig," Ambrosia explains. "It's an old family recipe, secret spices and all that." As she bites into her cracker, she makes little moans of pleasure. Every movement of her mouth fascinates me. She dabs at her lips with a cloth napkin, sets it aside, and fixes her attention on us with an individual nod to each.

"I called you," she says warmly. "You came."

I stuff the last of the cracker into my mouth.

She lifts a book off her desk. It's a journal or scrapbook, and she unties the bow of gold ribbon that holds it closed. I catch a glimpse of the calligraphed title, *The Book of* something. She takes her time leafing through pages. The paper looks old and in danger of crumbling. I notice clippings from newspapers, drawings, and passages in ornate handwriting. Ambrosia's so engrossed that for a minute I wonder if she's forgotten that we're still here.

"Ahhhh. Here it is. Just the thing for this occasion. Listen carefully."

She reads aloud and I know that she's speaking English, only the language is so dense and poetic that I can decipher only sections of it. There's something about somebody's hand

and a drawn sword dripping in blood, and a description of women who aren't really women. *A hideous sight.* I catch that. And how their moods and breath are foul.

Ambrosia closes her eyes and explains, sounding a little blissed-out as she does. "Those are the words of the ancient Greek playwright Aeschylus. Lived 525 BC to 456 BC. Considered the father of tragedy. In my opinion, he's the father of it all—tragedy, comedy, truth, falsehood. Nobody, then or since, has expressed it better."

So that's what this invitation is about. Greek theater. Our Western Civ project, schoolwork worth 25 percent of our grade. I feel disappointed—and yes, a cringe of humiliation—for thinking that Ambrosia could have any other possible reason for inviting me. Raymond was right after all, and speaking of Raymond . . .

"If we're working on our school project, why isn't Raymond here, too?" I ask.

Ambrosia's eyes open—*thwop*—like two black, spring-loaded umbrellas. She gives me her own look of disappointment. Her voice turns breathy, thick with concern. "Meg, my dear Meg. Always hanging out with the same person. It's so limiting to your personal growth."

I leap to my best friend's defense, the defense of our friendship. "Raymond is . . ."

She interrupts before I can figure out what exactly I was going to say. "Your loyalty is very commendable. Touching in its way. I value loyalty, too. But the two of you are very different. Day and night."

"Well, yeah," I admit. "But we're alike in the ways that count."

"Trust me. You're too close to see it."

"See what?"

"How you're changing. Surely you've noticed some of that. I certainly have. You're feeling things so much more deeply. The pains of your life, the love that doesn't ever get returned. This unfairness shakes your soul. Crying all the time now, aren't you? Your lows are so much lower. Ever since your hormones kicked in and you got your period and the blood . . ."

Alix snorts at that, a few cracker crumbs exploding into the air. Stephanie, on the window seat, sits straighter and leans slightly forward, looking very interested, *way* too interested in my personal problems. I can't believe that Ambrosia is talking about my hormones, my period, my soul, and my crying. But how do I stop her? I'm so flabbergasted that I'm not even capable of hearing full sentences right now. I take in only isolated phrases. "Full potential . . . late bloomer . . . finally had enough . . . waking up."

By then she's come full circle back to the subject of Raymond, and how different we are. "He is exactly whom you see, nothing buried inside, nothing to coax out and discover, nothing stuffed down and left to ferment. Within you, on the other hand, there are layers waiting to be revealed."

There's a big vase of white flowers on her desk, roses. A petal drops. She picks it up, eats it. "In you, Meg, there are untapped complexities. You know that. In this way you're more like Alix, as deep as the ocean."

Alix starts a little when she hears her name come up. She's trying to look indifferent to the comment, but her eyes dart and her gaze drops to her hands. I can't tell if she's embarrassed or flattered, maybe both. Probably nobody ever called her deep before. "Well, we might be alike a little," she says. "Meg hates everyone, too."

"But I don't really hate . . . not Raymond, not—" I protest.

Ambrosia stops me with a traffic-cop motion, the palm of her right hand held in my direction. She then swings her full attention to Stephanie. "Meg is also like you. Intense, passionate, eager, and willing to put aside mundane individualistic concerns for a greater purpose."

Stephanie scoots to the edge of the window seat in disagreement. "Like me? Not at all. No offense, Meg, and I'm sure you have lots of passion tucked somewhere inside your quiet little self. But other than that one weird outburst in Western Civ, I've never seen you stand up for anything. I don't have a clue what you care about. Do you even know?"

"That," Ambrosia says with a wistful sigh, "is the crux of our problem. We see the surface and assume that's the core. That may be true for most people, but not for us in this room. We have to dig before the others can see our true natures and understand the depth and breadth of what we share. Alix, why don't you ask Meg a question about herself?"

Alix groans, embarrassment or flattery over and done with. "What is this, some stupid icebreaker game? Are we in kindergarten?"

Stephanie, too, has an edge on her voice. "I have a question. For Alix. If you love surfing so much, if the ocean is so important to you, why don't you care when people treat it like shit?"

Alix doesn't miss a beat. "How do you know what I care or don't care about?"

"You're selfish!"

"Who made you the judge of me?"

"You only care about you."

"What do you know about me?"

The insults go on like this as Alix and Stephanie glare at each other. I'm sure Ambrosia is now sorry that she ever invited them. Only to my surprise, when I glance over, she actually seems to be enjoying their whole nasty back-and-forth. There's an expression of amusement, even excitement, on her face. She turns to me with a sparkly smile.

"So Meg, a question for you. Whom do you hate more—the foster parents who make money off of your misery or the mom who threw you away like garbage the day you were born?"

Her question catches me in the throat. I actually feel it lodged there, a shape that's huge and sharp and won't let me swallow. I can't believe that she asked that, that anyone would ask it. The question hangs there, grows and twists in me. I feel trapped, almost panicked for my life.

But then . . . but . . . and here's the truth. The question she just asked? It's the very question that I feel like I'm asking myself all the time, late at night, early in the morning, a question I keep stifling and never dare to answer, not even to myself. On the surface it's the rudest, meanest question, but it's also the most honest one I've ever been asked.

Alix and Stephanie have gone silent, waiting to see what I will do. Cry? Get mad? Answer?

When I turn to Ambrosia, I see encouragement in her. She honestly wants to know. She wants to get into my head and see what's going on there. She doesn't want me to lie or to pretend anymore. She wants to know who I really am—when I'm not faking, when I'm not scared, when I'm being totally true to myself.

The lump in my throat dissolves.

I give myself permission to answer: Whom *do* I hate most? In my mind, a blank face floats to the surface. No eyes, no nose, no hair. It's the mother I never knew. But to express the level of hate I want to express right now, a blank face isn't good enough. It won't let me focus. I need actual eyes and ears and the sound of a hateful voice. I need specific deeds where I was wronged. I push aside the blank face and let the answer to Ambrosia's question rise like scum on water.

"Foster mother," I say. "This one. I hate her. I call her the Leech. It suits her."

Ambrosia rubs a finger along the perfect polish of her thumb. "Should this leech be allowed to treat you the way she does?"

"No."

"Louder! More outrage."

"No!"

"Much better. And what would you like from her?"

I pretend to think about this, even though I've thought about it a lot. "I want her to feel sorry for how she treats me."

Ambrosia's voice drops. There's disappointment in it. "That's it?"

"Okay, I want her to feel really, really"—she coaxes me forward with her hands, like I'm trying to ease a car into a tight parking space—"*really, really* sorry. I want an apology."

Her body shudders like I blew it and hit the car behind me. "That's it? Words? Only words? Is this a wrong that can be erased by a little apology? That's all you think you deserve?"

"I want . . ."

Eager, a second chance for me to get it right. "Go on."

". . . to be treated the way she treats her cat."

Ambrosia slams her hand on the top of her scrapbook. "Is that seriously the best you can do, Meg? An opportunity for a wrong to be righted, for justice to be done. And all you can come up with is begging to be treated like a cat?"

"You should see how she treats the cat! Like royalty."

"Come on! Think big, Meg! You deserve it. What about some payback? Shouldn't a leech be punished for the blood-sucking misery she's caused you?"

"Well . . ." I open to other possibilities. "She should pay back some of the foster care money she's been paid." Ambrosia's eyes go even dimmer with disappointment. I try again. "Or how about she goes to jail for a while."

Ambrosia shakes her head slowly, like I'm the biggest dimwit she ever met in her life, and now she has to provide the answer herself. "Meg, instant death or slow, excruciating torture?"

"Excuse me?"

"What do you want for this miserable leech? Death or torture?"

At that, Alix laughs hard and uninhibitedly. Ambrosia's

choices are so unexpected, so wild, that I laugh, too, a real giddiness flooding through me. Stephanie joins in, bouncing on the window seat. "Why not? That's punishment fitting the crime, all right! For being part of a system that abuses kids? Death, definitely," she says.

"Hold on!" Alix insists. "It's Meg's life of misery. Maybe she wants torture."

I giggle nervously as they wait for my decision. I've never allowed myself to consider getting even with someone to this level. But it's just a game, so why not? No one's going to get hurt. I reach down past my usual forgiving thoughts to a more primal part of myself. As Stephanie asked, Why not? "You're right! It's my revenge. I guess I do want some torture first."

"Excellent!" Ambrosia mimes writing my answer in her book. "Would you prefer the torture of actual physical pain or excruciating mental anguish?"

"Pick mental," Alix advises. Her eyes go hard like she's remembering something important. "Bruises heal, believe me. You can get used to bruises." She launches into a cheer-leading chant, giving it a hard rock beat: "Mental anguish, mental anguish, mental anguish."

I give Alix a thumbs-up, warming to the game. "Mental anguish it is."

This time Ambrosia actually does write it down. I get a jolt of satisfaction from watching her pen glide across the page and knowing that my deepest, meanest fantasy of revenge is down in ink and can't be erased. She addresses me with a solemn expression: "What is this leech's legal name?"

"Lottie Leach." I spell the name like each letter is drenched in oil.

"By the way, you're a natural at mental anguish," Ambrosia compliments me.

I feel myself blush. "Thank you."

She writes the name and closes the book.

We've gotten so lost in my revenge fantasy that we haven't noticed how dark the room has become, even though it's still afternoon. The new storm is rolling in fast, the sky almost black except in one spot, as if an invisible moon has come up and is sending down a celestial spotlight. The all-white garden with the stinking plant glows in the center.

Stephanie leans against the edge where the wall meets the window, and she yawns. "Wow, I'm tired," she says. Alix's face and the muscles in her back and arms are slack and relaxed. I've never seen her look so . . . peaceful. There's no other word for it.

"Good time," she says dreamily. "Too bad it's fantasy."

I, too, suddenly feel tired, like years of tension have drained out of me. Maybe it's the aftermath of the revenge game. Maybe it's the low pressure of the unusual weather. Maybe it's something else.

Ambrosia starts humming a tune. I know that tune. It's *the* tune, and I want to ask her about it. I try. My mouth opens, a question forms, but I go limp, so limp, too limp to even talk. Nine notes rising and falling. I count them. I hum along. Alix and Stephanie's soft voices join in.

I let myself drift off thinking about the Leech, her cat, and my revenge. I feel exhausted in a totally satisfied way. Like when you use up every minute of your day, not wasting time by wishing that you had done something else or regretting where you are or who you're with or what you did or didn't say.

When you're totally aware that this is your life, and for the first time, you know exactly how you're supposed to be living it.

Time for the *stasimon*. *In Greek tragedy, a musical interlude, a helpful aside to make sure you, the audience, understand what just transpired, a face-to-face so that we can be mind to mind.*

In times past, it would be up to the chorus to sing the stasimon. But that was then. Big choruses and girl groups are a thing of the past. We now live in a culture of solo acts, live journals, celebrity autobiographies penned by those who are known around the world by one name only.

Jesus. Madonna. Tupac.

Ambrosia. I fit right in.

In case you're wondering, Ambrosia is not some nom de stasimon to hide my identity. I am not unavenged Clytemnestra, nor her wronged daughter Iphigenia, nor Cassandra whose woeful story echoes so perfectly with mine. Why Aeschylus didn't jot down my tale for all eternity is a mystery to me. But his literary snub hasn't stopped my need for revenge. That remains endless, enduring, immortal.

So given my longevity, who is better suited to make sure you understand how the plot is congealing and thickening?

I've called them and they've done their first experiment. It's written down in my book. So for now, I let them sleep. But not for long. Too much rest and they will not feel enough rage for what I've endured. Sleep can suck the strength of the serpent.

Awake, awake, awake, you artists of pain. Ugly and beautiful, that potent and combustible mix.

FIRST STASIMON, THE BOOK OF FURIOUS

I couldn't have been asleep for long, maybe only ten minutes, but when I wake I feel refreshed, like after a full night's sleep. We laugh a little about my revenge fantasy. It was so much fun. After that, Stephanie takes off on her bike. Alix gives me a lift down the hill in her old car, and even though the drizzle has turned to steady rain, I ask to be dropped a couple of blocks away from the Leech's house. I want to walk the rest of the way. I wish I could walk forever and avoid the reality of what's waiting for me. I know that what we said and did in Ambrosia's bedroom was just a silly game, but I'm still pumped and not ready to give up the feeling.

I turn the corner and there's my living nightmare waiting for me: Lottie Leach in one of her old flowered muumuus on the front doorstep. This is not a good sign. As I tentatively approach the house, her eyes narrow hard in my direction. I know that look. She's going to kill me for being late.

Gone is any hope of an apology. Gone is any hope of my life ever changing.

I hang back, trying to forestall the inevitable. She shifts

her weight, moves one foot down a step and brings the other to meet it, another right foot, another left. For her, this qualifies as a rush toward me. I have plenty of time to run in the other direction, but my usual feelings of helplessness whoosh back and take over. Where am I going to run? Whom can I run to?

Her features look contorted. She's yelling. She flings open her arms, and I flinch in memory of the last time those arms came in my direction.

Only this time she doesn't slap me. She's not screaming at me. Something drops from her arms, a black puddle that lands at my feet.

"Worthless!" she says to it, and then as an afterthought to me: "Both of you!"

He-Cat takes off running down the street.

What was that about? I'm not going to ask any questions and tick her off even more. I rush past the Leech into the house and close my bedroom door behind me.

Raymond! I forgot! I promised to call him as soon as I left Ambrosia's house.

I check my cell and find a series of increasingly urgent texts from him.

First message: *?*

Second message: *???????????????*

Third message: *You're not still harboring ill feelings, are you??????????????????*

Fourth message: *Meg, did you get my messages of rapidly multiplying question marks that reflect my atypical lack of patience?*

He picks up on the first ring and says something that takes a while to decipher: "About time!"

"What's wrong with your voice?"

"A cold. So, what happened? Spill all."

"She hates the cat."

"Ambrosia? What cat?"

"No! The Leech. He-Cat. I came home and she was going ape on him."

"Ape on a cat?"

"I don't get it." I hold up my phone in the direction of the locked bedroom door. "Hear that?"

"Hear what?"

"She's stomping around the living room complaining about how the cat is eating her out of house and home. It's weird. She's treating He-Cat just like . . ." They come to me, my own words: *I want to be treated the way she treats her cat*. I laugh aloud.

"Meg, what's so funny?"

There's no doubt about it. "She's treating the cat just like she treats me. And vice versa, I guess."

Raymond blows his nose. "That qualifies as hilarious?"

"Not ha-ha funny, bizarre funny. You had to be there."

"Be where?"

"Ambrosia's house."

Another nose blow. "Finally! We're getting to the heart of the tale. Tell me all about it. Spare no detail."

I prop myself up in bed, comforter around me, and let the particulars flow out in no special order, whatever pops into my mind: the red walls, the almost hypnotic taste of the fig-and-olive dip, the all-white garden with the awful smell, and the broken jack-in-the-box. I have a hard time describing the snow globe and get frustrated because I am in no way capturing the disgust that drained into my fingertips when I held that thing. I tell him about the squabble between Alix and Stephanie and the question Ambrosia asked me and how she ate a rose petal and how tired we all got and when Alix . . .

"Wait, wait, wait, stop, stop, stop. Back up. Ambrosia asked you what?"

"Who I hated more."

Raymond sneezes and makes me repeat the exact words of the question.

"She actually used those words: *threw you out like garbage*? I can't believe she did that. Rude!"

"That was my first reaction, too, but . . ."

"Cold!"

"But . . ."

"What did you say?"

"I . . ."

"What did you do?"

"I . . ."

"You know me, Meg, turning the other cheek is my specialty. We definitely have that in common. But what Ambrosia asked you? That's hard to forgive."

I give up trying to explain how I didn't mind at all. It's too complicated.

Later that night, I'm in the bathroom with the sink faucet running to do the experiment Mr. H assigned as physics homework. I hold a spoon lightly by its handle and slowly move the rounded bottom toward the water. You'd think that a gush of liquid would push the spoon away, but instead it draws it into the fast-moving stream.

"Bernoulli's principle," Mr. H said. "It explains how birds and airplanes fly."

The way I understand it is this: Moving air creates low pressure. The faster the movement next to you, the lower the pressure and the quicker and harder a slower-moving object gets sucked into its void. It's why a big rig passing you on the highway pulls you into its lane and causes a crash. What does Mr. H call it?

The attraction of curves.

I hear scratching at the bathroom window and look out on a face with whiskers and goop in the corner of one eye. Poor ugly He-Cat. I actually feel bad for him. What a shock to go from being the center of someone's life to being a total outcast without having a clue why or what you did to deserve the terrible treatment. I let him in, and he allows me to pick him up without getting scratched. He's not so bad. By the way he's purring, I know he's grateful to me. I sneak him into my bedroom, where he wanders around, sniffing at my things in an appreciative way.

That night He-Cat, my new buddy, sleeps in my bed. He has no trouble falling asleep, but I toss around until way after midnight. It's hard getting comfortable. It's impossible to slow my thoughts. I'm sure that what happened with the cat is total coincidence. I'm certain that I had nothing to do with it. How could I?

Why, then, do I have a sensation of being drawn into something that's moving very fast and is very dangerous?

The next morning I still can't shake the feeling. I'm totally freaked out. I need to talk to someone who knows about things like coincidence and the probability of something that can't happen actually happening.

At the end of first-period physics, I stand awkwardly in front of Mr. H's desk. He's got the absent-minded-professor thing going on, so it takes a few seconds for him to notice me standing there. He's fooling around with his desk ornament, a Newton's cradle, which is five shiny metal balls hanging from strings that he uses to demonstrate various science concepts. He looks up at me with curious eyebrows. "You have a burning question, Ms. Meg?"

"Let's say you want something to happen. You've secretly prayed for it and imagined it for a long time. Nothing ever happened. But one day out of the blue, it actually does. Well, it kind of does. Only it's a little messed up, but it's close enough to get you thinking. What do I make of it?"

"If I understand your drift, this is an excellent question given our current class topic of cause and effect."

Mr. H holds one of the shiny steel balls out to the right and releases it. There's a bright, clanking sound of metal hitting metal. The three balls in the center stay still, while the sphere at the opposite end is thrown into the air. "Explain what's going on here."

I watch the end ball hit the line again and transfer its

energy, back and forth, *clang, clang, clang*. "It's demonstrating conservation of momentum and kinetic energy in a mechanical system. The ball on the opposite side gets the energy of the first ball and swings out in an arc."

"Thank goodness *someone* wasn't dozing during class. Exactly right! There are a few more things that come into play, but that's it, more or less."

The balls slow down, the arcs get smaller. I toss in some formulas that further impress him. "Momentum equals mass times velocity. Kinetic energy equals one-half mass times velocity squared."

"Someone's going to ace the next pop quiz, which— hint, hint—is tomorrow." He starts the balls swinging again. "Back to your question. Show me the energy of this praying and wishful thinking. Put it in my hand. Make it burn something. Send it over a wire or transfer it from one of these balls to another."

"I can't."

"Exactly! So without cause, there's no effect."

"But it happened!" I work hard to quickly calm my voice so I don't sound like a maniac. "Hypothetically, of course. Something must have caused it."

He reaches out and stops the balls. "Don't make the mistake of confusing cause with coincidence. Most likely it was a totally random blip-blip, just two of the gazillion events going on in the universe that day. This hypothetical *you* just happened to notice it and made an incorrect assumption that tied things together. Make sense?"

Me, disappointed: "I guess so."

"Remember. Blip-blip." He checks the clock. We have a

few more minutes until the next class. "Now, Meg, a question for you. Where does bad light end up?"

I shrug.

"In a prism."

At the end of next period, still unsatisfied, I take my puzzle to Mrs. H. She's making a pile of the essays we just turned in. A few papers flutter to the floor, but she ignores them because she's thrilled with my question. "Ah! One of those amazing, glorious moments to cherish. A glimpse into the true nature of what is."

"So yes? The praying caused it? We can do it again?" I catch myself. "I mean, wishing for something can make it happen?"

"What is wishing, Meg? What is cause? What is knowable? There are things that we can never understand fully, forces that are too complicated for our simple human minds to ever fathom and unravel. But that doesn't mean they don't exist. A tiny beat-beat of a butterfly's wings can set off a whole complex chain of events that results in a tornado. Yet we don't see the connection."

I bend down and pick up the essays.

"Remember. Beat-beat. Any more questions, Meg?"

I have so many of them, but I'm not sure what they are. I fumble, give up. "Yes, where does bad light end up?"

She sighs. "You've been talking to my beloved husband."

Blip-blip or beat-beat. I'm no closer to understanding than I was before.

Raymond is home sick with his cold, which means that along with being baffled about the Leech and He-Cat, I'm faced with the dreaded lunch-seat question. Without Raymond, where do I sit?

Ambrosia comes to the rescue. She spots me standing in the middle of the cafeteria like a little lost soul with a tray of chocolate pudding, and she waves me over. Today her hair is up in some kind of beehive style from the 1950s. Alix and Stephanie are already at the table, looking skeptical at this lunchroom seating arrangement. Doing a school report together is one thing. This overrides every social rule in the history of Hunter High, and it isn't going unnoticed. Many eyes are on us. Pox's eyes. Ambrosia's friends' jealous eyes. *His* eyes, Brendon's eyes. We're a real spectacle. The Double Ds walk by and try to eavesdrop, but Ambrosia shoos them away like they're a pair of pesky mosquitoes.

"So?" she asks. "Something happened last night?" It's a question, but not a question, like she already knows the answer. "You want to tell us. Tell us."

"How did you know?" I walk them through everything that happened with the Leech and He-Cat. When I get to the end of the story, I'm practically hyperventilating.

"Cross your heart that happened," Alix orders.

I cross. "I swear. It was like something got into the Leech's brain and rewired it with a message: *Treat Meg and He-Cat totally the same*."

"No shit! That's awesome."

Stephanie, too, is wowed. "That's what you asked for!"

"Exactly!" I say. "Only . . . you know . . . *not* exactly."

I feel starved all of a sudden. I want food and I want it now. I pick up my cheese-and-tomato sandwich, bite hard into the crust. "What do you all think? Is this coincidence or . . . ?"

Alix puts down her fork with an annoyed clang. "Too bad it didn't work the right way and give you what you wanted. She was supposed to feel guilty."

"I would have been happy with an apology," I agree.

Stephanie, lover of all animals, focuses on He-Cat. "I'm super glad nothing bad happened to the cat. You'll give him lots of love, won't you?"

Ambrosia has been quiet, but I notice her glowing at us the way most teachers look at Raymond, everyone's prize student. She taps her fingertips together, giving us a dainty but enthusiastic round of applause. "I want to say brava to all three of you. Good job."

I put down my sandwich. "What do you mean?"

"It's good for a start, a little introductory flex of your muscles. Don't fret about the unforeseen glitch. That's to be expected. You're new to this, and you're not on fire yet."

"New to what?" I ask.

"On fire how?" Stephanie says.

Without asking permission, Alix dips her spoon into my pudding. "You're telling us that"—she licks the spoon clean, drops it back on my tray—"it was us: me, her, and her? We messed with the Leech? We're witches? Yeah!"

I'm not surprised to hear Ambrosia's distinctive laugh dismiss that possibility. "Witches? Of course you're not witches!" She gives a dismissive puff. "A little something out of the ordinary happens, a female shows a talent for power, and right away she's branded as a witch!" She makes some exaggerated sniffs. "Have you smelled any witch's brew? That's not something you'd likely miss. Talk about stinking to high heaven, a mix between old Brussels sprouts and dried menstrual blood."

Stephanie gives a nervous laugh and we exchange quick, uncertain looks. Ambrosia must be joking, even though she's not the jokey type and it's definitely a creepy joke. Even her laugh sounds deadly serious. In fact, I get the feeling she was born without a real sense of humor. She goes on with her witch checklist: "Is anyone here cackling? Does anyone even have a warty nose?"

Alix's hand dashes to her face. "I've got a zit—a big, juicy one on the chin."

"We've all got zits," Stephanie says. "Except you, Ambrosia. I always wanted to ask: How come you never, ever get a zit?"

Alix stays with the subject. "So if we're not witches, how about vampires?" Her voice sounds light, hopeful.

Ambrosia also dismisses that idea with a stern shake of

her head. "What is it with you people and your fascination with the living dead? You have vampires on the brain. They are so overrated in terms of punishment. One bite and you join a crowd of others just like you. It's a regular party every night for eternity. Where's the suffering in that?"

"I wouldn't mind being a vampire," Alix insists.

Ambrosia leans forward on the lunch table, hands folded, all business. "This is not one of Pallas's democracies, something you can simply vote on. Forget vampires and witches. Listen carefully."

She clears a space, hauls up her backpack, and pulls out the scrapbook from home, the one with the gold ribbon. She opens to a bookmarked place. She's come prepared. But prepared for what? She closes her eyes, revealing the thick line of deep-blue makeup ridged along her eyelashes. She doesn't actually need the book. She's got the section memorized.

"Mother who made me, Mother Night hear me, bred to avenge the sighted, the blind, bred to avenge the dead. What mortal feels not awe, nor trembles at our name, hearing our fate-appointed power sublime, fixed by the eternal law."

Her voice is even deeper than usual. It seems cut from the same fabric as her black-velvet jacket, thick and rich, swallowing up all the other sound and light in the cafeteria. I feel that everything, including myself, is disappearing under the spell of those words and her perfume. I want to hear more. But abruptly she closes the book, plants a big, loud kiss on the cover. "As I was saying the other day, Aeschylus almost got it right. Except for his totally unsatisfying ending. That ending! We can change that. The three of you can . . ."

Her sentence fades out. A frown. A flash of resentment.

I swivel to see the cause. Someone is coming up behind me. I take in the determined look on Ms. Pallas's face, the unblinking blue of her eyes, the swish of her iron-colored clothes, the way she's floating a few inches above the floor. *Blink*. Of course she isn't floating. In her hand she carries a long baton with a gold knob at the top, which makes sense only because she's the faculty advisor of the color guard that practices during lunch.

"Take my seat," Ambrosia offers with too much politeness. "I was just leaving."

Only that said, she doesn't get up. First she licks two fingertips and smooths the sides of her hair into place, even though it's already perfect. Then, very slowly and deliberately, she separates trash from things that can be recycled, returns the book to her backpack, arranges and rearranges the contents. She pulls out her iPod, debates between several songs, and slips the speaker buds into her ears. She takes her time doing all of this, while Ms. Pallas is forced to stand and wait.

"All yours," Ambrosia finally says, and way too loudly. I have the definite sense that the music's not blaring and that she is shouting on purpose to be rude. To the rest of us, Ambrosia mimes talking into a phone, thumb at her ear, pinky at her mouth. Her lips move, pomegranate red, and I read them: *I'll call you*.

When Ambrosia is out of earshot, Ms. Pallas sits and

says, "We have openings in the color guard. The three of you would be—"

Alix practically spews out her milk. "Me? Marching? Tasseled boots?"

Stephanie hands Alix a napkin. "Sorry, Ms. Pallas. No disrespect intended, but I definitely move to a different drummer."

Our teacher turns to me, the color of her eyes so unsettling I can't look away. She asked me to join the guard yesterday and the day before that and the day before that. At first I was kind of flattered and told her that I'd think about it. But she's gotten so pushy. Why does she keep asking? Can't she take a hint? What am I, her personal mission? Why doesn't she back off?

The bell rings and I'm glad. Saved again.

"Sorry," I mumble, and hurry off. "Guess I'm not much of a joiner."

Ambrosia texts each of us about when to meet (right after school) and where (at the cliff with the statue overlooking the famous surf spot). I'm first to get there, so I lean over the rail. My thoughts, as I sort through all that's been happening, feel as churned up as the ocean below. I'm hoping that Ambrosia will clear things up. Obviously she knows a lot more that any of us do. I wonder if there's some simple, logical explanation for everything that's been happening. Somehow I don't think there is. I have a feeling that what Ambrosia will tell us is more complicated than I can imagine.

I hear something that makes me turn away from the surf. My name, deep as a foghorn.

"Meg!"

A little down the path, someone waves. My name again, and out of the gray the figure comes toward me, walking and then jogging a little. It's Stephanie and her mouth is moving. I assume she's already talking about Ambrosia and Ms. Pallas and He-Cat, everything that's been happening. How could she be thinking about anything else? Only when she reaches me, she points an accusing finger to where a thick metal pipe juts out of the cliff, like the cigar in the Monopoly tycoon's mouth. A stream of gunk-colored water spews out of it and into the ocean. "The color of that ocean foam! Can you believe it? That's not from any natural causes."

When a wave hits the beach, it leaves behind a jagged line of foamy crud. Stephanie keeps talking, too outraged to take a breath. "Runoff. All kinds of crap—cigarette butts, dog shit, lawn fertilizer—washes right into the gutters and directly into the ocean. An otter can't shower off. Can you imagine the germ count right now? You have to be a nut to be in the water."

We turn together to watch the *nut,* suddenly visible in the haze, paddling hard through what I now imagine to be a wave of skin-eating bacteria that look like jaw-snapping Pac-Men. Of course, the surfer is Alix. She must have cut her last class to get here early. Her arm shoots into the air and we wave back, and soon she's washed onto shore, climbing the cliff, and standing next to us. I'm freezing just looking at her, but she doesn't seem to mind the weather.

"Think she'll show up?" she asks, and when Stephanie

doesn't answer immediately, Alix turns on her. "Well, do you?"

"Do what?" Stephanie's eyes keep returning to the pipe that's coughing out the pollution.

"Ambrosia! She can't say the stuff she said and not explain."

Stephanie turns back to the pipe. "That's disgusting. Criminal!"

Alix pulls off her neoprene surf hood and shakes her head. Her saltwater-caked hair spikes out like underwater snake creatures, their hungry mouths probing the air in search of food for their insatiable appetites. "I'm with you on that. Think what it's like surfing out there, getting a mouthful of that crap every day."

Stephanie, her jaw clenched: "The people responsible? They should be forced to drink it."

From behind us then, a disembodied voice: "Wanting revenge but being helpless in the face of injustice. I know the unbearable ache of that."

We see her now, Ambrosia, a figure in the fog in a black raincoat, her hair hidden in a man's-style hat. She's standing at the surfer statue and runs her fingernails along the bare metal feet. I notice that one of them, the pointer finger on her right hand, is painted black while the others are red.

No hello, no small talk, just:

"You three want to know what you are? I'll be direct. I'll say what I know. And if you look into your hearts, you already know it, too."

Something shifts in the light. I can't see the ball of the sun, but the rays must be bending through the nasty-looking clump of clouds to produce so many sparks of gold, orange, pink. The Prince of the Waves takes on a sickly greenish glow. If this were a disaster movie and the ocean and sky looked like this, everyone would be yelling and crawling over each to get to high ground fast.

Ambrosia rubs her hands together like sticks for making a fire. She shows us the palms. In the unnatural light, those hands appear to have no love lines, no life lines, few lines at all. Her words seem to emerge from some bottomless pit: "O Furies, born of sky, ocean, earth, and blood, mothered on foul human emotions, nursed on the tainted milk of greed, hate, and delusion, nourished with an appetite for ancient, twisted karma. Those Who Walk in Darkness, ceaselessly hunting and haunting those who have gone unpunished. Ferocious, powerful, unstoppable."

Alix's legs start vibrating and she drums her hands against the thighs of her wet suit. She's either freezing or unnerved. I know I am. Both. Her lips drain of their ordinary color, turning blue.

Ambrosia addresses her directly: "Alecto the Unceasing. Restless, endless maker of grief who revels in war and quarrels."

She faces Stephanie: "Tisiphone the Avenger. The retaliator who punishes those who harm the guiltless, the vulnerable, the innocent."

She swivels and her eyes lock onto mine like suction cups.

"And Megaera the Envious . . ."

Not me.

"Angry, untrusting, resentful. The undisputed master of holding a grudge."

Everything on the periphery of my vision—the pelicans overhead, the crashing waves, a hunched-over man walking his dog, the surfer statue—disappears into even thicker fog. I feel light-headed, like the time I guzzled wine on an empty stomach. *This is a dream. I'll wait until I wake up,* I tell myself. Only, a dream has a certain quality to it, and it's not like this. This is real. This is happening.

Overhead, the strangled cry of a gull. Within me, something peeks out of its dark hole and demands to be acknowledged.

Angry, resentful. Yes. Underneath, that's what I am.

Ferocious, powerful, unstoppable. That's what I want to be. I'd give anything to be that.

Ambrosia breaks eye contact. The world returns. A seabird drops like a dagger to snag an unlucky fish.

"There you have it, ladies. Ring a bell?"

What are you supposed to do with information like that?

Alix, Stephanie, and I explode in laughter. Ambrosia just told us that we aren't ordinary human teenage girls with massive social problems and some of the worst frizzed-out hair at Hunter High. We are straight out of mythology, goddesses who avenge, retaliate, punish, haunt, hunt, and don't stand around being victims, but make things happen. We are kegs of untapped, unstoppable power. What else did she say? We walk in the dark, or something insanely insane like that.

It's so ridiculous that I start pogoing around the surfer statue. I don't believe a word of it.

But at the same time that I don't believe it, I *do* believe it. I want to believe it. It explains not just about He-Cat and all the strange things at school but something even more important. It means that everything I want to believe about myself, what I hope for and pray for, is true. I am blossoming. There's something strong and powerful ready to come out. A *me* who can stand up for herself and who can right wrongs and who never has to be afraid. The real me, a Fury me.

I think that Stephanie and Alix are also bouncing between the two poles of not believing a word and total certainty. We keep dancing and shrieking a thousand *oh my Gods*, and under a darkening sky we pump Ambrosia with questions:

"Are you nuts?" (Alix)

"What exactly are the Furies?" (Stephanie)

"How do we use this power?" (Alix again)

"If we are Furies, who are you?" (me)

"Who else knows about this?" (Alix again)

Ambrosia gives us one straightforward and four not-exactly-straightforward answers:

"No."

"You have a lot of soul-searching to do to answer that question."

"You harness it."

"I am the one who called you out of your sleep."

"Me and a certain busybody."

Ambrosia hands us each a few sheets of paper. "Your job description. FAQs about Furies. For future reading," she says. "But now, dance, celebrate! Enjoy the cosmic moment."

So that's exactly what we do. By the time the sun sets, I'm charged with an exciting new energy, a sense of hope and optimism that maybe my life truly has been turned upside down. I am not who I think I am. We aren't who we think we are.

What do we do next? What happens after you get information like this?

"You're not putting us on?" Alix asks again.

"Don't take my word for it," Ambrosia says. "See for yourself. You need to test your powers, play with them, learn what they can do."

"I have another question." Stephanie's dreads are puffed out, like they gorged themselves on salt air and our energy. "Is anyone else starved? I mean, really starved?"

"Yeah," Alix agrees. "I gotta get home and make dinner for my little brother. It's burrito night, his favorite."

This doesn't seem like an appropriate ending to a day like this one, but I guess it's what happens after any event that blows apart what you think you know about life and about yourself. Everything changes. Maybe we really are Alecto, Tisiphone, and Megaera.

But right now we are also Alix, Stephanie, and Meg, who have chores and homework. I, for one, am going to get in massive trouble with the Leech for being so late.

We wind up doing what ordinary girls do. We promise to call each other. We make plans for tomorrow and then, after one more squealing oceanfront dance, we head off in our different directions to think about what just happened.

I can't go to the Leech's house yet. I'm not ready to face her. This is too wild not to talk about. I duck into a deserted playground, sit on the bottom of a slide, and phone Raymond.

Even though he's coughing and his ears are clogged, I make him shut up and listen. My words gush out. I know I'm not making total sense.

"It hasn't sunk in yet, but I think it's true," I say.

"What hasn't sunk in?"

"What I just told you! What Ambrosia said."

"Slow down, Meg! She said *what*?"

"I'm the undisputed master of holding a grudge."

Cough. "You?"

I pace the playground. I need to keep moving. Too much energy. "She said that I have to practice more than the others because everyone boils at different degrees. When it comes to fury and outrage, Stephanie and Alix are hotter cauldrons than I am."

"That's for sure."

"But I'm at a breaking point. Plus, I have all the raw talent. Nothing to worry about. She said so."

"Gee, that's a relief."

"Are you being sarcastic?"

Sneeze. He changes the subject. "Ambrosia's role in all this is . . . ?"

I sit on a toddler rocking horse, some sort of made-up creature, part dinosaur, part giraffe. It's purple with big yellow spots. "She's the one who called us. That's what she said. Plus, she's in charge of the paperwork."

Raymond snorts, and I get a flash of irritation. He's already made up his mind and thinks it's all a crock. "Don't snort! You think this isn't possible!"

"I don't think anything yet. I don't have all the evidence."

"You think Ambrosia's messing with me! You think I'm gullible. You think I'm what you see is what you get."

"Meg, calm down. I'm trying to keep an open mind without my brains spilling out. By the way, that wasn't a snort at you. It was a big hunk of phlegm."

"Gross."

"Imagine what it tastes like. Tell me more about the paperwork."

I move to a bench with an overhead streetlamp and read something random from a section titled "Anger Exercises." The typeface is small and tight. "If you feel your mind softening or taking pity, don't listen to it. Don't sympathize."

"Why wouldn't you listen to your own mind? What's wrong with sympathy? Why would . . ." Another sneeze.

Another flash of irritation. I shouldn't have to explain this to Raymond. A best friend should understand without me needing to spell it out. "I shouldn't listen because *my* mind keeps telling me to put up with being treated mean and unfairly."

"That's not what I—"

"Because if people do something wrong, they should feel guilty about it. They should be punished."

"Of course! But—"

"But not by me? That's what you're saying! You don't think I have any special power."

"You think you do? You actually believe what Ambrosia says?"

I hate Raymond's tone. I don't like it at all. He can be such a know-it-all. That's why he gets on everyone's nerves.

And his sarcasm! He's making fun of me. He's putting me down. When I don't answer right away, he changes the question: "Do you *want* to believe what she says?" Pause. " 'Cause Meg, if you do, I want to believe her, too."

And just like that, the anger drains out of me. It's gone. My pulse settles down. I move from the bench to a swing, wondering why I got so pissed off at him. How did that happen? It came on so fast, flared up, and I felt so right and justified. But then he said the right thing in the right way, and it all evaporated. I'm so glad. I don't want to be mad at Raymond, not ever. He's my best friend. He's there for me. He wants what I want.

"You still there?" he asks.

"I understand why you're skeptical," I say, my voice softer. "I'm skeptical, too. I'm not a total fool."

"Of course not!"

"We're not supposed to take Ambrosia's word for anything. She did her part by calling us together, but now it's up to us. We need to play with our power on our own, test it, figure it out."

"She said that?"

I nod even though he can't see me. "She said that's the only way we'll really accept who we are and what we're capable of doing."

We talk a little more, and then after saying good-bye I inch my toes behind me on the swing. I let the momentum take me, just like a ball in the Newton's cradle on Mr. H's desk. Only I don't bang into anything, except gravity. My energy is all mine. It carries me forward, and at the highest point I pump my legs to go even higher. I tilt backward, practically hanging upside down. The ground whooshes up to meet me.

Luck is with me tonight. I get into the house without a Leech attack, sneak into the bedroom, and lock the door. She hates locked doors and will probably come pounding on mine soon, but right now I don't care what she hates. He-Cat is curled up on my pillow. Poor thing. Mistreated little guy. I bet he hid out here all day to avoid her nasty temper. It's so unfair. When I sit on the bed, the cat snuggles closer and turns into a purr machine.

I eat some peanut-butter crackers, brush the orange-colored crumbs off my lap, and boot up my computer. I've never been this excited about homework. I've never had homework that has so much to do with my life.

Internet search: **The Furies.**

Definition: In Greek mythology, the Furies are female earth deities of vengeance and supernatural personifications of the anger of the dead. From one website, I learn that they are also called the Erinyes, which translates as "the angry ones" or "the avengers." Avengers! From another website, I discover that they are sometimes referred to as "infernal goddesses" who pursue, persecute, and represent regeneration and creation. In the *Iliad*, they are described as "those who beneath the earth punish whosoever has sworn a false oath."

The pictures I find are especially awesome. It turns out that the Furies are all over classical art. On some statues, their heads are wreathed with snakes and their eyes drip with blood. On one old vase in a museum, they have the wings of bats or maybe it's birds; on a piece of pottery, the artist portrays them with the bodies of dogs.

There are so many cultural references to the Furies.

They are major characters in the final part of the *Oresteia*, a trilogy of Greek tragedies written by Aeschylus, which concerns the end of the curse on the House of Atreus. There's a film, a Western from the 1950s, called *The Furies*, and a 1976 historical novel by someone named John Jakes. And it's the name of the newspaper of The Furies Collective, a Washington, DC–based organization. I'd like to know more about that.

At femalefury.net, I learn about an all-girl third wave proto-punk band, based in Athens, Georgia, that's now defunct. Discography: 1986: Debut album: "The Furies Rise." The title track and another cut, *Born from the Balls of Uranus*, received strong airplay on college radio stations and the band toured (small clubs and campuses) until disbanding due to personality and artistic clashes. Rumors persist that the group is planning a comeback. They maintain a small but passionate cult following. It's too bad they broke up. I wonder if I can find a video or their CD.

There's lots more. Furies. Infuriated. Furious. I stroke He-Cat's fur as my printer spits out everything I can find. I want to be prepared for tomorrow, our first scheduled practice session, even though we haven't figured out a place to meet yet.

The lair of the Leech is obviously out of the question. When I call Stephanie, she complains that her parents work at home a lot. Alix says no way are we meeting at her place. No explanation why, and she's cagey about it. I get the sense that she's embarrassed about where she lives.

"You *want* me. You *need* me," Raymond says with a clogged nose when he volunteers to host what he is calling *The Great Power Shift*. "To your gathering I will bring a healthy skepticism, a runny nose, and a mom who will serve her world-famous triple ginger cookies."

So that's how we wind up at Raymond's house the next day after school. When we step inside the front door, a cascading scale of violin notes from upstairs greets us. Raymond must be feeling better. His mom makes a special point of giving me a big hug and asking how I am. She does that every time she sees me, and I'm getting used to it. It's not phony at all. Then she hands me a plate of cookies and leads us to Raymond's room. She blows each of us an individual kiss before shutting the bedroom door behind her.

"Gawd, I just love my mom," Raymond says. He's propped up in bed, pillows fluffed, violin at his side, and wearing his favorite pjs with the retro cowboy pattern. I notice Alix and Stephanie exchanging glances. That's one more thing we have in common: none of us has ever publicly declared love for our mom, and not because it's an uncool thing to do but because we don't have moms like Raymond's. I'd give anything to have a parent who feels about me like she feels about him. She gets a kick out of Raymond being Raymond, exactly the way he is. You can just tell that she doesn't want to change a thing about him.

Sneeze. Cough. Raymond doesn't waste another minute before getting down to business. "My research on the matter in question," he announces. "There's a lot to be said for being home sick. School can definitely get in the way of an education." He opens a computer file and reads, "Those Who Walk in Darkness, blah-blah-blah. Alecto, Tisiphone, Megaera."

"Tell me something I don't know." Alix reaches for one of Raymond's stuffed animals, a cross between a bear and a chicken, and puts it behind her head as a pillow.

"Hold on, Ms. Patience. I have more. Female deities of vengeance and anger. Horrible to look at. Blood dripping from their eyes. Snakes in their hair. What they lack in good cheekbones they make up in horrendous BO."

"Hey!" I protest.

Raymond mimes giving me a reassuring hug, and then explains that the horrible part is only one aspect of the Furies' image. Artists and playwrights throughout history sometimes portray them as gorgeous temptresses, a trio of luscious-smelling goddesses.

"That's more like it," I say.

"And what personalities! Sheer determination. Without mercy, they punish all crime. They mess with your mind. They leave no foul deed unavenged. They are"—he picks up his violin and plays a dramatic, high-pitched *da-da-da-da*—"the Furies."

I add an interesting tidbit from my own research. "Furies, as in *furious*. And *infuriated*. Derived from—"

"Enough grammar." Alix is on her third cookie. "I don't care what they call them or why. I wanna know if it's true about us. What can we do and when can we start doing it?"

"*If* we can do anything," Stephanie emphasizes. "I obviously want it to be true, but I'm not totally sold."

Alix, chomping into ginger cookie number four, fans her mouth: "Spicy! Compliments to the chef. Anyway, we'll never know anything if we sit around like a bunch of motor mouths."

Raymond agrees. "Despite my proclivity for blabbing, I'm in full accord. Let's turn to the scientific method, and commence the Great Power Shift experiment."

He nods with extreme seriousness in my direction. I take it as the signal to begin reading from Ambrosia's recommended exercises. "Practice number one. Start small. A bug perhaps, some worthless member of a particularly despicable subspecies whose minuscule size is in inverse proportion to the amount of irritation and pain it causes."

"In plain English?" Alix asks.

"A flea," I say.

"Or a dung beetle," Alix suggests.

Stephanie looks unhappy. "I value all creatures large and small. Each and every one has a role to play in the environment. Without the dung beetle, there would be—"

Alix interrupts by grabbing the paper from my hand. For someone who's submerged in water so much, her nails are incredibly dirty. She squints like she's reading the fine print at the end of a legal document. "Tell any friend of the dung beetle that sometimes something has to be sacrificed for the greater good. Tell her that by doing one little experiment on a stupid bug that nobody will ever miss, she might discover her power to save an endangered llama or even the whole planet."

Stephanie lunges for the paper, misses. "Where does it say that? It doesn't say that."

"Naw, it doesn't," Alix confesses. "But let's say you can save only one thing, an endangered llama or a flea. Which lives?"

"Llamas aren't endangered."

Alix hurls the stuffed animal at Stephanie. "You know what I mean! Would you sacrifice Mr. Itchy Welt Maker to save Never Hurt Anyone Little Llama?"

Stephanie thinks hard. She's running her tongue along her braces. "This is tough. It's not just about one bug. It's a whole moral and political question about power."

"Give me a break." Alix groans. She notices an ant crawling on the nightstand. "How about that?" With the tip of her fingernail, she nudges it to the center of the table. "One stupid little ant," Alix insists. "We don't even know what's going to happen to it."

"Probably nothing, right?" Stephanie nods a reluctant okay, and Alix pumps her fist in triumph. Raymond volunteers to read the directions so the rest of us can concentrate. Ambrosia's paper doesn't say to lock the bedroom door, but we do it anyway. It doesn't say to sit next to each other, but the three of us move closer to the table, the sleeves of our shirts touching. We're ready. This is it. Raymond reads Ambrosia's directions:

"Step one: Isolate the victim. Step two: Follow the victim's movement. Put all your hate on it. Then double that hate. Triple it."

Honestly, I don't start out feeling any special hate for the ant, definitely not the double-triple variety. There are plenty of things in life that deserve to be hated, but how do you hate an ant? Still, I decide that I want to try this, and that means putting aside any resistance and not listening to my doubts. I want to give it my all.

If you feel your mind softening or taking pity, don't listen to it.

So I don't. As indifference comes to the surface, I replace it with contempt. As sympathy for the ant arises in my mind, I dash it away. It's like setting a radio in my head to station HATE. I turn down the volume on acceptance and crank up the blame. I think of picnics ruined and food wasted. I imagine ants crawling all over me, their filthy feet and disgusting segmented bodies. Someone has to take revenge on them. Ants would take over the world if we didn't.

It turns out that hardening my mind—moving it in the direction of judging, despising, detesting—is a lot easier than I thought it would be. It's a snap. Once I let go and give it permission, I feel myself go there naturally.

Step three, step four. I follow the sound of Raymond's voice until his words lose focus, just as my vision does.

That's when I hear a hint of static, far away but moving closer, deeper, louder, and, embedded in the chaotic sound, I can pick out a melody. It's *the* tune. Notes rising and falling. I hear a voice join in, and it's strong and clear, and it takes a while before I realize that it's my own voice. The others are humming, too. There are words now with the song.

Our binding dance. The malignant music unfolding the terror.

I know that I haven't moved from Raymond's bedroom, but I also know that I'm somewhere else, somewhere I've never been before.

In.

Deep *in.*

But not alone.

In. With them. My others.

Their voices, the swirl of their hair against my arms, legs, and face.

I need them. We need each other.

To do what we were born to do. To move things to our will. To punish. To control.

My hair. It has come undone, the strands twisting with other hair, twisting with our voices, with the music, to create an inescapable net.

We trap the target.

We spin him with confusion and delirium.

We never touch. We never push.

And yet . . .

And yet . . .

Two words reach in and yank me back to the surface of somewhere.

Out.

Raymond's bedroom. I touch my hair, surprised to find it still clipped back and braided, tight against my scalp, under control.

The two words are "Holy crappola!" and Raymond is yelling them over and over. "Holy crappola! Look at this. The ant is going nuts."

We lean in and watch the bug. It runs left, stops short,

then runs right. Then it begins moving in tighter and tighter circles, as if all its instincts have been short-circuited.

"So it's true," I say.

"I'm convinced. I've seen enough." Stephanie hugs the stuffed animal to her chest. I know she's feeling badly about the ant, but there's also a conflicted look on her face. She's fighting it, but it's winning. Like me, like Alix, she's proud of what we just did. And I know that also like me, she's wondering what else we can do. And to whom? How far can this thing go?

Alix slams her palm on the table, crushing the ant, putting it out of its misery.

Raymond tunes up his violin. His slack jaw and dim eyes tell me that he's slipped into deep concentration. He plays the tune that he heard the three of us singing. The nine notes played twelve times, the malignant music, the binding dance.

Nine notes in their binding song. Nine notes repeated twelve times. One hundred and eight in the melody. Three digits—108—that add up to 9, the product of three 3s.

Divide 108 by 3 to get 36; 3 plus 6, another 9. Another 3 to that ordained third power.

I bow to the malicious music.

You are expecting your stasimon, the curtain down between acts, the promise of clarity and comment. And here I am, your guide, going off on wild, arithmetic tangents.

What I want to say is this: I sure know how to pick 'em. Don't you adore those three lovely, ugly girls? I do.

How quickly they learn. I'm thrilled to see the light come on behind their eyes as they begin to understand their capabilities. The way they got into that ant's brain, twisted and tweaked it. They taught it a lesson: There is no escape from the terrors of the mind. Brava!

Let me reiterate where we stand at this point in time. And yes, it is only a matter of time.

Alix. Alecto. I hardly have to tempt her. Her fury has been so fine-tuned by others for so long. I ought to send her parents—and her parents' parents and even her parents' parents' parents—fruit baskets for instilling in her so much animosity toward humankind.

And Stephanie, Tisiphone, sheer delight. We can thank so many for shooting down her earnest, peaceful attempts to bring about change. She's a product of the whole world with its endless greed, materialism, lies, and unabashed self-interest. The warlords and presidents of countries; the lying media and corrupt priests; the insatiable real estate developers and corporate polluters; the autocrats, plutocrats, and bureaucrats; the fascists, communists, and every other ist—*there's no end to those who deserve my utmost and sincere thanks for creating Tisiphone. I could give them all hugs.*

Which brings me to Megaera—quiet, still-developing Meg—with the potential to have the most fury of all. Abused by both individual and society, cast aside by parent and the system's so-called parent substitute. Look what the human race is doing to her.

She is my third, the one I have been waiting for.

But she's got this one blessing—a curse, in my view—that she manages to keep things in perspective. Damn her open heart and mind. Damn her optimism, the way it dilutes her well-deserved anger. I must get those moccasins off her feet, not allow her to walk the proverbial mile in someone else's shoes.

I must keep her away from that meddlesome goddess of justice disguised in teacher's clothing. You know who I mean.

Plus there's her little friend, Raymond. He's a question

*mark. Will I have to do something to keep that interfering ray of
light from fiddling sunshine notes into her ear?*

*Three plus one is four, and four is not an acceptable number.
Never four. Never two. It's always three.*

SECOND STASIMON, THE BOOK OF FURIOUS

With one less ant in the world, we leave Raymond's house. Alix, Stephanie, and I decide to walk the long way home through downtown. We could talk for the next month non-stop and not get everything said and sorted out. *What happened? What exactly did we do to the ant? How did we do it? Can we do it again? Can we do it any time we want? Whom can we do it to?* We need so many answers and I'm not even sure we have the right questions.

I zip my hoodie and shove my hands into the pockets. It's not raining for once and it feels more like the usual October weather in this part of California, warm in the day but chilly as soon as the sun sets. Alix takes a black knitted watch cap—basic headgear for surfers—out of the back pocket of her baggy, low-slung jeans and pulls it hard over her ears. Stephanie buttons up her cardigan, which is worn thin at the elbows. Between the bells on her belt and the metal beads threaded into her dreadlocks, she makes music as she walks. She's dominating the conversation.

"Let's each pick our top candidate, the number one

person who deserves a lesson from us. Can we call what we do a lesson? *Lesson* sounds so professional. I'll start." Pause. "It was in the news today. There's this coal company in West Virginia that thinks the Clean Water Act doesn't apply to it. The boss dumps chemicals into the town water supply. And that gives people cancer and kidney damage. Little kids get open wounds, just from taking baths. I'll show you the pictures. They're awful."

It's a big joke at school how easy it is to make Stephanie cry. Mention a toxic spill or an endangered species halfway around the world, and boo-hoo-hoo. I overheard the Double Ds in the bathroom say that they think it's all a big phony act, and that Stephanie only pretends to be oh so sensitive because it's the only way a geek like her can get any attention. They *would* say something cruel and shallow like that. Stephanie sniffs, and even though I'm not looking at her directly, I know there are tears.

"You really feel for those people, don't you?" I ask.

She stops so suddenly that we almost collide, and she puts herself right in my face. "How can you *not* care? How can anyone *not* feel?" She starts walking again, picking up the pace. Alix and I take giant steps to keep up with her. "What can someone our age do about it? About anything? Write letters? Hold a fund-raiser bake sale? Make speeches in class that everyone makes fun of? Try to tell the truth in a blog that nobody reads? I can't even vote. I have no power. There's nothing I can do."

"Until now," Alix says.

Stephanie perks up, remembers. "That's right. Now I finally have power."

"*We* have power," Alix emphasizes.

"Power that we can use to undo the injustices in the world. To make things right and fair."

"Right for us, too," Alix points out.

We turn the corner and get hit by a mind-blowing sight. The moon. It's low on the horizon but full and huge, vibrating white and sharp around the edges. It's like a cutout moon taking up a whole section of dark construction-paper sky. I stare at it with awe. Stephanie asks Alix whom she would put first on her list to teach a lesson. Alix mumbles a name.

"You want to punish someone named Simon?" I ask.

She turns on me so fast that I stumble backward. She shouts in my face, the Ps popping. "Not punish *him*! Punish anyone who lays a finger on him, anyone who gives him any shit or takes advantage when I'm not around to stand up for him."

Stephanie unclips her stainless-steel water bottle from the side of her backpack, takes a drink. "Who's Simon?"

"My brother. He's nineteen, but he's like a little brother. He's . . . um, retarded."

A disapproving groan from Stephanie. "Alix, the word *retarded* is a derogatory term. You mean developmentally different."

"Whatever. I'll tell you who's *different*. The rest of the world. Simon's awesome. Except for how dumb people treat him."

Stephanie passes her the water bottle, and as I watch Alix throw back her head and guzzle, I realize that even though she's not afraid to hurl herself into fifteen-foot waves, even though she's got a scary reputation for not putting up with anything from anyone, when it comes to her brother—and other things that I don't know about yet—Alix feels helpless and frustrated, too.

With the moon rising, we begin the descent down Laurel Street, a steep hill treasured by the town's radical skateboarders that brings us into the downtown area. It's past rush hour, so traffic has slowed a little, but there are still plenty of people on the streets. That's when I notice something. We're on everyone's radar. I'm not used to that. It's subtle at first. For example, a middle-aged mom type stares at me with a puzzled look, like she can't place where she knows me from and it's going to drive her nuts until she figures it out. Then two girls in their twenties stop an intense conversation and drop their eyes when they pass us. A group of loud, obnoxious middle-school skateboarders go mute and step aside respectfully so we can pass through the center of them. All this could be coincidence. It could mean nothing.

But then, get this: a bald guy carrying a briefcase almost trips over the curb, that's how hard he's gawking at us. And what about the little girl throwing a fit in front of the Cookie Company because her mom won't buy her a chocolate chip one? It's like someone flips the Off switch on her. Suddenly she's Little Miss Manners, holding her mom's hand and giving us a look that says *I'll be good. Promise.* And the cop who stops traffic to let us cross against the red light. And the homeless guy sitting on the corner who usually never says anything to anyone, never even makes eye contact. When we pass he stands up, salutes, and bows from the waist. And then . . .

Just ahead on the corner, I spot him. Brendon. A curl of

his dark hair twists over one eye. He brushes it back with a hand. I've become a little fixated on this frequent gesture of his, because when he does it there's a moment when he's unguarded and I catch a glimpse of that other Brendon that I want to believe exists. A Brendon who isn't like all his vile friends. A Brendon who will see something special in me. A Brendon I don't have to hate. When he brushes aside his hair it's like a curtain going up, but then it quickly comes back down.

At the same corner I also spot the big wall of Pox standing next to Brendon. On the other side of him, chugging from a giant-sized plastic bottle of soda, is blond, buzz-cut Gnat, who is half Pox's height and weight but twice as hyper and just as mean.

It's too late to cross to the opposite side of the street. There's no way of avoiding them. All that power that had been surging through me? I feel it draining away, and the feeling is so strong and real that I glance to the ground, almost expecting to see a puddle of something on the concrete.

Why did we walk this way? Why do we have to deal with them? Why didn't I do something with my hair before we left Raymond's?

Gnat spots us first, lets loose with a big fart as soon as we're close. "Why do my farts stink?" he asks no one in particular. "So deaf people can enjoy 'em, too."

The light is red, so we're forced to stand there as Gnat chokes with hysterical laughter at his own lame joke. Pox then makes a big show of crumpling an empty Cheetos bag and tossing it on the ground. Bait for Stephanie. *Don't take it,* I plead silently. *Don't lecture him about the sin of littering.*

She mutters disapproval. He puts his hand to his ear, egging her on to scold him aloud so he can make fun of her even more. Radiating silent tension, she picks up the bag and lobs it into the nearby garbage can.

"Two points for the cousin of the monkey," Pox says.

More Stephanie bait, and this time she takes the whole thing. "Pox, we're all descended from monkeys. And considering your intelligence, it's the monkeys who should be insulted by the relationship."

Pox pounds his fists on his chest, Tarzan-style. "Not me, monkey girl. I'm human and humans rule. Top of the food chain. Survival of the fittest."

Stephanie's bells jingle in frustration. "Are you a complete moron, Pox? How can you quote Darwin—survival of the fittest—and not understand evolution?"

"Evolution sucks." As usual, Pox doesn't let facts get in the way of his beliefs. "Humans are the alpha dog." He launches into an exaggerated bodybuilder routine, flexing his biceps and triceps, thrusting a hip, bouncing his tilted pelvis.

Meanwhile I'm doing everything I can to sneak peeks at Brendon and not get caught doing it. I'm fixated on him, I admit it. He's wearing faded jeans and a brown-and-beige plaid flannel shirt, the top three buttons undone so I can make out the shape of his collarbones and the hollow between them. I sense him maybe looking at me, so I quickly inspect my feet. I study my hands. I turn my attention to the sky, but just my luck, I glance back right when Pox happens to swing around in my direction. My eyes land directly on the zipper of his jeans, and that's all he needs to target me as his next victim.

A knowing smirk. I want to punch that smirk right off his face. He puckers his mouth and makes a loud smacking noise at me. It's like his lips are moving in slow motion, which should give me plenty of time to look away in irritation. But I don't. I am so lame. I can't. I'm stuck on Pause, and I'm fully aware that Brendon is taking all of this in.

What if he thinks that I actually have the hots for Pox, who is now wagging his tongue at me, heavy-metal style? It's wide and coated with bright, Cheeto-colored orange. Gross. He steps closer to whisper in my ear. "Tired of hanging around with Gay Ray? Want a taste of the alpha male?"

Brendon then, to my amazement, steps between us and puts a hand on Pox's big, square shoulder. "Hey dude," he says. "Lay off a little. She's not . . ."

She's not . . . I'm not . . . what? What does this mean? Is Brendon standing up for me? Why would Brendon stand up for me?

These questions and thinking of all the possible answers make my cheeks explode with heat. I want to pound the traitorous things, but that would only make them more pink.

For a second Pox looks at Brendon, puzzled, and then glares at the hand on his shoulder like it's a mortal threat. But his sharp, warning look disappears as soon as Brendon finishes his sentence. "Dude, she's not . . . worth the energy."

Pox scans me head to feet and dismisses what he sees with a shrug of boredom. "Yeah, yeah, right. Bigger fish to fry."

I feel like a scrawny minnow, no good to anyone, thrown back into the ocean.

Why won't the traffic light turn? What's wrong with the light? The red finally changes, but only to a green arrow, so we're still trapped while a long line of cars makes left turns. But at least some other people are gathered at the corner now, and I'm grateful for that. Regular, normal people, grown-ups, a mom with a baby. Surely this crowd will keep Pox in check. In another minute we can cross and it will all be over.

Pox starts humming something, like a jingle, and drifts to the back of the small group, maneuvering until he's right behind Alix and practically singing into her ear. The humming turns to a song. I'm close enough to make out some words. It's a nursery rhyme.

"Met a pieman going to the fair . . . let me taste your ware."

The light finally switches to green and I tug on Alix's arm. "Come on, Alix! Ignore him," I practically beg, but I know it's pointless. She's not going anywhere. She doesn't even hear me. Her anger at Pox has shut down her ears, her eyes, her brain. All the regular people cross the street. That leaves the six of us and we drift into a semicircle.

Alix, her chin jutting: "What did you say, asshole?"

He puffs out his chest. "You heard me."

"Say it again and I'll . . ."

"You'll what?"

He turns to his friends with a mocking tone. "She'll what?" He repeats the rhyme, taunting. "Simple Simon met a pieman going to the fair."

I sense Alix's body poised to spring forward, and I guess Brendon senses it, too, because he tries to maneuver Pox out of the way. But getting Pox to do something that's not his idea is like trying to move a bear.

"Leave it be," Brendon urges. "Why get into it with some girl over nothing?"

"Go on, beat it. You too, Gnat. This is between her and me."

Brendon hesitates, still trying to figure out a way to defuse the situation. I'm grateful to him for that, but it's no use. When the light turns green again, he crosses the street with Gnat reluctantly following.

That's all the time we need. That's our cue. I feel Alix's anger drawing me to her. It sucks me in and feeds my own. We don't discuss the next step, or even make eye contact with each other. Our agreement is wordless and without thought, beyond the usual ways of communicating. We don't think, we just do. The three of us surround him and cut him off from the curb. We edge in, guiding him backward until his back presses flat against the bricks of a building.

He throws up his palms. "What the hell are you doing? Am I gonna have to smack all of you? Don't push me."

Alix takes the lead. This is her injustice, her wrong to be righted. She hooks her elbow into the crook of my arm and Stephanie does the same on my other side. I am the center of the chain and I squeeze them close to me, feeling the pressure of Stephanie's long thighbone and Alix's solid hip. She sounds the first note. I join in on the second, Stephanie the third.

"Singing? What the hell? Why are you singing?" Pox asks.

That's the last we hear of his repulsive voice. After that

it's nine notes, *our* notes, the amazing melody repeating itself. We're in perfect harmony. We're . . . in.

In.

I embody the true meaning of that simple preposition, two letters that are the source of all our power. This is what we do and how we do it. We are in his head. Dark and light and color and colorless and flashes of storm.

We know the direction to take, as if we've been handed a drawing of his brain that shows all the wiring.

We override his thoughts, reroute his feelings, hijack his emotions.

From our fingertips we shoot him full of regret.

He covers his ears, but he can't drown out the voices.

With our combined breath we pump him full of guilt.

We punish him by making sure he punishes himself, the worst sentence of all.

He shakes his head, but he can't shake off the knowledge of his own wrongs.

We use the strands of our wild hair to cross the wires of his thinking and shock him into seeing his true, hateful self.

We sing.

He moans.

He's lost and we're found.

One hundred and eight notes, and then we feel satisfied. We've done our job. It's over.

A final shiver returns me to the ordinary world. I shake my head a couple of times to clear it. Everything is the way it was before—a full moon, a busy downtown, a traffic light that's green again. A small crowd has gathered and they applaud politely. We must have sounded pretty awesome. A little girl, coaxed by her mom, lays a couple of quarters at our feet.

"That's different music," a man says, scratching behind his ear. "Can't say whether I like it or not." Some college kid asks: "You guys got a CD for sale?"

"Show's over!" Alix announces. They see she's not messing around, and everyone scatters.

Not everyone.

At a downtown corner on a perfectly ordinary October evening, Kai "Pox" Small, death-defying big-wave rider, major hypocrite, unapologetic insensitive sexist pig, stands with his shoulders caved in. He blinks several times, trying to get his bearings. He's sweating through his T-shirt. He takes a step toward Alix, who throws up her fists in defense.

Only there's no need for that because he bows his head and lets his arms dangle slack at his sides. "Alix, slug me, go ahead. I deserve it."

At this point, Gnat—without Brendon, I note with disappointment—returns to collect his fearless leader. He assumes the apology he just overheard is some big joke. Only when he starts yucking it up, Pox whirls on him, tells him to "shut the hell up and apologize, too."

"Dude!" Gnat snaps. Then, puzzled: "Dude?" With a swirl to us: "What the fuck did you do to him? Something! You did something."

Pox ignores his friend and continues to apologize, peering earnestly into Alix's face. He runs his fingers through his hair, practically tears at it. "I'm such a jerk. I can't believe I made fun of some retard kid. Your brother."

"Not retard! Don't call him that. Developmentally . . ."

Alix checks with Stephanie, who nods in confirmation. "Different."

"Don't hate me, okay?" Pox is pleading, and in his open expression I see what he must have looked like as a little kid, the first time he got caught being naughty and couldn't live with the shame and guilt. "Forgive me?"

Together, the three of us answer as one: "Maybe."

I wonder how long this new Pox will last. An hour? A day? A week? Could it be forever?

The light is red, but Alix, Stephanie, and I cross anyway. We don't even bother to check both ways. We know the cars will stop for us, and they do. No one even leans on a horn. It's our turn.

As we continue down the street, I take a long drink from Stephanie's water bottle. Being a Fury is dehydrating. When we pass an empty store window, I catch a glimpse of our reflections in the dusty, warped glass. We are three figures attached at the shoulders, stretched, distorted, and unrecognizable.

I wake the next morning after ten hours of dreamless sleep and remember again with wonder everything that happened yesterday. The song, joining with the others, the ant, the anger, the power, Pox groveling at our feet.

It's true, then.

I'm not who I think I am. I'm not who I used to be. All my life, I've been waiting, listening, hoping to find this *thing*—some special talent, something unique—that tells me why I am me and not someone else, why I was born, why my life hasn't been like everyone else's, and what I'm supposed to be doing with that life. Now I've gotten exactly what I wished for. True personal discovery. This is forcing me to reconsider everything I think I know about myself, every assumption of who I am and where I came from and what my future will look like. I no longer have to be secretly terrified that there is nothing special brewing inside of me and that my life will never, ever change.

I can change. I have already changed. Life has changed. I have a special purpose, a destiny. There's no doubt about it. I'm Megaera, a Fury. This is the new normal.

Don't you think a personal revelation of this magnitude deserves a day off from school?

It does, doesn't it? This tops a fever. I should get to turn in a note that says: *Please excuse Meg for the day because she needs to contemplate the idea that she is the reincarnation of a mythical being, quite possibly capable of ridding the world of wrongdoing and injustice.*

But no such luck. While I am lolling around in bed with He-Cat curled at my feet, my phone vibrates with a text from Ambrosia, like she can read my mind. Come to think of it, maybe she can: *No cutting today!*

Right after that, a similar message from Raymond, another mind reader, pops up on my phone: *Up and "Atom," my powerful friend.*

They're right. There's so much to figure out and so much to do. With a sense of purpose that I've never felt before, I perform my usual morning rituals: tooth-brushing and face-washing, backpack-loading and cat-feeding. It's sweet the way He-Cat follows me everywhere now. I pick him up, and as I stroke his fur and listen to his grateful purr I wonder if people will immediately sense the enormous change in me. I feel so different. How can the world not recognize it? When I enter the kitchen a few minutes later, I take special satisfaction when the Leech doesn't immediately order me to rub her gross feet or clean the dishes. She's studying me with a perplexed expression.

"What?" I ask, certain that I have a new, un-ignorable Fury glow.

"Did you do something different with your hair, Meg? You look . . . You seem more . . ." She fumbles for the right word. In my mind, I provide several that I've always wanted to hear attached to my name. How about poised? Self-assured? Positive, confident, endowed with a whole new set of amazing, superhuman mental powers?

"Taller," she finally says. "That's it. You probably grew a whole inch lately. Don't you dare think that means I'm gonna buy you any new clothes. Am I made out of money? You're going to have to make do with the ones you already have."

So much for my glowing radiance. It's more than my height that's changed. How can she not see it? This isn't about a stupid inch; it's about ten thousand million megawatts of power that I don't fully understand yet. I want her to notice, and I'm annoyed that she doesn't. I have courage this morning, a hangover from yesterday, and that stops me from pushing down my anger the way I usually would. I put a sarcastic edge on my voice. "Did I grow, Lottie?"

Her head snaps around at the unfamiliar challenge in my tone.

It feels good, *so* good, to confront her this way. "What else have you noticed, Lottie?"

Her lids flutter, like something sharp and painful flew into her eyes, and I think for a moment it's because she's finally getting a glimpse of the new me. But then her features bunch tight in the center of her face as she reaches for the closest object, a ceramic pitcher, and hurls it in my direction. I duck. He-Cat springs out of my arms and pottery shatters on the wall behind me.

Everything *has* changed. But in the reality of my life, where my life must be lived every day, everything is still exactly the same.

For now.

Before I leave the house, the new me, the powerful me, the furious avenger me, is on her hands and knees silently picking up every little sliver.

Most people who find out their best friend is part of an ancient trio that possesses the incomparable and penetrating power to get inside the minds of wrongdoers in order to make the world a more just and fair universe for all would probably have a real solo pity party. I know I would. I'd try to be excited for my friend and make a big fuss. I'd say something like "Awesome!" and hope it passed for sincerity. But in private I'd lock my bedroom door, throw myself on the bed, and start moaning, *Why don't I get to be a Fury, too?*

Not Raymond, though. That's another way that he's different from me and from most people I've met in life. He doesn't seem to have dark, jealous, resentful thoughts like that. On our way to school, when Stephanie, Alix, and I jump all over each other's words to tell him about what happened downtown and what we did to Pox, he is genuinely thrilled about our new powers.

"But you are pissed off not to be one of us, right?" Alix asks.

"Jealous?" Stephanie tries. "Just a little?"

Raymond's response? Totally supportive, but not in a syrupy and gushy way. That would be creepy. "Meg, here, she's definitely ready for a power upgrade. It's long overdue. But personally, I like me the way I am: busy with my violin and contemplating a long, brilliant career in law, perhaps. Or music. No change necessary. What I lack in—"

I slide my finger across my throat, the universal cease-and-desist sign, which makes Raymond laugh. That's another example of what I mean. He's able to laugh at himself instead of taking offense like most people do. We're halfway across the school lawn when his laugh turns into a nervous titter. He points out that a large, square human being is rushing our way at full speed.

Pox.

Alix widens her stance, a linebacker ready to take a hit. Stephanie, fists bunched, moves to her side for backup. I try to determine if Pox has anything in his hands, such as a newly sharpened meat cleaver. He is holding on to something. A plastic bag. It's definitely big enough to hold a cleaver. I look around anxiously. Where is school security when you actually need it?

"Hey guys!"

Well, he looks like Pox, he smells like Pox, but he sure isn't acting like Pox. Not the old nasty Pox who would never in a billion years say "Hey guys!" with an open, eager, and uncertain smile plastered on face. His eyes are also blood-shot, and his skin is flushed but pale underneath the high color, like he didn't sleep at all the night before but still got up and ran for miles. He positions himself in front of Alix and thrusts the plastic bag in her direction.

She's suspicious. She stares at it without touching. I can't blame her. Anything could have happened overnight. The old Pox lives to torture on land and sea, so this could be one of his sick tricks and he's faking this cheery nature and the bag contains a big load of dog crap. I wouldn't put that past him. Maybe our magic or our spell or our lesson—whatever you call what we did—lasts no longer than a typical change of heart. I see that all the time. Someone feels terrible about something they did and they vow never to do it again, but then break their own resolution the next day. That kind of thing happens every January 2.

"What's in it?" Alix asks, still hands-off.

Pox assures her. "It's okay. Peace offering. Go ahead. Take it. It's for Simon."

"You stick your face into it first," she orders, and he does. Then she looks, too, and emerges with a half smile. "What is it?"

Pox, perky as a five-year-old girl at her own birthday party, pulls out a gadget still in the plastic shrink wrap. "It's a Six-in-One Outdoor Survival Mini Kit." He ticks off each item on a finger. "Whistle, compass, magnifier, flashlight, thermometer, and something else. I had one just like it when I was a Cub Scout."

Alix smirks. "You were a Cub Scout."

Pox looks sheepish. "Yeah, until I got kicked out for my bad attitude." Pox, eager to please: "Do you think Simon will like it?"

"It's cool. He'll go totally nuts over it."

"Nuts! That's great!"

The warning bell for first period rings. We start walking across the lawn toward the front entrance, Pox in front facing us, moving backward, practically skipping. "So Alix, anything else Simon might like? I can't stop thinking about what a jerk I am. I couldn't sleep last night."

I get an idea and tell everyone to hold up a minute. "Pox, there's something else you should do."

"Of course!" he gushes. "Anything."

I motion to my left. "You should apologize to Raymond for . . . for what, Raymond?"

The look on my best friend's face shifts from detached amusement to personal interest. Raymond has done so much for me; this is my chance to finally do something for him. He deserves it. He's described some of the awful stuff Pox did to him starting in middle school. Raymond tries to make it sound like it wasn't that big of a deal. He can turn anything into a joke. But I know that he downplays just how bad it got. I picture a younger version of Raymond—still Raymond, but even more trusting and not as sure of himself, Raymond before he learned not to care what other people thought about him. Pox must have made his life hell back then.

"There are so many grievous insults in our shared history together," Raymond begins. He motions Pox to his side, like he's calling a disobedient puppy, and that's how Pox responds, shamed and repentant, with an invisible tail tucked between his legs. "How about the time you pushed me into my locker and superglued it shut? When was that? Seventh grade?"

Pox winces at the reminder. "Gee, Raymond. Super-glue. That was a super jerky thing to do. Will you accept my apology?"

Raymond puts his hands on his hips, exaggerating the stance of a disappointed teacher. "That was such a pedestrian act of bullying, definitely not your finest moment. I exonerate you for the prank, Pox, but not for your lack of imagination."

Pox turns to me, puzzled. "Did he accept?"

"Not quite." Raymond's features shift again, this time into something darker and more serious. His voice no longer has its playful, sarcastic edge. "Pox, it's not only me you tortured. I got over your bullying. I figured out how not to let it hurt me. But there are other kids, kids who never get over it and walk around ashamed of who they are, and they have no reason to be ashamed. They hate themselves. Because of you. That's who you need to apologize to."

I think I see tears forming in the corners of Pox's eyes. His chin drops to his chest.

"Start with the gay kids. And then the kids you call homo or faggot even if they aren't gay. And the short guys. And the flat-chested girls. And the handicapped kids. And the Danish foreign exchange student. And the geeks and the freaks and the Mexican—"

"And you, Meg!" Pox adds. "What I said about you and your family. I'm an asshole." He bangs his forehead with his palm. "Asshole! I will apologize. I will! I won't miss anyone. Promise. And after that, Raymond, will you forgive me?"

When Raymond nods, Pox lets out a big puff of air. "It's gonna feel great to get this off my chest."

The late bell rings, so we make a mad dash to get to first period just in time. Raymond slides into the seat next to me. "That was my dream come true. How many times did I rehearse that conversation in my head?"

"A million?"

"It was even better than I imagined. Thank you, Meg."

I raise my fists over my head, like I'm Winner and Still Champion. "You're very welcome, Raymond."

In Western Civ, Ms. Pallas gives us the first half of class to work on our projects, so Stephanie, Raymond, Ambrosia, and I drag our chairs to Alix's spot in the back of the room. It's a wasteland back there, which is perfect. We don't want anyone overhearing our conversation. This is a prime opportunity to talk about our cosmic destiny.

I can tell that Raymond has something important on his mind. He laces his fingers together. Is he growing a little mustache? No, it's just a smudge of ink on his upper lip. I point it out and he wipes it away.

"The fact is," he says, "I do see a place for myself in this turn of events."

Alix, smug: "Knew it! You want in. You're jealous."

"This is more of an offer. An exclusive offer of myself. Every power trio needs a manager."

At the mention of a manager, I check Ambrosia's reaction. Today her dark hair cascades over her head and ends in a long braid that lies against the front of her coal-black sweater like a hibernating snake. She must have added some highlights, because there's a definitely flash of auburn when she flips that braid so hard that it slaps Raymond on his cheek. I'm not surprised to see irritation bloom across her features. Raymond is pushing it. If anyone should be our manager, it should be Ambrosia. She's the one who recognized us and called us together. Without her FAQs and exercises, we wouldn't have gotten started.

Raymond, though, has an amazing ability to ignore glares of animosity. He slaps the back of his hand into his open palm. It's a gesture he must have seen in an old movie, a salesman offering the deal of the century. "My services come to you totally pro bono."

"Pro what?" Alix asks.

"Free. Out of the *goodness* of his *heart*." Ambrosia does something with her voice that makes the word *goodness* sound distasteful and dirty. The word *heart* sounds even more revolting. "What pro bono service could *you* have that could possibly be of any benefit to *them*?"

Raymond makes another offer-you-can't-refuse slap. "My dear friends, a manager would remember that today, third period, this very instant, our project description and outline are due."

"Shit." Alix pounds her desk. "I need to pass this class to graduate."

Raymond gives her a *there, there* pat on the shoulder. He opens his backpack and pulls out a stack of papers. "Four pages, six copies, meticulously researched, facts from multiple sources, spell-checked and collated."

"No argument from me," Stephanie says. "You're hired."

Raymond makes a seated bow. "At your service. Please note my usual obsessive-compulsive's delight with thoroughness and order. I also narrowed down our topic. Is everyone okay with it?"

I take my copy of the outline and pass the others along, noting how Ambrosia reads each page slowly, every word. She's trying to find fault with it. When she's done, she pronounces the title aloud: " 'The Furies—Eye for an Eye in the Ancient World.' I have to admit that despite my initial skepticism, I'm pleasantly surprised. I'm *very* okay with this."

Since Raymond did all the work, it makes sense for him to present our outline to the rest of the class during the second half of the period. Our group is scheduled second, right after the Double Ds giggle their way through their presentation, titled "Glam Makeup Ideas That We Got from the Egyptians."

"So, to sum up," DeeDee says, "there was Cleopatra with her hoochie-momma eyes and flawless skin. How did she and other ancient hotties get their unique look? Makeup, of course, and most of it was made out of lead and arsenic."

"Totally toxic," Dawn adds.

"Fantastic colors! And it only did minor damage to the nervous system."

"Unless you were stupid enough to eat some, and then it killed you."

"So that's our thesis. Very often in this world, you have to suffer for beauty, and it's worth it. A message from the past . . ."

". . . that rings totally true today."

The twins are clearly psyched about their topic, and Ms. Pallas agrees that it's the perfect subject for them, "though you should adjust the thesis a little," she suggests. They collect compliments in the form of air kisses from their friends on their way back to their seats.

Raymond is up next. He hands a copy of the outline to

Ms. Pallas and then spins quickly on his toes, Michael Jackson–style, to face the class.

"In the beginning, before Greece was even ancient, there was the Father. This was a very bad father who hated all of his children. True, the kids were total monsters. Literally. There was the one-eyed flesh-devouring giant and the towering creature with a hundred hands and fifty heads. But hey, kids are kids and family is family. He brought them into the world, monsters or not. Yet this father—this Father Heaven, aka Uranus—hated his offspring so much that he imprisoned them in a secret place in the very bowels of the earth. Only one of his kids—the Titan Cronus—had the cojones to stand up to him."

The room is silent, riveted. No one makes a crack about Raymond using *bowels* and *cojones*. No one even whispers *Your Anus*, the sixth-grade alternative pronunciation for Uranus that high school kids still find hilarious. That's how well he's telling the myth.

"After eons of this shameless child abuse, on a fateful day that will live in infamy, Cronus waited in secret for his abusive, deadbeat dad. With a chop-chop of his mighty sword, he hit below the belt and castrated Uranus. Then Cronus threw his father's entire mutilated package of genitalia into the churning, swirling sea."

"Ouch!" someone says.

"No kidding," Raymond continues. "The wound, as you can imagine, was terrible. When the blood hit the water it created a mighty trio, conjured them right out of Father Heaven's pain, blood, and desire for revenge. The Furies, aka Creatures of Darkness. Aka Sisters of the Night. Aka the Erinyes. They have writhing snakes for hair and eyes that weep tears of blood. Their job is pursuing and punishing sinners, avenging the innocent, and taking care of injustice."

Ms. Pallas, I can't help but notice, cringes at the description, actually shudders in distaste when Raymond mentions the name, the Furies. She's seated at her desk, and even though it's dingy inside and outside the room, she seems to be splashed in a pool of light, the strands of her thick crown of hair giving off sparks of it. I glance around for a source of the light. There's nothing external. It's an internal glow, which tells me something important: My instincts are right. Our teacher has something to do with what's going on. I can no longer ignore that. She knows. She probably knows everything. She's part of this somehow. She's no more *just* a teacher than I'm *just* another student and Ambrosia is *just* another girl. Ms. Pallas—if that's even her real name—has a crucial role in all of this—whatever *this* is.

Her voice, when she finally speaks, seems to come out of the light, rather than from the throat and mouth of a normal human being. It vibrates with barely contained anger, and everyone in the room shifts uncomfortably in their seats.

"Those Furies had the gall, the unbridled audacity, to take up residence in the sacred temple of a goddess. I don't care who they were after, or what their target supposedly did. How dare they? A goddess's space is a sanctuary, a shrine of light, no place for the dark ugliness of revenge."

I thought I'd gotten used to Ms. Pallas's intensity, but this takes teacher pontificating to a whole new level. A layer of nervous sweat pops out on my forehead and in my armpits.

Ms. Pallas places her hand on a copy of the Aeschylus plays, hard, like the book is alive and dangerous, a vicious animal that requires all of her strength to keep it down and in its place. She closes her eyes. She recites, like she's soaking up the passage through her fingertips:

"'Monsters, who lap the blood of live men's bodies, this temple is no place for such as ye. But there where criminals are slain or mutilated is meet abode, and the feast ye love, ye loathsome goddesses.'"

In the unnerving silence that follows, I hear my breathing quicken. Her eyes pop open, her voice demands an answer: "Raymond, how do we get rid of these Furies?"

Flustered in a way that I've never seen Raymond flustered, he runs his finger down his outline, flips some pages. "As far as I can tell . . ."

"Go on," she orders.

". . . as long as there's unfairness and injustice happening in the world, they can never be driven away, not like other monsters."

"Never?" someone blurts out. It takes me a second to realize that this someone is Brendon, whose voice sounds dry and slightly strangled.

"That seems to be the situation." Raymond is still hesitant, so unlike him. "They go to sleep for long periods of time, until a powerful person who has been wronged summons them again. Conditions need to be perfect, the stars in alignment, the Furies ripe to go, that kind of thing." He turns to Ms. Pallas. "Did I get it right?"

It's Ambrosia who responds without being called on. Her tone manages to combine reassurance and threat. "Don't fret, everyone. There's nothing to fear from the Furies if you behave yourself. You're perfectly safe if you don't act stupid and get in their way."

One of the Double Ds giggles nervously, but it quickly dries up.

Brendon's arm is in the air again. I study his profile, which is still and solemn, unreadable. He directs his question to Raymond: "You called them monsters, right? Creatures of darkness?"

Raymond nods.

"But you also describe them like they're heroes? They avenge the innocent and combat injustice. How can these Furies be both monsters and do-gooders?"

Raymond's face empties with the question, and it makes me wonder, too. Why are we called loathsome goddesses when we are doing what's right? Why so much talk of blood and snakes and tears when we are standing up for the innocent? I know that artists have sometimes portrayed us as beautiful, but more often we are shown as vicious hags. Why so hideous and loathsome if we're on the side of fairness? Why did the goddess want to banish the Furies from her temple? Why are we hated so much?

I see Raymond thinking hard, and I know him well enough to know that he's stumped, too, lost in the same questions I am.

Ms. Pallas's voice, sharp and penetrating, snaps him out of the reverie. She fires her own set of questions. "What is punishment? What is revenge? Who has the right to determine what is just and fair? Who decides when justice has been served? Well, Raymond? What happens when an eye for an eye goes on and on unchecked?"

"I don't—"

"Take it to the conclusion! Everyone winds up blind. The Furies can be called up. But then what? Who can put them back to sleep?"

The light around Ms. Pallas flickers before fading out, casting her into shadow. "You're only at the beginning of your research. This is what Raymond"—she aims a stern look at the rest of our group—"what all of you have to figure out. You have your work cut out for you. Don't take it lightly."

"We're up for any challenge," Ambrosia says. "We aim for the highest grade."

"I've no doubt that you do." Ms. Pallas rubs her temples, like she's fighting off a headache. Maybe she already has one.

"Agreed?" Raymond asks.

"Agreed," I say.

"All of you. No backsies?"

"Agreed! Wow, you're a pain," Stephanie complains. "For about the twenty-fifth time, we promise not to get carried away and overdo it. We promise to use our powers only for the good of mankind. That's what my whole life is about. You want us to sign a document?"

"In blood would be nice. With a clause about turning over your firstborn if you renege," he suggests.

"Raymond!" Stephanie puts her hands on her hips. She turns very preachy very fast. "I took a vow in ninth grade. I'm never having any children. You should take the same vow of nonprocreation. We all should. The world's overpopulated enough as it is."

Raymond gives a thumbs-up. "Stephanie, going for the literal! What you lack in a fine-tuned, subtle sense of humor, you make up for in unsmiling solemnity of earnest purpose."

"He's just being Raymond," I translate for Alix. "He was only joking about turning over our firstborn."

He pushes through the double doors and holds them open in a mock-gallant manner as we exit. We're more than ready to get out of school today. It was torture sitting through classes. Physics, trig, poetry, and all the rest suddenly seem like pointless busywork for little kids, given that we have real, substantial, grown-up work. The world is already much better with Pox in his place. We are ready to keep making a difference.

Ambrosia is last out the door, and Raymond lets it swing closed behind her. He goes on: "I'm just saying that Ms. Pallas has a point. Self-control is a good and noble quality."

Ambrosia huffs in annoyance. "Control? Pallas is the one who's a complete control freak, like most of those in a high position. Her kind doesn't like it when young people have minds of their own. People in power don't like sharing their power. She hates the competition."

Alix is in total agreement. "Yeah, Pallas does like things done her way. Teachers—most grown-ups—treat us like we only have half a brain and—"

Raymond tries interrupting. "They do have a somewhat valid point. Teenage frontal lobes aren't quite fully formed yet, and—"

Alix doesn't want to hear it. "They treat us like we can't be trusted. Like we don't know right from wrong. It's a pure power play . . ."

". . . designed to keep the new generation down," Stephanie finishes for her. "They want to keep the status quo."

Raymond again. "Far be it from me to discount—"

This time it's Ambrosia who cuts him off with "You can bow to Pallas if you want, but not me, not us."

"Who's bowing? I'm not bowing to anyone," Raymond protests.

"Good to hear that," she says, and flips her braid so that it hangs down her back almost to her tailbone. "Let's keep walking, then. Being a Fury is not a nine-to-five job. It's not for slackers. These girls have things to do, people to see."

Despite her rant about Ms. Pallas and the little snip at Raymond, Ambrosia is in a noticeably good mood this afternoon, and so am I. I'm happy to be out of school for the day and stretching my legs. I'm happy to be discovering new talents in myself. I'm happy to be surrounded by new friends. I'm happy that Raymond is so supportive. I'm happy that . . .

A rumble of thunder—rare in this part of California—rolls over above us. The first big splats of rain hit me on the head. I don't put up the hood of my rain jacket. I let the cool water soak into my hair. We run for the bus.

I'm happy that it's raining.

I'm happy that I know exactly where we're going right now.

I'm positively and completely happy.

The scenario that greets us: the Leech in the living room. The Pepto-Bismol pink of her housecoat clashes with the red plaid print of the couch. She reminds me of a big, rectangular bolt of fabric tossed randomly on top of another in a fabric store. She's chewing a big wad of gum. I see the others glancing around, taking it in. This is my home, and it's a depressing sight. The pink bolt speaks: "What the hell is this about?"

"Friends," I say. "We have . . ."

I have practiced for this moment in my mind. My friends have given me a pep talk, but I feel a familiar timidity taking the power out of my voice. I sense myself sliding back to the way I used to be, just yesterday. I flood with doubt. The whole thing is probably a bad idea. I could wind up just making things worse for myself. She's not so terrible. I can live with this. I want to give the Leech a last chance. Raymond nods with encouragement, and that's enough to help me get out the rest of the sentence. "We have some work to do, Mrs. Leach. Schoolwork."

With a moan she pushes herself to a seated position, fixes me like a bull's-eye in her sight. "Does this look like a library? Do I want a bunch of hoodlums hanging around here?"

"Hoodlum? Me?" Raymond asks. He sounds pleased by the idea.

I'm tingling with anticipation and my fingers are jiggling by my side and my leg vibrates, like I'm the lead singer of some overcaffeinated girl group that's standing in the wings about to perform in front of thousands. Only I'm not sure that I can go on. I'm not sure I have what it takes to be the leader.

He-Cat enters the room. He must have heard my voice and that was enough to overcome his dread of the Leech. When she hurls the remote control at him, any hesitation that's left in me evaporates. Poor thing is too slow. Hit, he meows in pain and outrage before scampering back to the safety of my bedroom.

The Leech is pleased with her aim. "Worthless!"

The cat. Me.

Ambrosia, by my left ear, doesn't even bother to whisper. "Justice delayed is justice denied."

Raymond is by my right ear. "Go for it. Just don't overdo it."

I suck in my breath, and for some reason the lyrics to an old Doors song rush through my mind: *The time to hesitate is through*. But it's a different first note that makes its way from deep in my belly, up my throat, and out through my lips. And another note and another and all my stage fright is gone like it never existed, and I'm singing and humming my way—our way—to the core of her.

To where she hides in lies and denial.

We turn loose her memories and force her to experience the hurts and sorrow that she's caused. She tries to retreat. We don't let go. She shivers. We shake the truth in her face. And as shame and regret for how she treats me and how she has treated others course through her, I experience the taste of something sweet and rich, like the first bite of food after you've been hungry for a long time.

Satisfaction. Justice served. It's wonderful.

I remember Raymond's warning. *Don't overdo it.*

This is enough. This is perfection.

I sound the last note to alert the others and lead them back out.

Here's what we return to: There's a couch. There's the

Leech in her pink housedress, and her eyes are big. "Please, please, Meg, can you forgive me? I want to change."

"A wise choice," Alix says.

"Things will be different. I promise. You have to believe me. What do you want?"

All eyes turn to me, Stephanie's elbow in my ribs as encouragement. The possibilities unfold. What do I want? I slide my gaze to her feet. "I don't want to ever touch those feet again. Ever."

The Leech scoots her feet under the edge of the couch to hide them. The move is so quick and compliant that I realize something: I could ask her to take a hatchet and whack them off at the ankles and she would happily turn her legs into bloody stumps and then perform a tap dance, if that's what I wanted. No questions asked.

Of course I would never suggest that, but I feel bolder now. Ambrosia urges me with her eyes to ask for more. She's right. I deserve more. Why stop?

"Never order me to do *anything*."

Alix and Stephanie exchange approving smiles.

I hesitate. Dare I? "I want a nicer room. I want clothes when I need them, even if I don't really, really need them!" I turn to the others. "I can ask for that, right?" I don't wait for an answer because I know what they would say. I'm on a roll now. One by one, I rattle off my demands:

"The money you get from foster care you spend on me."

"My friends can hang out here whenever they want."

"The way you talk to me? Be polite."

He-Cat wanders back in, and when I call him by name

he responds like he's a dog and rushes to my side. I pick him up. "Another thing—the best kibble that money can buy for He-Cat. No skimping."

The Leech actually takes notes, writing down my wishes on a piece of paper. He-Cat purrs, and I feel like purring, too. For so long I've been starved for justice, and now my appetite has been satisfied.

That is how we Furies spend Monday afternoon.

TUESDAY

We stand on the cliff as Alix paddles into the ocean to join the lineup of other surfers. With her mass of wild hair and a green-striped board, she's the most flamboyant one in the water. I'm not being biased because she's my fellow Fury. You can't keep your eyes off of her, the way she appears everywhere, cutting back and forth. Before she left land, Alix told us exactly what to watch for.

"It'll happen," she assured us. "Guaranteed. People never change."

"That's right," Ambrosia agreed. "Nobody will give you justice, Alix. You need to take it."

Stephanie points toward a wave that is building into a classic shape, large and rolling. The pack of surfers angles for position. Only one of them will be able to ride it, and it's an unspoken rule that the first surfer on the wave stays on and the others drop away.

I see the green board setting up, just as the lip of the wave begins its breaking curve. She's at the perfect spot to catch it. Alix's arms paddle hard and then she's up, she's standing. The way her hair flies behind her, dark as smoke, makes her look like a burning candle moving fast on a watery road.

But then, seemingly from out of nowhere, another surfer drops in directly in front of her and cuts back suddenly, a motion that takes her by surprise and sends her hurtling off her board.

Nasty. That was a mean, vicious, intentional move. She tumbles over the peak of the wave and is clobbered by a wall of churning white that comes down hard on her. She's tossed around like a rag doll.

For several moments we can't see anything, and then her board pops to the surface, but it's straight up and down, like a gravestone in the water, and we know that Alix is buried somewhere under it—who knows how deep?—connected to the surface only by the long leash around her ankle.

Raymond grips my arm and we wait, wait, wait, until finally her head emerges, her mouth open and gasping for air. I'm so relieved. We all are. She coughs and quickly gets her bearings. She's shook up. Only it was worth it. This is what she wanted us to see. The evidence. The culprit. The outrage to avenge. How many other times has this happened? She points to her right, stabbing her finger at the surfer who cut her off. Our target.

"Is that who I think it is?" Ambrosia asks.

The light's tricky, and under the tight wet suits everyone looks similar, all the bodies appear lean, strong, and muscled. Is it someone we know?

Ambrosia, her black hair ironed straight into a metallic

sheen today, moves to a different part of the railing. She drags her hand along the base of the surfer statue. She lets it linger there, closes her hand around the bronzed ankle as she studies the moving figure in the water. "Yes, of course it is. It would have to be one of that Plague crew. They're all like that. Every single one of them. Vicious backstabbers not to be trusted."

What if it's . . . a name passes through my mind, and I quickly dismiss it. It can't be him. Sure, he's part of the Plagues, but deep down he's not that sort of person. I know he's not. I don't know how I know, but I know. He wouldn't go out of his way to intentionally hurt Alix.

"I'm thinking," Ambrosia goes on, "that it's Brendon."

My heart pounds as I narrow my eyes and home in on more details. I don't want Ambrosia to be right. This figure has a bulky frame. Brendon is narrower than this. At least I think he is. I hope. Brendon also has lots of dark hair, and even if it were wet and slicked back, he wouldn't look like this surfer. I now recognize the eyes and the sneer on his lips as he paddles past Alix and flashes his middle finger in her direction.

It's not Brendon, definitely not! An embarrassing amount of relief whooshes through me, and I can't contain it.

"You're wrong, it's not Brendon!" I say with too much excitement. They look at me puzzled. "I mean, I know who it is. It's Bubonic."

"Oh," Ambrosia says with a dismissive glance into the water. "So it is. My mistake."

Stephanie waves at Alix, who again points at the surfer.

I feel her anger starting to filter through me, not just from today's injustice but from so many years of being cut off, bullied, harassed, hounded, and frustrated in the surf.

I'm ready when you are, Alix.

My vision goes dark for a heartbeat, and there's an explosion and the zillion pieces that emerge from it look like dust particles, rising and falling and swirling in a shaft of light. They're beautiful because they are pure fury and they have purpose. I follow them.

We sing. We unravel his defenses. We show Bubonic his own greed to give him the lesson that he deserves. This should have happened long ago.

When we're done, I shake myself out of an exhilarated daze and land back in the here and now. I squint past the glare on the water to see Alix, pleased, sitting up and straddling her board.

Bubonic on his board next to her folds his hands in prayer as he grovels for forgiveness.

A harbor seal, sleek and mottled gray and brown, breaks through the surface near them, its head like a bowling ball with whiskers bobbing in the surf. I see movement around its mouth. There's a struggling fish gripped between its sharp, pitiless teeth.

WEDNESDAY

In physics, two kids in our class—notorious grade grubbers who wreck every curve by getting As—rush to the front of the room and stun Mr. H by confessing that they cheated

on the last test. They have tears in their eyes. They beg forgiveness, saying they can't live a minute more with their
guilty consciences.

THURSDAY

The three of us link arms and walk down the hall against the
oncoming flow of students. We hum our song softly, work
lightly, and cast our power widely but gently, like tossing
wildflower seeds across a big meadow.

Each person we pass gets the same look on his or her
face, a bloom of shame. They're remembering some hurt
they caused—the time they ignored their grandma's birthday, how they talked trash behind a good friend's back, the
way they sneaked cash out of their parents' spare-change jar.
What a flurry of regret and guilt! Everyone's desperate to
apologize and get rid of the awful feelings.

FRIDAY

You know that mom who seems to be in every supermarket,
the one who yells at her kid, tells him to shut his mouth or
she'll give him something to wail about? And then she gives
him a big smack across the butt, and the little kid doesn't
know which is worse, the sting of the slap or the public
embarrassment.

You know that mom? You know how you always want
to do something to make her stop picking on her own kid?

We did something. She will never, ever hurt or humiliate anyone again.

SATURDAY

This is Stephanie's day to be in charge, and she's very deliberate in her choice of target. It turns out to be so rewarding that she writes a blog post about the incident. Of course she eliminates any mention of our role in the course of events. Raymond and I read over her shoulder as she types her newest post.

Green from Tenth Grade to Death:
One Student's Struggle to Save Mother Earth

There are many places that make this blogger infuriated: standing in a new housing development that sits on top of former wetlands; venturing into a redwood grove that's been logged into oblivion; standing by a cliff that's crumbling from man-caused erosion.

But above all, there's one place that instantly throws me into a state of despair and hopelessness: Surfside Mall on a Saturday afternoon.

Today I ventured into this fortress of shameless capitalism and soullessness. My heart sank as I watched my fellow humans suckered into buying useless stupid crap. But hope showed its bright shining face.

I was standing outside of Britches Boutique, a chain known for its complete disregard of fair labor practices and its overpriced schlocky jeans. Two twins of my acquaintance passed by, their arms loaded with bags from The Clothing Goddess.

Suddenly their arms dropped their packages. If shame has

a color, I saw it as the blood drained from their cheeks. Their faces went white with a tinge of blue, like the anemic shade of no-fat milk.

In that moment, on the outskirts of the food court, in the artificially recycled air, standing by the fake fountain, two new activists were born.

In impassioned, pleading voices, they recanted their ignorant consuming ways.

"I've been blind to avarice!" one declared, using a word not formerly in her vocabulary. "My shopping is killing Mother Earth."

"Take it all away!" the other begged. "I don't want these bloodstained goods. I can't live with the guilt."

Their friends pleaded with them to stop being so weird and embarrassing.

But they wouldn't. As one of them explained to this blogger: "I'm so sorry that we ever made fun of you. You've been right all along! We need to do something to save Mother Earth. Tell us what to do and we'll do it!"

It was when the twins started to take off their clothing and give it away that the heavy hand of the law got involved and put an end to their brave demonstration. It took two security guards to quiet these half-naked speakers of truth.

"You did get a little carried away with the nudie part," Raymond says, but he's grinning at the memory. He shows us some photos of the Double Ds that he took with his cell phone. They are priceless.

"Should I put those on the blog?" Stephanie asks.

Raymond wags a disapproving finger. "That would definitely be over the top."

"I'm so glad to be living in a world that works this way," I say.

Raymond deletes the incriminating photos from his phone. "What do you mean?"

"This is a world with order to it. It makes sense. There's right and wrong, good and bad, and the line is clear."

I nod my approval of the post. Stephanie clicks Publish.

SUNDAY

The Furies rest.

I am nothing like my birth parents. I never even met them and I can tell you that we have nothing in common. Nothing! If by chance I ever do meet them, for example if they decide to track me down because suddenly after all these years they get curious, I'll try to be polite but I'm not going to hug them. Maybe they'll start sending birthday cards, but we will still have zip to say to each other because we're totally different, poles apart in our values and dreams, likes and dislikes. How do I know this even though I never met them?

They gave me away. That's all the evidence I need.

When it comes to other people, though—regular kids with typical, everyday families—I have a whole different idea. I expect most people to be more or less like their parents and to have lots in common besides hair color and the shape of their eyes. Take Raymond and his mom. I get a real kick out of them, how they have the same body type and the exact same philosophy of life, which goes something like this: If you expect the best of people, you usually find it. If you expect the worst, that's what you get.

I'm pretty sure what I'm going to see at Stephanie's house. We're heading there to hang out on Sunday afternoon. Furies need downtime, too. After a week like we had—the strangest, most extreme days of my life—I'm ready to kick back with an all-organic, home-brewed sassafras tea or something equally healthful and environmentally aware that I'm sure Stephanie will serve. Alix is driving us north toward the outskirts of town. In the front passenger seat, Raymond adds a mouth-violin harmony to the hard-core surf music that's blasting from the car radio. He's into it, until Alix tells him to knock it off because he's wrecking the vibe.

Stretched out in the back seat, I envision what we'll see when we get to Stephanie's. I'm thinking a cozy house with basic hippie parent décor, the back door leading out to a woodsy area, solar panels lining the roof, a kitchen pantry packed with quinoa and tofu. A dog, I definitely imagine a dog, a big, hairy, happy mixed breed that's been rescued from certain death at the pound.

What I don't expect: a left turn into a gated community. A huge, white box that looks more like a bank than a home. No trees at all. A long, rolling lawn that's as iridescent green and smooth as a golf course. A gardener with a leaf blower on his back walks the perimeter. Another gardener tosses handfuls of white powder to keep the lawn so perfect. They stare suspiciously as we rattle into the driveway and Alix parks her battered Volvo behind a black SUV. It takes me a second to decipher the license plate: REL S T8.

Real estate. Tate. Stephanie Tate. Of course! The Tate Company is the biggest developer in town. They're the ones who constructed a three-story combination conference center/hotel/restaurant/bowling alley/parking structure that completely obstructs the view of the ocean for two solid blocks.

Stephanie opens the front door before we can knock. "Guess you found it." She sounds totally mortified. My "like mother, like daughter" myth is shattered. I'm not the only one who must feel like a complete alien from the person who gave birth to her.

We enter the house and I'm hit with the combined smell of lemon furniture polish, floor wax, and bleach, a hospital clean that makes me want to gag. How does Stephanie, who won't even pollute the air with perfume, live with this? Every piece of furniture is white or chrome, glass, shiny, new, and very uncomfortable looking.

Stephanie's mouth twists in distaste. "You know how Ambrosia said that her family doesn't like anything contemporary? My parents *live* for contemporary, basically nothing older than a few years. After that, my mom gets bored and it's out with the garbage."

Cue the mom. The front door opens and a woman with short, very auburn hair and pointy, very red shoes charges into the room. She's involved in an intense conversation on her cell phone. It's one of those hands-free devices, so she looks like she's shouting to herself. Stephanie resembles her a little around the eyes, but other than that they look nothing alike. Stephanie's face is round, and when she smiles her cheeks puff up like little crab apples. Her mom's face is so lean and tight, it's like she does special exercises just for her cheekbones.

"Mom," Stephanie says, "these are—"

"Yes, yes, nice to see you again, girls." Back to the phone: "I told him we're not budging on commission. We're a development corporation, not a charity."

I notice Stephanie's face register a range of feelings—ashamed, hurt, disgusted, sad, mad, lonely—all of them appearing and disappearing in a few seconds. She ends with a sigh that harmonizes with the hissing sound of furniture polish spewing from a can, the housecleaner at work. Her mom leaves the room the same way she entered, talking into the phone and with a little wave to us.

"Wow," I say. "You and your mom are so opposite."

"She used to be just like me. I didn't believe it until she showed me pictures of herself when she was just a little older than us. Can you believe she lived in a commune that protested logging in the redwood forest up north? She even spent a night tree-sitting to keep it from being cut down."

"Not in those Versace ruby slippers she didn't," Raymond interjects.

Alix stares at the front door. "No way."

"Way. Believe it. Let's go to my room."

"Where's Ambrosia?" I ask.

"Got a text this morning. Apologies all around. Guess it's just us today." Stephanie grabs a couple of apples and a jar of peanut butter from the kitchen. We follow her up the stairs and she introduces us to her room by saying, "My parents hate how I decorated it, of course. But it's my room. I'll live the way I want."

It's a whole different world in there. Beige carpet, old but still clean. A single mattress on the floor with a pretty piece of yellow cloth, probably from India, laid over it as a bedspread. There are posters of famous activists on the wall—Jane Goodall, the Dalai Lama, and the girl who changed her middle name to "Butterfly," who's pictured hugging a tree. Stephanie resembles her, and when I point that out she brightens. "Really?"

In a corner, a philodendron plant has been trained to climb a string and is spreading its big green leaves against the ceiling. Alix whistles when she checks out Stephanie's walk-in closet. It's huge. I've lived in bedrooms smaller than that. But there are hardly any clothes in it. Stephanie rarely buys anything until she's worn out whatever she already owns, and even then she hits the resale and import stores.

I plop down in a corner, lean my back against the wall, cross my legs in front of me. Raymond sits next to me and Alix takes the mattress, tucking her hands behind her head like she's in a hammock. To be truthful, if I had a lot of money like Stephanie's family does, this is not how I would decorate my room. I'd be more in the School of Ambrosia Home Décor. I'd buy beautiful things—down comforters and cut-glass lamps and . . . but I do understand this simple taste from Stephanie's perspective.

"So what happened?" I ask. "To your mom, I mean. What changed her?"

"They cut down the tree she was trying to save."

"That sucks," Alix says.

Stephanie clears off a spot on her desk for the peanut butter and apples. She opens her Swiss army knife. "Not according to my mom. She says that was the best lesson of her life. It taught her that things don't change, so why try? Why go against the grain? Why not devote your life to making yourself happy?"

She cuts the apple in half with a hard, solid chop. "She says I'm going through a phase and that I'll grow out of it the same way she did. But it's not a phase. I'll never become cynical and selfish like her." As she continues talking, she cuts each half of the apple in half and then in half again, and I wonder if she'll keep going until it's minced into a thousand pieces.

"Whoa," Raymond says. "Take it easy with that knife, samurai master."

Stephanie gives an uncomfortable laugh and divvies up the small pieces. She starts over with a new apple, makes four even cuts, smears them with peanut butter, and passes them around. While we eat, I wonder if the others are thinking what I'm thinking: Stephanie's mom belongs on our to-do list. We wouldn't hurt her, of course. We would make her see how much she's hurting the land and the air by all the overdevelopment in town. Plus, she's hurting Stephanie. We could show her that, and I bet that she'd even thank us in the long run. It would make things so much better for everyone. Stephanie deserves a mom who understands and supports her passions. That's only fair. That's the way a mom and daughter should be. A team. We would make that happen.

I think Alix is going to suggest exactly that, because she shifts with agitation. But it's only to get her cell phone that's vibrating in her back pocket. She checks the info about the incoming call.

"Shit," she says. She answers by shouting into the receiver: "What?" Then: "Oh, it's you. He can't even call himself. He makes you do it."

She listens, shaking her head in disgust until she's too worked up to sit still. She hits Speaker, tosses the phone onto the mattress, and paces, glaring at the voice that fills the room.

"Honey, you know how much your daddy loves you. You're the apple of his eye."

Alix gives the phone the finger.

"And Simon, too—your dad adores him."

"Screw you," Alix mutters. Then loud enough to carry to the phone: "If Dwayne adores him so much, why doesn't he ever see him?"

"Oh honey, you know your daddy. He has the best intentions, but he's got so many health issues, poor guy."

"He's got drunk and stoned *issues*."

"Is that a nice thing for a daughter to say about her father? His back went out today. The pain! That's why he didn't call you himself."

"Listen! What's your name again?"

"Tabitha. You know that."

"I get Dwayne's girlfriends mixed up. They come and go so fast."

"I resent that. We're engaged. Practically."

Alix puffs her cheeks, letting her lips vibrate noisily as she releases the breath. "Dwayne's bailing on his promise to take Simon to the boardwalk today. Tell Mr. Sensitive I'll take Simon myself."

"Oh, you are such a sweetheart. Next week. He promises—"

Alix presses the Off button and explains to us: "Gotta go. The kid is gonna be crushed."

Raymond stands, brushes some lint off his pants. "We'll go with you. I must meet this Simon. Besides, I love roller coasters."

Alix, her mom, and Simon live in the Sleep Tight, an old beach motel with blinking neon that's been converted into one- and two-bedroom apartments. You'd think that a place that's walking distance to the beach and has a great view of the boardwalk rides, where you can hear waves crashing and sea lions barking and ride your bike to the best surf spot in the state, would be where everyone wants to live. But the motel sits in the middle of the Flats, the part of town with a reputation for crime, drugs, and gangs.

"My parents have been trying for years to get permits to bulldoze the whole area to put up expensive homes and hotels," Stephanie says as we pull into the parking lot. One of the letters in the sign has burned out, so it says S EEP TIGHT.

Alix shuts off the engine. "What would happen then to the people who've lived here all their lives? Like me? I know what most people think of the Flats. You can't walk through without being robbed, raped, and murdered all at once by some drug addict. But it's not like that. The neighborhood's kinda tight."

A homeless person with his stuff in a shopping cart walks by and calls hello to Alix by name. Two little kids are playing outside door number five, and they show us their drawings.

"This is me, us. Number seven." Before Alix even turns the key in the lock, the door flies open and a pair of arms wrap around her waist.

"Happy, happy, happy!"

Obviously this is Simon. He's as tall and wide as a full-grown man, but his voice is high-pitched and full of giggles. He's dressed in clean jeans, a flannel shirt, and a Boy Scout neckerchief. He's holding the six-in-one gadget that Pox got him as a peace offering.

"Whoa, big guy. Glad to see you, too," Alix says. Then to us: "He's obsessed with his neckerchief and roller coasters."

"My kind of guy," Raymond says.

Simon turns to the sound of the voice and his eyes grow wide like he's taking a deep breath through them. "A dude!" He swirls his big frame and wraps his arms around Raymond in a full-press hug.

"Oh yeah, he's also obsessed with dudes. He's with my mom and me so much. And his teacher at school is a lady. That's why when *you-know-who* flakes out, it does a number on him. If we didn't come, he'd spend Sunday all day alone in this friggin' room." To Simon: "And that wouldn't be fair, would it, big guy?" To Raymond: "You still breathing okay in there?"

Raymond peeks out from a corner of Simon's big squeeze. "I am honored to be a dude."

Stephanie sits on the couch, moving aside a couple of pillows and a folded-up comforter. The living room must double as Alix's bedroom. Even I don't have to sleep on a couch. Even I get to close a door behind me for privacy. I look around. "Where's your mom?"

Alix coaxes Simon to let go of Raymond for a minute by dangling the promise of an awesome roller-coaster ride. Together the three of them set off on a search around the room for Simon's shoes. "My mom's working. She's always working. It's not easy for her. Mom's okay, except for her totally crappy taste in a father for her kids."

Sneakers found. Simon holds one up to Raymond's face like it's a trophy. "You like my new shoes?"

Raymond makes a big deal over checking it out, turns it upside down, squints inside, holds it to his ear like he can hear the ocean. "Size twelve. My favorite flavor."

This sends Simon into a fit of laughter. We're all laughing as we leave the apartment, say bye to the little girls who are coloring, and head across the levee toward the boardwalk. You can hear the excited screams of roller coaster riders from blocks away. Simon won't let go of Raymond's hand.

"Too slow!" he says, and pulls Raymond ahead of the group. As they pass us, I hear Raymond say, "Cotton candy? Now you're talking my language!"

We walk another block, turn the corner, and that's when Alix comes to a sudden stop. She freezes there, arms hanging at her sides but with her fists bunched. She blinks once, twice, as if she's trying to clear away a film from her eyes to make sure she's seeing what she thinks she's seeing.

"I can't believe it."

"What?" Stephanie asks.

"A new record for low. Even for him."

We follow the line of her vision across the street to the front door of a nasty-looking bar called the High Dive. Country-rock blasts out of it. Two people just stepped outside.

"Hahahahahahaha," the guy laughs. He is short and square with long hair in a graying ponytail.

"Hehehehehehe," the lady laughs back.

"Yo, shithead!" Alix yells.

The couple look over. The man's upper lip curls and I bet he's picturing himself charging across the street and getting in the face of whoever dared cross him. But the woman puts her hand on his shoulder to hold him back. She squints hard. Quickly she leans in and whispers to the man, whose whole body jolts upright and then slumps. I can see him reminding himself of something. He puts his hand on his lower back. With his face wincing in pain, he raises his hand and waves limply in our direction. As an actor he's truly pathetic.

Dwayne. Her dad. The shithead.

Alix chews at her lower lip, and I feel a pull to do the same on mine. I bite down hard and taste a pinpoint of blood. I take in her anger like it's a living, breathing thing, a virus that's entering my body through my mouth, my nose and eyes. I start to sweat. She sounds the first note. I sing. My vision blurs, and I know that Stephanie, too, feels her muscles pulsing, her bones vibrating, the world of the bar and the boardwalk, the ground beneath us coming undone.

Alix's rage is our guide, our rope and ladder. We enter a space, but this is not deep enough, so we plunge even deeper—deeper than we've ever been, much deeper than with Pox and the others. We don't hold back. Why hold back? On the way down we break things apart, rip and tear, until we burrow into the nucleus of something dark and dank.

We present Dwayne with our true face—not just the

terror of three, but we fracture into a million furious fractals that are smaller than no-see-'em bugs and we are everywhere. We swarm, hissing in a million undeniable, inescapable voices of torment:

You're worthless.

You're a coward.

Your life is meaningless and hopeless.

Worthless, meaningless, hopeless.

Worthless, meaningless, hopeless.

Far away I hear shouting, but I push it aside. Let them shout.

Off in the distance I hear sirens. Let them tear the silence apart.

I hear "Stop!"

I hear my wronged sister Alecto urging: "Don't stop!"

Another voice: "Stop!"

"Don't stop!"

"Meg! Stop!"

This last voice somehow reaches in and loosens my grip like my fingers are being pried from around someone's throat. "Enough! Meg, that's enough!"

I have to fight hard to clear my head and come back into ordinary consciousness, and when I do I'm blinking into the terrified face of Raymond, who's shaking me by the shoulders. "Meg! Stop!" Simon is sobbing, his neckerchief is wet, and his arms are wrapped around his sister's waist, begging her, "Come back!"

Alix, glassy-eyed, rigid, empty. Stephanie, pale and shivering.

Across the street there's chaos. I see a cluster of police

cars and people being questioned. There's an ambulance, and two paramedics lift someone—I look closer; it's Dwayne—onto a stretcher. His girlfriend glances at us, bewildered and scared, and quickly turns away.

Alix is slowing coming back to life, *this* life, the ordinary life. She gives Simon a sisterly rub on the top of his head. "All's okay, big guy. I'm not going anywhere."

"But you left! You were gone," Simon insists. "And Daddy! The car hit him."

I pull Raymond close and whisper: "Did anybody see us? Does anybody . . ."

"Drunk." Raymond takes a step back from me, like I smell bad. "He started wobbling. Talking crazy. They assume he was so drunk that he accidentally walked in front of that car."

I have a sick, panicked feeling and an awful thought. "He's . . . Is he . . . ? He's not . . ." I try to ask.

Raymond gives me a push, a real shove, nothing friendly about it. I've never seen him so upset. "No, Meg, he's not dead. Not this time. But I don't know what would have happened if I couldn't reach you."

"I'm sorry," I stammer. "I—"

"Why are you sorry?" Alix interrupts. "Dwayne's the one who lied."

She has Simon by the hand, and he's pulling at it, perplexed about the situation and where his loyalties should be. With his dad, being put into an ambulance? With his new best dude friend or his beloved sister, who are yelling at each other? I motion for Stephanie to distract Simon, and she takes him aside.

Raymond waits until Simon is out of earshot before unleashing his anger. "Just because your dad happens to be one of the biggest nitwidiots who ever walked the planet doesn't mean he should be roadkill two blocks from the boardwalk."

Alex remains certain, unmoved. "He needed a lesson."

"A lesson? That was attempted murder with a moving vehicle."

"We didn't touch the dickwad! Let someone try and prove we did."

"Nice rationalization, Alix. You made him so crazed with guilt that he jumped in front of a car."

Then Raymond whirls on me, even madder: "That wasn't justice. That was revenge. You did what you promised you wouldn't do. You went out of control."

The next day after school, Raymond invites himself over. I don't want him to come, but I can't figure a way out of it. His excuse is that we need to catch up on the huge amount of homework that we let slide the past week. But I know what he's up to. The visit is a ruse, another opportunity to lecture me on a subject that, in my opinion, we've already talked to death. He just can't let go of it, the whole Alix's dad fiasco. That's what he calls it: a *fiasco*.

What more can he say? I *know* that he's not pleased that we went a little overboard. I *know* that he's not pleased that I keep putting the adjective *little* in front of *overboard*. I *know* that he doesn't think I admitted my part in it enough and that Alix and Stephanie aren't treating what happened seriously.

The only good part of the afternoon so far is that we're not cramped together in my old, depressing former bedroom. I let the Leech know that I would be much, much happier if she swapped her big, sunny bedroom for my small dungeon, and she assured me that given her previous disrespectful behavior toward me, she was only too glad to trade. It would make her feel better, less guilty. She cowered when she said it, and even gave me a ton of money so I could buy a brand-new mattress, ditch the old sheets and curtains, and redecorate the room to my own taste.

I'm propped against the headboard with Raymond sitting next to me on the big, cushy queen-sized bed. He takes one of my pillows and fluffs it behind his head. When he once again launches into his latest lecture on the dreaded subject, I try to wear a contrite expression. I do! I don't want him to be mad at me. But the truth is, I'm tuning him out and instead admiring the lace curtains that I paid full price for. I like the way the light filters in and makes patterns on the wall. I like the way they set off Francine, my ceramic frog planter. The curtains are white, the sheets are white, everything new is white, Ambrosia style.

Meanwhile.

Raymond's voice is at its most irritating. "Do you remember the promise you made? Do you want me to take your firstborn? Didn't you listen to that description of the Furies that Ms. Pallas read?"

"Uh-huh."

"Monsters. Lapping blood."

"Uh-huh."

"I think she knows."

"Uh-huh."

"Meg! Uh-huh what?"

"Uh-huh whatever you just said."

"What did I just say? Tell me."

There's an open bag of spicy-sweet pretzel mix on my lap. I take a piece and crunch into it. These days I am starved all the time and notice that I'm finally putting on some weight. I feel a little bad about not listening totally to him, but I also don't feel bad at all. Why should I have to explain myself to him again? "Okay, you caught me. Shoot me because I was a little spaced out after getting the same lecture ten times!"

He pivots on his bottom so that he's sitting in front of me cross-legged. His back is poker straight and his nose is about a foot from my face. No way to ignore him now. This is his favorite body position for giving serious advice.

"For one minute, stop admiring all your possessions and listen to me. This is important. You called it earlier. Ms. Pallas is part of all this."

"Duh."

"Don't duh me, young lady. When did you start saying *duh*?"

I shrug. "Of course Ms. Pallas knows something."

"Good then, you agree. That passage she read in class— monsters who lap the blood, loathsome goddesses—totally creepy, right? It obviously has deeper meaning. I think it was a warning."

At least we're off the topic of Alix's dad. For that I am grateful. Plus I am curious about Ms. Pallas and what she knows and who she really is. I wonder what Raymond knows. "A warning about what? Why would she warn us? Who is she?"

I see him weighing the decision whether or not to tell me. "Raymond, spill!"

"I'm not sure exactly, not yet. I have an idea, though. But at this point it's only one step above pure conjecture.

She's not exactly forthcoming with the juicy personal details of her life. I mean, what do we know about her? Nothing!"

"You've been prying!"

His eyes tease me back. "Yep, I admit it. Guilty as charged." He slaps the top of his own hand. "Shame, shame on nosy me."

I smile and relax. The way we're talking now, the banter and the teasing, sends a rush of nostalgia through me, a longing for the good old days of only a week ago when it was just him and me laughing, plotting, telling each other everything. Him and me, nothing more complicated than that. "Yes, you are terrible," I scold playfully.

"You'll know everything as soon as I'm certain. Until then we should proceed with certain assumptions."

"Those assumptions being?"

"That you don't want to piss off Ms. Pallas. And she would be very, very unhappy with what you did to Alix's dad."

Oh no. Nostalgic moment over. How many times do I need to hear this? How many times do I have to agree that we made a little mistake and that it won't happen again? We're just human. Well, not really just human. But Dwayne is the bad guy; we're the good guys, and I'm tired of having to justify that to Raymond. And now I'm also supposed to care about what a teacher—or whoever she is—thinks.

"Ms. Pallas should mind her own business," I say.

He-Cat jumps onto the bed, sniffs at the pretzels, does a bread-making motion on my thigh. Raymond has gotten me all worked up. I'm not in the mood to be pawed and purred at. I hiss at the cat—*sssssss*—and he moves away. Raymond takes pity and settles He-Cat on his lap. I try to explain myself again. I want Raymond to *get* it. For a smart person, he can be very thick and stubborn.

"You're going to feel differently about Alix's dad when you hear this next part. Alix says that Dwayne's so-called terrible injuries have turned into one more excuse to bail out on poor Simon. We didn't begin to touch his mental attitude."

The bedroom door swings open then with a hard thrust that sends the doorknob slamming into the wall.

"Knock!" I yell at the Leech, who is taking up three-quarters of the doorway.

"Sorry," she says.

"Didn't I tell you before? You knock if you want something. I decide if and when you get to come in. Get out!"

The door shuts quietly behind her.

After that, things remain tense between Raymond and me. Yeah, I suppose I didn't have to yell at the Leech like I did, but what does he expect? I'm all agitated, and it's his fault for making me lose my temper. He's so annoying. He never knows when to stop pushing. For the next half hour I pretend to do homework while he practices violin. Usually I don't mind listening to him play. Usually I like it. But he's been going over and over the same few measures, stopping and starting, speeding it up and slowing it down. It's driving me nuts.

"Enough!" I toss aside my physics book. "Are you trying to torture me?"

"Not so good, huh?"

"What is it?"

"Opus number something by yours truly."

He plays it again, and I offer an honest critique: "It's awful. Chuck it and compose something else."

He looks at the bow like there's something wrong with it, like that's the problem. "I tried, but the tune is a mind worm. I can't stop thinking about it. I'll move past these few measures eventually."

Before I go back to my problem, I say, "You better."

Western Civ class. We're in our project group, circled in the back of the room. Ambrosia passes around pictures of the Furies that she copied from books and the Internet. I try looking through them, but Alix, who's sitting on my left, distracts me with her low, irritated muttering. We follow the jut of her chin. "Him. Gnat. Makes me sick. I can't stand that he's walking around untouched. I hate his face. His arms. Ears. Brain."

"What brain?" Stephanie asks.

"Put him on the to-do," Ambrosia suggests with a toss of her hair. She has another new style, this one a mass of long sausage curls that tumbles down her back.

Alix squeezes her fist. "We should take him down, give him a message he won't forget."

Raymond looks up from the pictures he's been studying. "Excuse me, but what's your name?"

"What do you mean, what's my name? What are you talking about?" Alix responds.

"I was thinking that your name is Dirty Harry. Listen to yourself: Take him down? A message he won't forget? I thought you girls were Team Justice, not a vigilante squad."

Ambrosia, patting the air: "Simmer down, Raymond. You're losing your calm. You sound positively furious."

Raymond takes a slow inhale and exhale, hands in prayer, overdoing a monk imitation. "Attention please. I'm going to quote Benjamin Franklin."

Ambrosia shoots a hard look in his direction. "Of course you are."

"'Whatever is begun in anger ends in shame.'"

Ambrosia explodes into tinkling laughter, like that's the silliest thing she ever heard, the ramblings of a child. "Raymond, chill. It's just the girls toying with semantics. Look around at the better world they've already created. You have to admit that life is a little more peaceful here at our Hunter High. A lot less mean-girl antics by the twins formerly known by their breast size. Pox and Bubonic aren't totally groveling anymore, but they aren't bullying anyone either."

We survey the room, admiring our work. I swell with pride. No one can deny that things are better. Pox, for example, has abandoned the Plagues to work on his project with the Danish foreign exchange student and the dorky president of the Future Leaders of America. Boy, he must feel really guilty about something he did to them.

Ambrosia addresses Alix. "It makes you stop and think, doesn't it?"

She is chewing on a pen, takes it out of her mouth to respond. "Think about what?"

"With the track record you've racked up, why limit yourself? Gnat? Natch. But why stop there? Why not all of them, all that smug surf royalty? Give them a taste."

I am definitely with her on Gnat. He's a nasty little bug who needs a complete personality makeover. The world would be better for it. But the *all* part? All as in *all*? Every single one of that crowd? That includes Brendon. What if we change him when he doesn't really need to change? What if we turn him into someone completely different and that person isn't Brendon anymore, at least not the Brendon who makes my heart thump every time I think about him?

I squirm uneasily and realize too late that I just blurted, "Not all."

Ambrosia frowns. "Excuse me?"

"Maybe not all of them."

Her frown deepens. "Who among that lot doesn't deserve it? Who would you leave just the way he is?"

I pretend to be thinking hard. Then I try to sound casual, completely random. "Gee, maybe . . . maybe Brendon?"

"Brendon?"

"I'm just saying," I fumble. "I just happen to notice that he's not so bad. So why waste our energy on him?"

"Energy, huh?" Ambrosia asks. "This is about energy?"

I go with that explanation. "Yes, energy conservation. A very good thing. Ask Stephanie."

I'm hoping that Ambrosia will leave it alone and move on to another topic, but no such luck. "I notice that you notice Brendon a lot."

I avert my eyes to my lap, like there's something very interesting in it, a fascinating piece of lint perhaps. But nobody gets away with ignoring Ambrosia. "I said"—*tap, tap, tap* on the desk with her one black fingernail—"that you notice Brendon a lot."

I aim for a super-casual lilt in my voice, pretending that my heart isn't pounding like I've been chased and cornered. "Notice him? What? No way! No more than I notice anyone else."

A big, gross snort from Alix. "Yeah, right. We're not blind. You have a crush on the creep."

"I don't have a crush on the creep!" I protest.

"Remember mini-golf," Ambrosia points out, as if I could forget.

I turn to Raymond for backup, but I don't think he's heard a word of this. He is genuinely lost in the pictures of the Furies that Ambrosia brought in. He's going through them one by one. He doesn't have his usual *duh* expression of deep thought, but the space between his eyebrows is wrinkled like an accordion.

What should I say about Brendon? Keep denying the crush? They're waiting for me. I try to smooth out the quiver that I know sits right beneath the surface of my voice. "Brendon didn't . . . I don't think he hurt my feelings on purpose. Brendon's not . . . Brendon's not a creep like the others."

There. I did it!

"He . . . I get a sense . . . There's something good hidden in him. I just know it."

Ambrosia toys with her pearl earrings, gives them a spin. "And your evidence for this glowing character reference?"

I hesitate, then take another chance. They're my friends and they'll support me on this, help me understand it better myself. "He gets this expression, something about the crinkles around his eyes."

It's a good thing that Alix isn't drinking milk, because it would have come flying out through her nostrils. "Bite me! You trust someone because of that. He gets a pass for wrinkles?"

"Crinkles," I insist.

"Sucker."

"Looks lie, Meg," Stephanie says, as if I'm an idiot and haven't lived my whole life getting screwed by people who look one way and aren't that way at all. I want to say something in my defense—about how I don't usually trust people. So then how do I explain about Brendon? I can't. I keep all the adjectives attached to his expression—deep, private, sexy, secret—to myself. It's an effort. Ambrosia notices the color rushing to my cheeks.

"Ah, I see what's going on. You have hormones now, Meg. This is a little new to you. Hormones can't think straight." She runs her hand over my hair, and the sensation of that, the way it sends a shiver straight to my stomach, my legs, my everything, makes me think about Brendon again. "Your hormones have given you a crush. A crush blinds you. You feel compassion when compassion isn't deserved."

She leans in even closer, and I get a strong whiff of her perfume, the soil and mint. I think she's angry, but the edge suddenly leaves her voice, turning it unusually soft and understanding. She pats my hand. "You don't have to take my word for that, Megaera. Come to think of it, it's actually better if you learn about these things firsthand. That will be a more powerful, lasting lesson that will serve us well."

A lesson about what? Serve us well how? I don't get a chance to ask because she changes the subject.

"A party," she says abruptly. "I'll throw a little gathering. Halloween is coming up, the perfect occasion to bring everyone together. We should all be there for this fling."

Ms. Pallas has been making the rounds of the project groups, and she's gotten to us. Stephanie fake coughs and bounces her finger on her lips in warning. I figure we're done talking about parties and crushes. To my embarrassment, though, with Ms. Pallas towering over us, Ambrosia returns to the subject of me. "Meg, a crush puts your best instincts to sleep. It keeps you from seeing how manipulative humans can be."

Only then does Ambrosia look up at our teacher. Her smile is a big, fake flash, quickly gone. "The Furies. I was explaining to Meg how people try to elude them. She needs to understand why a little taste of guilt doesn't make a dent in most people. Human nature doesn't change that easily."

Ms. Pallas's eyes widen. The blue is so deep and steely it's hard not to feel sucked into them. "What *does* make a dent? What is enough?"

"When justice is done," Ambrosia answers. "When there's true satisfaction."

"And when is that? When does payback finally stop?"

Ambrosia does a counting motion with her fingers, mimes like she's thinking hard and adding up all the considerations. Her hands clap. "Never. For some crimes, no punishment is ever enough."

"There must be compassion," Ms. Pallas insists. "And forgiveness."

Ambrosia scoffs, turns to Alix for reinforcement. "What has forgiving ever gotten you?"

Then to Stephanie. "Has compassion for your enemies brought you satisfaction?"

Ms. Pallas moves until she's standing right behind me, and I feel her hand firmly cup the dome of my shoulder. The pressure makes me feel very small and powerless under its grip, and I don't like the sensation. I don't like it at all. Reflexively I knock the hand from my shoulder, and Ambrosia laughs so hard that everyone in class looks our way.

"It's so tempting to hold on to self-righteous anger and never let go," Ms. Pallas says, her braid tight, her lips just as tight. "That brand of justice can taste so good!"

"Scrumptious," Ambrosia agrees.

"Without forgiveness, it gets stuck in your throat. Justice becomes revenge—endless, hateful, spiteful, soul-rotting revenge." She starts to say more, but changes her mind and settles on a single word: "Raymond."

He's been so quiet and un-Raymond-like that I've almost forgotten about him. I think that he also lost track of where he is, because he looks up startled, ripped away from another time and place. Something unspoken passes between him and Ms. Pallas. What was *that* about? He gathers the pictures of the Furies and slides them across the desk, spreads them out especially for me so I can take in all the images.

I let myself float off into the world of the pictures. There's a black-and-white etching of three naked, sexy, winged women hovering in the atmosphere. A carving on an ancient vase of a trio of hags with long, matted hair and limbs intertwined, a real nightmare. A photo from a theater production of an Aeschylus play: masked, bloodstained figures, a different nightmare.

And in every picture there's also a man, a young man not any older than I am. In the etching, his hands cover his ears as he pleads in anguish. In the carving, he's bent over, huddled in misery, defeated, as the creatures hiss in his ears. In the third, I look hard but see only a foot sticking out from the mound of wings and hair.

I study these Furies and their victim, and sense something and someone very familiar.

"Look at their victim, Meg," Ms. Pallas says. "Look at *them*! They start out beautiful, but turn as hideous and as dangerous as poison gas."

MURDERER ON PAROLE MURDERS AGAIN

KILLER WALKS FREE

When you hear news like this, doesn't your blood boil?

I place the blame squarely where it belongs. On Athena, the goddess of light and justice, aka Minerva, aka the Virgin Goddess, protector of so-called civilized ways. And here at Hunter High in her newest incarnation of authority figure, color guard advisor, and teacher of third-period Western Civ.

One look at her clothes and you know she's the original goddess of weaving. She may have been born right out of her father Zeus's skull, but she's our splitting headache now. Blame Pallas Athena for bogging down the world with courts, judges, lawyers, hearings, appeals, bail posts, and probation departments. Blame her for all these abominations.

I'm an old-fashioned girl longing for justice, old-school style—the simple, satisfying acts of revenge and retribution, the eternal locking together of victim and perpetrator with blood spilling everywhere.

No jury of anyone's peers.

No compassion for anyone's so-called sad childhood.

No extenuating circumstances.

I actually heard of someone hugging someone who once did them wrong. Please. What's up with that?

That someone needs to take a tip from the Old Testament—eye for an eye, tooth for a tooth—but without the wimpy back-pedaling section about showing mercy. I aim for a different ratio: ten thousand eyes for an eye, revenge with daily compounding interest.

Here's my story. It starts back in ancient days when things were so much simpler. Someone killed someone, so someone in his family killed that someone, and so on and on until it got to me.

Someone killed my father, and I had to avenge that murder. It was a given. Poison worked nicely. Poison was very popular in those days.

But then someone was obliged to kill me. The duty fell to a certain prince, a deceptive young man who lured me—so luscious and desirable, a princess in her prime—into his arms. He was smooth all right, but I should have stayed on guard.

For my naïveté I got a knife in the back, along with a quick taste of his lusty lips. While dying a slow and torturous death, my only solace was knowing that someone—a bloodthirsty uncle, perhaps—would avenge me in the old way.

But no!

Athena came down from her mountain on her high horse and read them the riot act: No more vengeance. Let's all join hands and sing the ancient version of "Kumbaya." Let's have peace among enemies, invite lions to lie down with lambs.

So because of Athena's meddling, no one picked up a vial of poison on my behalf. Both sides buried the hatchet—right into my eternal rest.

With no one to avenge me, I wandered alone in a hot, stuffy, miserable netherworld humming the same song over and over. I kept at it until they finally heard me. One hundred and eight notes until they could no longer ignore my misery. My righteous need for vengeance woke them out of their deep sleep.

They came and licked at my wounds, fed themselves on the injustice, and drank up the unfairness of my unavenged, un-mourned, unsanctified death. They drove my princely killer stark, raving mad.

Only my killer had a son, and as soon as that spawn of my enemy hit puberty he lost his baby fat and got the same princely profile and curly hair—the spitting image in killer smile and killer instinct of his father.

I could not get him out of my head. The knowledge that he breathed robbed me of my long-deserved peace. I summoned up my next batch of Furies and sent them off to work.

I was dead and deadly.

Only then came a son of this son, followed by a son of that son and soon a son of a son of a son—each of them a son of a bitch with thick hair and great cheekbones. All these grandsons and uncles and cousins many times removed, all of them good-looking, popular princes.

I dispatch them now whenever I can, whenever the stars and human suffering allow my Furies free rein.

I set aside a section of my book for a history of these joyous events that ease my rage, at least temporarily. My successes cluster around certain historical eras. I need the worst of times to spark the awakening of the Furies.

Now is such a time. There's so much anger, fear, hostility, greed, wars, corruption, racism, genocide, fraud, assassinations, vice in the highest and lowest places, oil spills turning the oceans into slippery graveyards. Just driving on a crowded freeway and listening to the hostility of blaring horns sends my spirits soaring.

In pencil I've added my newest target. This scion of a scion of a scion, dark-haired and handsome, and as despicable to me as all the others.

This prince. This Brendon. This Prince of the Plagues.

Arise, my furious ones. Don't let Athena and her teacher's pet with the fiddle seduce you. Ignore their offers of a warm bed and a cool head. Cast off all of their tempting poppies of Hypnos.

Stay awake!

THIRD STASIMON, THE BOOK OF FURIOUS

"Are you sure I won't kill myself?"

"Naw. This is the beginner's break."

"But I'm a wimp. And a klutz."

Alix spreads her arms, throws back her head, and makes a dramatic motion of appreciation to the sky, which is cloudless and blue, an increasingly rare sight lately.

"Perfect conditions today. Warm. Actual sun. Surf's as smooth as glass. So don't sweat it. No fear when the Big Kahuna Alecto has got your back."

What was I thinking? Why did I confess to Alix that I envy her fearlessness in the water? Why did I tell her that I stand on the cliff and fantasize about riding waves? Why did I let her talk me into taking my first surfing lesson?

We're standing by a set of steps that lead down to the ocean. As I gnaw nervously on my upper lip, I taste the thick layer of coconut sunscreen that I smeared everywhere. Two of Alix's surfboards are propped against the railing. This isn't the famous surf spot with the terrifying walls of water. That's about a quarter mile up the coast. We're taking on a far easier break known for its gentle and uniform waves, the place in town where everyone first learns to surf.

I peer over the railing, relieved to see that the waves are hardly cresting above the waist and there's plenty of slack time between them. Even so, an obvious newbie loses control and I cringe as a wave clobbers him on his head and his board goes airborne before landing with a smack right where the wave took him under. I don't like the panicked look on the surfer-wannabe's face when he breaks back to the surface, coughing. Even beginner waves pack tremendous power.

Plus I'm dreading the temperature. I've dipped my toes into the surf on sunny summer days, and it's cold even then. What's it going to be like now? This time of year, it never gets above the fifties. And there are the sharks to worry about, the ocean's ruthless, deadly eating machines. I will not think about the sharks. You don't actually see them, but everyone knows that they're lurking beneath the surface. I won't think about the sharks. People call this section of the coast the Bloody Triangle, and even to me all these flailing people in sleek, black wet suits—what real surfers call kooks—look like sick, slow seals. They must look like an all-you-can-eat buffet to a nearsighted shark.

"Trust me. You're gonna love it," Alix promises. "Makes you feel like a million bucks. I'm a big fan of salt water. The ocean, breaking a sweat—salt water is the cure for whatever's bothering you."

"Tears, too," I add quickly. "That's salt water. I can just stay on land and cry."

"Never thought of that. I'm not much of a crier, though, but I hear it works for some people. Surfing's a lot more fun."

"Promise?"

She motions for me to spin around so she can zip up my wet suit, which closes around my throat like a set of thick, rough hands. "I'm choking. This is misery. I can't even stand a turtleneck sweater." I pull at the neck.

"Stop that! It's supposed to be tight. How do you think it keeps the water out?" She swats my hands away. "Actually, this suit is too tight on you. I thought you told me your size."

"I did. I guess I put on some weight recently."

"I'll say. And it's all in the right places. You have hips all of a sudden, and a waist."

I'm normally horribly self-conscious and would squirm over any mention of my weight or body. This time, though, I don't scramble to change the subject because I've noticed what Alix has noticed. It's not just wishful thinking. I put my hands on my hips and run them along the sides of my torso. This has nothing to do with the tension of the wet suit. Something has changed not only *in* me, but *on* me. There's a deep indentation, a curve where there wasn't a curve before.

"I've never had a shape in my life. It's weird 'cause I'm not exercising. I'm hungry all the time—starved—and I keep eating."

"Like a shark. Same here. I'm really into the rocky road ice cream. And it's all becoming muscle." Alix lowers one of the surfboards and gets on her knees to demonstrate how to put zigzags of wax on the surface. "This will keep you from slipping off when you stand up."

"*If* I stand up."

I lower the other board to the ground and go to work on

the edges, imitating what she's doing. The bar of wax smells nice, like the peppermint gum Raymond is always chewing. It meshes with the scent of the coconut sunscreen, and makes me think of fruit drinks and tropical islands. "So your body is changing, too?"

"Yeah. I figure it's connected to what Mr. H taught in class the other day. What's that law? The conservation of energy."

"I thought you slept through physics, Alix."

"Naw. I just look asleep. Stuff sinks in even with my eyes closed." She stops waxing to give me her full attention. "Here's how I figure it. What we're doing takes energy, right? And energy's got to come from somewhere. It doesn't just grow on trees, right?"

"Well, energy does kind of grow on trees."

"You know what I mean. Not *our* energy. It must be coming from us. Messing with people's minds is exercise, maybe like running a marathon."

"The Fury Diet!" I suggest. "We could write a best-seller and make a fortune from it. We need a motto."

Instead of drawing more zigzags, I use the wax to write in my elegant handwriting *Get Mad! Get Fit!* along the length of my board. Alix nods approval and balances her board on her head. "Ready to tackle the ocean? Yeah, you're ready."

I take my time following her down the steep, rocky stairs. The board isn't quite as heavy or cumbersome as I thought it would be. Thank goodness for that. Alix, too, is being very patient with me; I didn't expect that from her. I figured she'd make fun of my fear and get irritated with how tentatively I'm maneuvering the steps. That's exactly the attitude I couldn't handle right now. When I know someone is watching and judging me, I just get more fearful and clumsy. But Alix is giving me the same respect for my limitations as she shows her brother, and I appreciate that.

When we get to the edge of the ocean, I flash her a nervous look and then force myself to step into the knee-high water. When I dunk up to my neck, there's a slap of cold as some water finds its way past the protective barrier of my wet suit. But quickly my body heat warms it up, and no more water gets in.

This is amazing. The ocean is freezing. I feel the sting of the icy salt as I splash some on my face. Only, my core, the center of me, doesn't feel it. Putting my belly on the board, I paddle away from shore exactly as Alix instructs. She stays right next to me, giving directions and shouting encouragement.

I try for a few waves, but they pass right under me. "You're not working hard enough," she shouts. "Paddle!"

Another wave and another and another. All misses. I feel the ocean energy slide away beneath me.

Then one wave, bigger than the others, comes right at me and I panic. I can try going over it. Maybe I can get out of its way. But I hear my name again, and that gives me confidence. This is my wave. It's meant for me.

I turn the board and point it toward shore. My arms dig into the water and I can feel—I can actually hear—the building swell of a wave getting closer. That's when Alix gives my board an extra push.

It's exactly what I need.

I slide down the front of this liquid wall, and when I get

to the bottom I actually manage to spring to my knees for a second—a whole, wobbly, terrifying, thrilling second— before losing my balance and falling into a swirl of foam. The air disappears. Cold water goes up my nose, tosses me around, and holds me under. I don't know which way is up.

But unlike the usual me, I'm not afraid for some reason. In my mind I replay Alix's instructions: Stay relaxed. Go with the flow of the wave. Don't fight it.

I pop to the surface in calm water and see Alix's worried face looking down into mine.

"Are you okay?"

I lick my lips, enjoying the sting and taste of salt already drying on them. In answer to her question, I get right back on the board and start paddling back out to where it's deeper and dangerous.

I loved catching that wave, and even getting tumbled. I loved the roughness of the break and the stillness when I was underwater. I loved paddling hard and going over the top of a wave.

I love being out here with the gulls overhead and the seals nearby.

Alix could be right and the ocean is a cure. If I keep try- ing. If I don't give up. If I have faith in myself and my sister Furies. Maybe from now on, things in my life won't be as hard or as scary or as impossible as they used to be.

At school the next morning, I'm going through my locker to get ready for class. I find an envelope that was pushed through the vent, and open it to find an ornate, professionally printed invitation to Ambrosia's Halloween party.

"Hey."

Even though my back is to him, I recognize the voice. Brendon. I'd know it anywhere, even underwater, I bet. Right now I want desperately to channel Ambrosia, to remain calm and aloof, to turn slowly and meet him with lowered eyes and a breathy greeting, to say something like: Hey yourself.

I whip around like I've been shocked with electricity.

The book I'm holding—one thousand textbook pages of Western Civilization—jumps out of my hand and lands hard on his right foot, sending him into a one-legged, hopping dance. Meanwhile the party invitation and pile of papers in my other hand—research on the Furies—fly through the air like confetti on growth hormones. I fumble to get them. He tries to help, but he's off-balance and I'm off-balance because I'm so close to him and I can't believe he's talking to me, and I can smell his piney, oceany smell. We knock shoulders and bump heads, and it's a total, horrible disaster.

This encounter firms up my double reputation as a klutz and the girl who hates everyone. I wouldn't blame him if he ran off screaming. So I'm surprised and relieved that he helps me pick things up. His eyes glide over the invitation. "I got one of those, too." He comments on the papers. "Furies. Interesting."

"I'm not always like that," I blurt.

"Not always like what? Interesting?"

"No, clumsy. Well, actually I am. Clumsy, I mean, not interesting."

Idiot! Shut up!

He flashes one of his rarely given grins. I almost drop the papers again. Eye crinkles appear, which cut off any possibility of me responding. Brain dead. Lips numb. My mouth won't do a thing except to smile back way too broadly, a creepy clown grin that makes the muscles in my face hurt. Several more uncomfortable smiling seconds pass, and then, thankfully, he picks up the slack.

"I saw you in the ocean yesterday."

"I was in the ocean yesterday." This is the brilliant response that I manage to get out.

"Looking good on that board."

Does he mean *looking good* as in *I look good to him*? My hands begin a mad dash around my body. I can't stop them. They scratch my upper arm, rip the elastic band out of my hair and put it back in, cover my mouth in a fake cough, and then massage the back of my neck. *Stop fidgeting!* My left arm finally goes limp at my side and the right hand lands on my hip. I feel the brand-new curve of my waist in my hand and hold it there like a good-luck charm.

"You like to surf?" he asks. "I didn't know that."

"I like to surf."

"Been surfing long?"

"I haven't been surfing long." More brilliance by the brilliant conversationalist.

"Maybe you'd like to . . ."

He hesitates. His eyes drop. He's shy. I didn't know that about him. But I imagined that he might be shy. Why not? Popular people can be shy, too. That's what I saw in his expression! I'm glad he's shy. I like that he's shy. It makes him even cuter. So what is he trying to say? Maybe I'd like to what? What? What would I like to do?

". . . to go surfing sometime."

Be cool, Meg. Steady, girl. "Surfing? Me? With you? Together?"

"Yeah, with me. I want you to know . . ." He jams his hands into the pockets of his jeans. "I'm sorry."

"About what?"

"About the mini-golf thing. The way you asked me . . . your invitation was pretty random. 'Cause we never talked before or anything. You took me by surprise."

"It was weird."

Something happens to his face then. It scrunches in on itself, a wince, like he's reminding himself of something he'd rather forget. "No, I want to be more honest. I wasn't just surprised. I was rude. I was an asshole. When I get uncomfortable, that's sometimes my default mode."

My hands start their flutter dance again. "Oh, that's okay. I didn't actually expect you to say yes, even though I asked. I'm always doing things like that."

"Like what?"

"Like . . ." *Shut up!* "Like nothing. I had the coupon and I saw you and I thought . . . anyway, it was just a whim. Dumb."

"No, it wasn't dumb at all. It was kinda cool. Nobody ever does anything like that. We stay with the same group of friends forever, never step out of our comfort zone. You tried. I'm flattered."

I feel my cheeks getting hot. Ambrosia is definitely wrong about him. Here's the hard evidence she wanted. He actually apologized for being a jerk. On his own. We didn't do a thing to make this happen.

A couple of his friends walk by. Brendon's right hand comes out of his pocket, and I figure that's that, now he's going to signal them to wait up for him. Apology over. Good-bye, Brendon. But instead, he pulls out a bag of jelly beans and holds it open for me. I take my time to select pineapple and coconut. He chooses the same piña colada flavors. I can tell he does that on purpose. That's so adorable.

Chew, swallow. "I also want to apologize for my friends—about the golf-club swinging. So immature. They can be real jerks."

I shrug. "That's okay. You're not your friends."

"I know, but it's no excuse." Another wince moves over his face. "My friends do things, and I just go along with them. Sometimes I don't think for myself."

I select a popcorn-flavored jelly bean and let it dissolve in my cheek. "Your friends, especially Pox, seem a little nicer lately. Bubonic, too."

"They are definitely different."

"An improvement for sure, don't you think?"

Brendon gets thoughtful, and I worry that he somehow senses that I have something to do with the increase in the niceness quota at Hunter High.

"Maybe we're all just growing up," he suggests.

"Could be. I hear that happens at our age."

He laughs immediately. A good sign. It would suck if he didn't get it when I was being funny.

"Apology accepted?" he asks, and when I nod he looks relieved. "Can I make it up to you? Want to go surfing together?

Let's both branch out. I have some favorite secret spots I can show you."

The way he says that—using the words *spots* and *secret*—I hope he's not just talking about surfing. My mind makes a wild leap, and I let the words follow my thoughts, let them right out into the air between us. "I like secret spots."

I. Can't. Believe. I. Said. That. I said that!

Then I can't believe that I lean against my locker with one of my hips thrust forward and my shoulders rolled back. Suddenly this is like a conversation between two sexy people in a sexy movie. I'm not sure if it's a good sexy movie or a stupid sexy movie, but I have to think it's at least fairly good because Brendon touches me lightly on the shoulder. I flinch, but he doesn't remove his hand. I'm very glad about that.

The bell rings for first period. His hand lifts. Sexy movie over. I turn away, slam my locker door, pick up my book, and fumble to get everything into my pack.

"So," he says.

"So," I reply.

"It's a date then?"

Date! He used the word *date*.

"When?" I ask it too fast and too loud, way too eager.

"I have an idea, but I have to check on something. I'll let you know." He hands me back my papers, checks out the title again. "The Furies. You don't want to forget these."

Did that conversation really happen?

Yes, it did!

Did Brendon ask me on a date?

Absolutely! At least, I think so.

Is it possible that he likes me? Me?

How could he like me? Why wouldn't he like me?

This question-and-answer session with myself goes on all day, through classes, during lunch. I'm totally distracted, but I don't tell anyone about Brendon, not even Raymond. I'm afraid that saying it out loud will break a spell of some sort. (No! We didn't do anything to him. He asked me completely on his own.)

I'm riding the bus to Stephanie's house after school because I promised that I'd help put together flyers and posters for her newest project—*Save Our Town's Last Greenbelt*. I also know that she and Alix want to talk about projects of a different sort: What should we do about Gnat? Who else needs a lesson from the Furies? What specific areas—cornering, singing, entering, exiting—should we target for more practice?

But Fury work is the last thing I feel like doing right now. True, Gnat is a serious contender for all-American pain in the ass, but right this instant I just don't care. I know I should, but I don't. I can't muster up any real anger at him. Rather, I want to drift off into about five happy hours of re-playing my amazing conversation with Brendon—what he said and how he looked when he said it and what I said in re-turn. I'm thinking about suggesting something besides surf-ing for our date. How about a movie with popcorn, sitting close to each other in the dark, someplace where we're not separated by double layers of neoprene and icy waves?

When I get to Stephanie's, one of the ever-present gar-deners with a weed whacker lets me in the front door and then a housekeeper with a vacuum cleaner points me in the direction of Stephanie's room. I enter without knocking. The room is a jumble of posters, papers, pens, markers, tape, and other assorted art supplies. Stephanie and Alix are sitting cross-legged on the carpet, huddled over a paper banner to color in bubble letters. I smell pot, which is a drug that Stephanie approves of because it grows in nature.

They don't look up. Things are too quiet. Something's wrong.

"Greetings and salutations?" I ask.

Alix gives me a halfhearted hello. She's got a smudge of blue marker ink on her chin, which clashes with the red of her stoned eyes. She arches one brow, a message to me that my instincts about a problem are dead-on. I've just walked into a major drama scene. Stephanie, I can see now, is crying. She's one of those near-silent criers, meaning that her shoulders are shaking and she sniffs pathetically every few seconds.

"I'm self-medicating," she says, showing me eyes that are bloodshot from both tears and weed. "She's driven me to this. That's how awful she makes me feel."

Alix puts down her marker, pats Stephanie on the back. "Nothing wrong with self-medicating. We all need coping tools."

"Who?" I ask. "Who makes you self-medicate?"

I'm using my most sincere caring and concerned voice, but, like I said, my heart isn't really into it. Is it so wrong to want to feel good, to not feel pissed off? All day I've been practically giddy about Brendon. I want to smell flowers. I want to giggle. I want to tell Stephanie, *Shut up! Stop crying. I'm not in the mood for negativity today.*

But I also know that when a friend is upset, the world should stop, so I plop down on the floor between them, trying hard not to show my real attitude. To cover up, I take Stephanie's hand and give it a light squeeze.

Alix offers me a hit of the joint, but I turn it down. I don't have anything against pot for other people. They can get as stoned as they want, but I'm wary of it. I can never count on how it's going to make me feel. Sometimes I get relaxed and friendly. But more often, I want to unzip my body and step out of it like I stepped out of the wet suit. I don't want to risk the feelings of paranoia and weird social vibes that I sometimes experience. Not today, not when I feel so happy.

Stephanie takes another hit, and her words come out with a cough and a cloud of smoke. "If she was just apathetic. In her case, apathy would be a treat. I could handle apathy."

"Who?" I ask again.

Alix makes a growl of disgust in the back of her throat. On the other side of the door the vacuum kicks on, so she has to talk loudly over the whirl of the motor. "Her mom. She called Stephanie a naïve, vapid hippie and told her to grow up. I heard it myself."

Stephanie's shoulders start shaking again. "And I told her she's a self-absorbed jerk who drives a gas-guzzling pig mobile."

"Ugly, ugly mother-daughter scene," Alix explains for my benefit.

Stephanie grips a black marker like a dagger and scribbles hard, dark lines on the poster board. When that brings no relief, she hurls the marker across the room and it leaves a line on the white wall. "Guess what real estate developer is going to turn the city's only green space into a new mall? Guess who said that her job feeds me and keeps a roof over my head and I have no right to complain about anything?"

As if to answer her questions, the vacuum clicks off and we hear the housekeeper say, "Missus, can I help you with your packages?"

"Let's do it," Stephanie says.

Alix takes another hit. "I'm game. Long overdue."

They look at me. "Um, I'm not sure."

Stephanie's features tighten, like she bit into a lemon. "What do you mean? Why not?"

"I've been thinking. Remember what Ms. Pallas said?" Stephanie gives me a blank look, so I explain. "The stuff about compassion and forgiveness."

Alix tries to push the joint on me again. "Sure you don't want some of this? Sounds like you need it."

I wave it away and focus on Stephanie. "I agree, your mom's awful. And her values suck."

Stephanie's head is bobbing. "She called me pathetic."

"But she's still your mom. That's got to count for something."

"And I'm her daughter! Doesn't *that* count? What about me?"

Alix, with narrow, bleary eyes: "You didn't have any problem teaching my dad a lesson. I'm a daughter, too."

I'm wasting my words. I see by the tension in Stephanie's face that she is already miles away on a train of anger. She stabs a finger at me. "There are only two people in the world that I can count on, Alix and you. Okay, three—Ambrosia, too. You owe me!"

Alix bounces her fist twice on her chest, finishes with her index finger pointed at my nose. "Remember how we helped with the Leech. It's Steph's turn."

I suck in my lips and hold my breath, as if that can ward off peer pressure that's about two hundred times stronger than any normal-variety high school peer pressure. I have to inhale sometime, and when I do I feel myself letting in Stephanie's anger.

She's right. They're right. I do owe them. I owe them the world.

The vacuum clicks on again and the whir provides the

background to the notes of our song. Stephanie begins; Alix and I join in. I don't want to let them down, so I try. I *really* try.

Only right from the beginning, something's missing. Each note sounds vaguely flat, and our harmony has an awkward tone. Even worse, I feel alone and lost. Where are they? Where are my others? Where am I? I keep trying, but the whole thing fizzes out at note number fifty. There's no sense going any farther. We all know it and give up.

We listen without comment as the front door opens and then slams shut. We watch out the window as Stephanie's mom gets into her car. Through the front windshield we see that she's whistling happily. Our song didn't touch her. The car comes alive with a roar, and she blasts music as she pulls away.

"What the hell happened?" Alix snaps.

Stephanie turns from the window, slides down the wall, knees to her chest, a disappointed and depressed lump. "It didn't feel right. Not like the other times."

Alix, also mystified: "Something felt . . . I can't explain it . . . it felt not angry enough."

Stephanie nervously bounces her palms on her thighs. "Exactly!"

My turn. I need to say something. They're waiting. "It could have been the pot. It made the two of you too mellow to be furious."

"I didn't feel mellow," Stephanie says.

I overexplain. "You know how pot is. Yeah, I bet that's it. It took the edge off your anger. Anyway, good try, everyone. We tried. We'll do better next time."

What I don't say: It takes a lot out of a person to whip herself into a rage, to hold tight one hundred percent and block out any soft feelings. You need to stew and wallow and burn the endless fuel of fury. And right now, this minute, I'm too happy, too full of hope and possibility and thoughts of Brendon. I'm not into so much hate.

"Yeah," Alix says. "We tried."

But her look—confused, let down, and skeptical—tells me that she suspects that a little pot had nothing to do with our failure.

Ding, dong, ding.

"Good afternoon, Mr. H."

"Good afternoon, Mrs. H."

It wouldn't be daily announcement time without a burst of static, the Thought for the Day, followed by the upbeat voices of Mr. and Mrs. H piped live over the loudspeaker.

"What are the Hunter High announcements today, Mr. H?"

"Well, Mrs. H, the SAT prep class begins after school and continues every Thursday for the next ten weeks."

"Mr. H, due to yet more rain, color guard will practice indoors today. Members should meet Ms. Pallas at the gym. Yearbook photo sign-ups begin next week for seniors. And to conclude, we offer these two words about in-school Halloween costumes for the upcoming holiday. Ready, Mr. H?"

"Be appropriate!"

Announcements end with another *ding, dong, ding,* followed by the bell sending us off to our next period.

"Wait!" I yell to Raymond, who's gathering up his books and obviously trying to get out of the room quickly to avoid contact with me.

To put it mildly, things suck between us. We're hardly talking. The list of taboo topics keeps expanding. Alix's dad, of course, but also how tight I am with Stephanie and Alix. Then there's what he calls Ambrosia's negative influence on me. Ms. Pallas. The Furies. Even the weather. What friends can't talk about the weather without pissing each other off? Raymond blames the Furies for all the storms. He says he doesn't know how and doesn't know why, but he's certain of it.

Well, maybe he does have a little point—not about the weather, but about Alix's dad. I'm ready to admit anything if it means smoothing things over between Raymond and me. The truth is, I miss my best friend. I'm dying to share the news about Brendon with someone who will be as thrilled for me as I'm thrilled for myself. I miss him in a hundred different ways. Not having Raymond is a huge gap in my life. No one can take his place. I hurry across the room and position myself in front of him. He doesn't give me a chance to say anything.

"I've given this serious thought," he begins. "I didn't make this decision lightly. You can't fire me as your manager, because I have already resigned."

I don't comment on his resignation and instead hand him a makeup present that I brought to school for the occasion. It's wrapped in yellow tissue paper with a green bow. He closes his eyes and feels it all over. Eyes pop open in disbelief. "No! Is this what I think it is?"

"Yes. To show how sincere I am about missing you. You know what she means to me."

He tears off the wrapping and addresses my ceramic frog planter by her given name. "Francine!" To me: "Are you sure you want to give this away? You know I'm a big admirer. I'll treasure her always."

"I know you will, Raymond. I miss you. I'm sorry."

So just like that, ninety percent of the tension between us drains away. It's amazing what a present and an apology can do. Everything's going to be better between us now. I just know it. I motion for Alix and Stephanie to go ahead to the next class without me. They exchange dejected looks, but they'll get over it. Raymond and I have a lot to cover in the few minutes between classes. We haven't talked—a real talk—in days. We're used to knowing everything about each other.

As we walk he tells me he's making progress on the violin tune that's been stuck in his head, and he hums it for me. I still don't like it. Something about the rhythm grates on me. I describe my first surfing lesson with Alix. He says that his mom misses having me stop by. I tell him I like his mom a lot. He wants to know what cute thing He-Cat did lately.

"And the Leech?" he asks.

"Some of our lesson has worn off. She's not begging my forgiveness anymore. But it's okay. She basically leaves me alone. That's a big improvement. I can live with that."

"Prepare yourself for my big news," he says. "Wait for it . . . wait for it . . . I joined the color guard."

"What?" My voice jumps an octave and at least ten decibels. "You hate marching-band music."

"Ms. Pallas kept on me about it. She said I could even

write a song for the band. You know how I've harbored a long, secret desire to wear a snappy electric-blue-and-white uniform with epaulettes. You should join, too."

"No way." I salute him and he snaps his heels together and returns the salute.

"But Meg, it's got high-step marching. It's got the John Philip Snooza version of music from *Zorba the Greek*. By Jove, it's got flags. What more could you want?"

We reach the section of hallway where we split in different directions. "Correction," he says. "I should say, 'By Zeus, it's got flags,' considering the band's Olympus theme this year, and your personal connection to all things ancient. Ms. Pallas said to encourage you to join."

"The woman's relentless. I swear she's made it her personal mission to get me into the guard. Ms. Pallas is . . . you know what I'd like to tell her to do?"

He breaks in, takes me by the arm. "Ms. Pallas is not someone to mess with. Seriously, Meg. Don't mess."

"What do you know about her? Are you still snooping? What did you find out? Tell me what—"

I'm stopped short by the way he is squinting hard at me, like he can't quite get me into focus.

"What?"

"You're thin, but only in all the right places."

"You've noticed. Yes, I am now the proud owner of hips and a waist." I show them off by doing a fashion-model spin.

"And boobs! Sigh. How quickly you children grow up!"

"Boobs? Me?" I drop my head to my chin and peek down the unbuttoned top of my shirt. What I see there takes me by surprise. When did *that* happen?

I raise my eyes again to find Raymond's pinky finger extended in my direction. "We're okay, then? You and me?"

I hook my little finger to his. "Friends forever." We pull and break.

"I have something for you, too." He removes a couple of sheets of paper from his backpack and hands them over.

My eyes skim the first sentence: *The law is reason, free from passion*. And the second: *The virtue of justice consists in moderation*.

"Promise me you'll read it."

"What is this? Are you auditioning for a guest spot on Hunter High's Thought for the Day?"

No snappy comeback, just an earnest "Promise?"

I make an *X* over my heart. I remember Brendon. "I have big news, too."

His eyebrows lift with interest.

"Too late to go into it now," I say. "There's plenty of time later."

> *Let me be blunt: The three of you are neither moderate nor free from passion.*

What I have in my hands is Raymond's official resignation as the manager of the Furies. It's signed and dated, and clearly influenced by Ms. Pallas. I recognize the tone, which is even more pontificating than Raymond's usual style. I'm surprised he didn't get it notarized.

> *Don't write me off as some super-naïve type who doesn't understand that society would be a mess if*

nobody gets punished when they do something wrong. I get it: you can't let everyone off the hook.

But who made three angry high school girls judge, jury, and prison guards? How do you know what's right? How do you know when the punishment fits the crime? How do you judge people clearly when you're all wrapped up in your own hate and delusions of world domination?

You say you want to punish people who abuse their power. Well, open your eyes, little missies! Guess who's in danger of abusing their own power? Do I need to name names?

Be careful! You are messing with forces bigger and more powerful than yourselves.

I hereby give my notice. I am cutting all ties with your endeavors. I will be devoting more time to my studies, my violin, and color guard practice. I will, however, fulfill my obligation to our joint Western Civ project. Ms. Pallas is blackmailing me into it. My other option is to take an F, and I've never gotten below a B-plus in my life on anything. I am not about to let it happen now.

Sincerely, Your former manager

I read his resignation twice. The first time through, it annoys me so much I start to crumple up the paper. Raymond just won't give up. What we did to Alix's dad hardly qualifies as having delusions of world domination. And what's wrong with passion?

I stew on his insults a little, but my mind quickly loses its grip on them. The warm feeling of having Raymond in my life rushes back to me. I don't want to be mad at him. I don't want to be mad at anyone. Life is too good right now for that. I have my best friend back. I have Alix and Stephanie, who are feeling more and more like the sisters I never had. Ambrosia looks out for me. My foster mother leaves me alone. He-Cat is the best pet ever. And, of course, I have my date with Brendon coming up.

The second time I read Raymond's resignation, it's a whole different experience. It's weird how the same words that made me flash with anger a minute ago now make me smile tolerantly. This is classic Raymond—the Raymond I love and who loves me.

I flip to the second page, which is his promised contribution to our class project.

1. *Our rage that patrolled the crimes of men, that stalked their rage, dissolves—we loose a lethal tide to sweep the world.* Aeschylus
2. Oedipus was tortured by the Furies for killing his own father, even though it was in self-defense and he didn't even know it was his dad. Fair?
3. The chorus swears to avenge themselves by setting loose all their evil powers on the land of Athens . . . They do not let up; they do not go home (Cliff Notes; Fourth Stasimon, Aeschylus, *The Eumenides*)

There are more quotes and ideas in a numbered list that fills the page. I flip it over looking for an explanation. It's blank. We can use this stuff in our project somehow. Who knows? It could come in handy.

I hear my name and whirl to see Brendon running down the hall to catch up with me. He's wearing his intense, serious expression, which, on the knee-buckling scale, comes in a close second to his grin. I order my heart to slow down and my books to stay in my arms.

"How about today?" he asks.

"Today?"

"After school. You and me."

"You mean, our . . . like, getting together?" I can't bring myself to say the D-word, because maybe that's not what he has in mind. Maybe he just wants to hang out like I'm one of his surfer bros. Except for the fact that I'm a lousy surfer. I'm sure he noticed that.

"Yeah, our date," he says. "But not surfing. I have a better idea."

No neoprene! I want to pump my fist in the air, but I restrain myself. "Like what?"

"It's a surprise. Meet me at—" He checks his wrist. He's wearing one of those mammoth sports watches with enough buttons and dials to navigate a ship. "At 3:47. At the board-walk in front of the roller coaster. Okay?"

"3:47?"

"3:48 is okay, too, but don't be late. It has to be close to that time. You said you like secret places."

Parrot Meg does her thing again: "I like secret places."

His expression explodes into that grin. "It doesn't get much more secret than this."

In autumn on a weekday afternoon, nothing much is going on at the boardwalk. I wonder why Brendon wants to meet me here, of all places. The shops selling tacky souvenirs and overpriced corn dogs are closed until spring, and so are the rides. At first I wonder if this is about mini-golf, but Poseidon's Kingdom is closed, too.

A deserted boardwalk on a dreary, gray day like this one can be kind of eerie. Most people think it's too lonely to hang out with games and rides that sit there doing nothing. They prefer the bustling summer crowd, to get lost in the energy, the pushing and laughing, the lines of hyper kids. I prefer the empty boardwalk. I guess I'm different that way. There's the sound of waves smashing on the beach, some-thing you can't hear when there's music blasting and sum-mer crowds. Overhead, the bright red and blue cars of the gondola sit still in the sky. I pass the motionless Pirate Ship ride and then the mechanical gypsy fortune-teller machine, whose eyes seem to follow me as I head for our 3:47 meet-up. Is the gypsy looking at me with pity or with a laughing, mocking expression? Does she know something that I don't?

What if Brendon doesn't show up? How long should I wait? What if he's playing me so he can laugh himself sick? I just know that's it. He's home, smirking to himself at the image of the pathetic, naïve girl waiting among all the boarded-up rides and games. He's going to tell his friends what he did, and they'll get a good laugh out of it, too. The perfect follow-up to my mini-golf humiliation.

Why did I agree to meet him? How could I have fallen for this? I am an idiot! Why don't I learn? Ambrosia is right! Don't trust him! Don't trust anyone. Embarrassment and anger, they both start building inside of me.

But when I get to the roller coaster, I see a hand waving from a little farther down the boardwalk. The distrust drains away. He didn't lie. He's here. He walks faster, breaks into a little jog. I steady my nerves, steady my everything.

"Hey!" he says, rushing up a little too close to me, then backing away.

"Hey!"

"You made it!"

"I made it!"

"I'm glad you made it. And all that!"

"Me too!"

He beams at me. I beam back. I play with my hair a little. He looks at his hands. What happened to all the exclamation points in our greeting? It's like they fell off a cliff. Could our date have turned any more flat and awkward so quickly? I'm a loser. He's sorry that he ever suggested meeting me here, meeting me anywhere.

"Hey." He starts again.

"Yeah," I say.

Thank goodness, in that awkward moment there's the sudden *clickity-clank* of the Giant Dipper behind us. It makes me start, and I have an attack of the nervous giggles. A workman must be putting the famous wooden roller coaster through its paces to find out what repairs are needed. Good distraction. Brendon and I study the train of cars inching up the tracks. When it reaches the high point and shoots over the edge and comes tearing down the first wild dip, I don't know why—we aren't even looking at each other—but we get the same reflex. We put our arms in the air and squeal, imitating all the thousands of summer and weekend riders.

That breaks the ice a little. We both like roller coasters. That's interesting. We can talk about that.

"I like roller coasters a lot," I say.

"I like roller coasters, too!"

"The boardwalk's fun when everything's open in the summer."

"But it's even better now."

I jump on that. "I was just thinking that! I'm glad you suggested meeting here. There's a certain feeling to the boardwalk when no one else is around, a sad happiness."

"Or a happy sadness," he quickly adds. "Most girls I know think it's too boring in the off-season. They get depressed by the whole ghost-town feel."

The cars make another loop, and I raise my voice almost to a shout to be heard over the rumble. "I don't mind depressed at all. I'm more of a ghost-town kind of person than most."

He's studying me, really listening, which I take as

encouragement to go on. "I like being the only thing moving here. When everything around me is still like this, I can almost feel the blood going through my veins. It makes me feel really alive."

When he doesn't respond—just more of his serious look—I want to take back my words. Why did I say something so bizarre? Blood through my veins? He doesn't have a clue of what I'm talking about. It's even worse when he *does* respond: "I can leave if you want to be the only thing moving."

"Oh no! That's not . . . I mean, I didn't mean . . . not at all. I'm glad . . ."

"I'm just teasing you. I'm not going anywhere. What you said about feeling alive? I feel it here, too."

He checks his watch and motions for me to follow him down the boardwalk. He has a high-spirited, skipping walk that I never noticed in school. Maybe he doesn't have it in school. There he has to act cool and aloof to fit in with those Plagues. He dashes over to the Tsunami ride. "When I was eight, I threw up my entire guts on this ride. The centrifugal force on half-digested cotton candy was awesome."

Well, that wasn't the most romantic memory for him to share, but in a strange way it is romantic. It's the sort of thing you tell someone that you don't want to pretend with, a person that you want to know the real you, barf episodes and all. To reciprocate, I point to the Double Shot, a tube of metal with cages at both ends.

"And on our left, we are passing one of my worst memories. I came here with a group of . . ." I start to say kids in my group home, but leave out the group home part. "At the first drop, I cried so hard they had to stop the ride to let me off. I still cringe thinking about that walk of shame."

"Care to indulge in some Dipping Dots?" He mimes purchasing a large bowl at the boarded-up stand, and as we walk we pretend to share the cold treat, oohing and aahing over the delicious flavors and chiding each other for being pigs and taking more than our half.

"Here's something you can't do in the summer!" Brendon makes a dash to a kiddie ride, a ring of wildly painted sea creatures that, when powered, go round and round and up and down. He scans for a security guard, then jumps into the seat of a purple-and-yellow whale with big green eyes. "Good old Bulgy!" He strokes the creature's neck. "This dude rocked my world when I was five."

Brendon looks totally ridiculous on that ride, a muscular surfer with his knees folded to his chin in order to squeeze in. But so cute. Playing with the steering wheel, making stupid little-boy driving sounds, he looks happy and open, just like the little kid he probably was in kindergarten. I wish I had known him back then.

I stand outside the gate of the ride and extend my hand in his direction. He slaps it like kids usually do with their parents. We touched. He gives me a sheepish look and hops out.

"What a dork. I haven't done anything like that in forever."

"It's my bad influence. I bring out the dork in people."

He thinks for a second. "That's a good thing. I'm happier being a dork than a jerk."

He checks his watch again. Why does he keep doing

that? Does he have somewhere else to go? Is he bored with me? He must be bored. He doesn't *seem* bored, but people can act one way and feel another. That's happened to me before. It's happened to me a lot. It embarrasses me to think that he's bored and is looking for a way to dump me. Then I feel kind of mad about that. I'll beat him to it. I'll dump him first. I wish I had a watch to check, too.

"Well, this was fun," I say, super peppy. "But I have to go now."

"What?"

"Thanks and everything. I liked seeing your secret spot."

It's Brendon's turn now to fumble for words. "But this isn't . . . you have to go? I thought. When I said . . . I want to show you . . ."

I am so relieved. He looks too disappointed to be faking it, so I must have been wrong about the dumping part. I backpedal hard. "I guess I can stay a little longer. I mean, I do have something else to do, like I said. I didn't make that up. But if you want me to stay . . ."

"I want you to stay."

"For real?"

He leans in closer and I think: *He's going to kiss me.* It's going to happen. He's going to kiss me on the lips in front of the Ferris wheel. But instead of lips, his finger moves gently over the corner of my mouth. "You had a little crumb there. Must have been an escaped Dipping Dot."

I blush. That was almost a kiss. It made my legs go weak. "I'm a messy eater."

"It's settled, then. You're staying?"

I nod.

"Good. Because this isn't the secret spot. This is just the boardwalk."

Again he checks his watch. "It's time." He reaches out like he wants to take my hand and I start to give it to him, but we both change our minds at the same instant. He walks quickly, and I take giant steps to keep up.

"Come on," he urges.

At the far end of the boardwalk, behind the Logger's Revenge ride, there's a hole in the chain-link fence that cordons off the boardwalk from the cliff above the river that empties into the ocean. Using both hands, Brendon widens the opening so it's just big enough for me to squeeze though. When I'm on the other side I do the same for him, and then we're both standing on a high, narrow cliff ledge.

"This is where you tell me, 'Whatever you do, don't look down,' right?" I say.

"Not afraid of heights, are you?"

I shake my head and give a nonchalant smile, even though I am not thrilled about being suspended twenty feet above the water on a ridge that's not much wider than my shoes.

"Don't worry. It's safe. I've done this a lot. Follow me."

With Brendon in the lead, we inch along the cliff and follow the steady downhill slope toward the open ocean. I don't look beneath my feet and I keep my back pressed against the solid rock wall for security. When we get close to the bottom, Brendon waits for a wave to recede and then he jumps onto the only small patch of sand that's momentarily dry. Everywhere else, there are nasty-looking boulders.

Then it's my turn. He must sense my hesitation, because he holds out his arms—"Want some help?"—and as much as I want those arms around my waist and my hands on his neck, I also want to do this on my own. I don't like being a helpless girl. Because I'm not. I'm a Fury. I should be able to jump a few feet. I tell him I'm fine on my own, and he gives advice:

"Time it right. Avoid these big rocks. Wait. Wait. Now! Jump!"

My knees buckle a little and the legs of my jeans get splashed, but other than that it's a perfect landing. I did it. Just offshore, though, I see another wave build and break. I glance left and right, wondering how we're going to avoid getting soaked or even bowled over. I panic as a flood of white, swirling foam rushes at me. Brendon's hand takes mine and pulls me backward with the water pursuing quickly.

It stops because it hit a barrier. We're in a cave, a small one but big enough for two to squeeze in tightly. I have my second attack of giggles of the day, and I'm normally not a giggler. Maybe it's the relief of not drowning. Or noticing that overhead, a dozen orange sea stars framed by clumps of dark seaweed cling to the ceiling. Maybe it's because I'm gripping tight onto the sleeve of Brendon's flannel shirt so we can both stay balanced on the same boulder, and there's no place else to go.

"Welcome to my humble secret spot," he says. "Like it?"

"It's amazing! How did you ever find this place?"

"Coincidence."

"There is no such thing as coincidence, young earthling.

There are only karmic lessons from the cosmos. Maybe you were supposed to find it."

"Yeah, well, I did a total klutz move surfing, and the *cosmos* ripped my board away from me. The current took it into here. I paddled after it. The cave is underwater most of the time—except for a short period when the tide is super low like it is today. I come here when I want to think."

"Think about what?

I catch him looking at me out of the corner of his eye, weighing whether he wants to tell me. "You know . . . stuff."

"That's descriptive."

"Sorry. It's hard to say it out loud. I think about . . . well . . . you, for one thing."

"Me?"

"How I treated you when you were gutsy enough to ask me to go golfing. And how I treat other people. I haven't always been the nicest guy in the world. I think about the person I want to be. And whether I can ever be that person. Do you think people can change?"

"Of course!" I'm not saying this just to be flirty. I think of what I discovered about myself recently, how so much is possible. I can't give him the details, but I want to say something encouraging. "Yes, definitely. From personal experience, I know that people change. You can, too."

I peek around the opening of the cave and get a glimpse of the famous surfing spot. There's a lineup of surfers, probably his friends, waiting for the next set of waves to roll in. "Cool angle on the surfer statue! This is how the seals, otters, and whales must see it."

I'm surprised at his reaction. He stares at the statue like he's scared of it, or hates it, or both. His voice goes flat. "Yeah, Prince of the Waves gazing out into eternity."

"That statue. It reminds me of you."

His body shifts uncomfortably. I feel it as a tug on the flannel in my hand. "What? Did I say something wrong?"

"You don't know? You really don't know?"

"Know what?"

His jaw tightens and the resemblance to the statue is even stronger. "My grandfather was the model. Big-wave surfer from way back. My father looks just like him, and I look like my dad did at this age. My family's been in this town for a long time."

"That must be something," I say. "To know where you came from. To feel connected to a place and to people. I wish I . . ."

I let the sentence run out. I don't know how much Brendon knows about me, and I don't want to turn this into a pity party about the poor foster kid who doesn't know her own parents or belong anywhere.

"There are some good things about it," he says. I wonder if he's going to say something else. He seems to want to, but he pauses. I want to know more about him. Anything. Everything. I ask: "That must mean that there are some not-so-good things, too."

"Expectations." The word comes out harsh, blunt. He motions toward the Prince, a gray silhouette against a gray sky. "I'm supposed to be just like him, and just like my father, carry on the oh-so-important family legacy. Never question it. Ride the biggest waves and tackle the hardest surf, win all the contests, be the biggest badass dude in the water. Have the coolest friends, the sickest board, the newest wet suit, the hottest girlfriend. What if I don't want the hottest girlfriend?"

"Every guy wants the hottest girlfriend."

Fierce. "Not this guy."

"You always date the hottest girls in the school."

"Because that's what everyone expects me to do. What if I want a girlfriend *I* want and she's not so hot?"

Now I'm the one who's fidgeting. He rotates on our rock and gives me a funny look. "Uh-oh. Did I just blow it? Yeah, I blew it. I'm not saying *you're* not hot. Because you are."

"Yeah, right." I lick my index finger, touch it to my bottom and make a sizzling sound.

He laughs. "See, that's what I mean! What if I want a girlfriend who makes me laugh and thinks about things in interesting ways? Maybe I want a girlfriend who's not in the popular crowd and who prefers the boardwalk in the winter and doesn't complain about hanging out in a cave and takes risks and . . ."

"And," I add, hopefully, "is hot, too?"

"Definitely. Smoking hot." Another laugh, but he quickly turns pensive. "I'm talking about more than just my choice of girlfriends."

"I know that."

"It's about my whole life. What if I don't want to carry on some stupid surfing family legacy? What if I want something else? What if I want to figure things out for myself?"

"Surfing? You want to give that up?"

"No way! I love surfing. Without it, I feel disconnected from everything—the air, the water, from myself. Coming down the face of a wave, the power, the explosion of colors, being eye to eye with an otter, being part of all that. It's the best. But for him"—he juts his chin toward the statue—"for my dad, for Pox, for all those guys, it's not about any of that. For them, it's about competition and winning and making new surfers feel like shit. It's about ruling the break, being royalty, the prince. They miss the point."

Everything he says meshes with what Alix feels about surfing and how Stephanie relates to nature, and what I felt during my short surfing experience. "No one can be prince of the waves," I say. "The ocean can't be ruled by puny people. It doesn't even know we exist. We're lucky it lets us hang out in it sometimes. "

He laughs again, though I wasn't trying to be funny. "Exactly. *You* get it. But if my dad or any of the Plagues heard me talking like this . . . It's hard to go against your friends and your family, against who they think you are and who they expect you to be. Sometimes I feel like I'm living a secret life. Prince of the Waves on the outside. Somebody else—I don't even know who yet—on the inside. But I want to stop pretending."

"So stop, then."

"It's not so easy for me. Not like for you. You say exactly what you feel."

"Me?" My voice goes up an octave.

"You stood up in class and said you hated everyone."

"Oh God, not that!" I try to hide my face in my hands,

but that puts me off balance and I almost fall into the tide pool below our feet. Brendon saves me by wrapping his arm around my waist.

"It was weird as hell, but I couldn't stop thinking about how you said exactly what you felt. I can't stop thinking about you. Meg, do you hate me, too? Please don't hate me."

I can't speak. I can only feel his hands.

"Is this okay? That I'm holding you like this?"

I nod approval and manage words, the right words, I hope. "Let the real you out. People will like that person. I really like him."

He's so close and I feel him wanting to get even closer. I want to confess my biggest secret to him, too: I'm not what I appear to be on the surface, either. But I stop myself. I don't dare. I can't.

With his free hand he takes my face by the chin, turns it in his direction. We are nose to nose, belly to belly. He kisses me, and he tastes of salt water and apples and a taste that's uniquely him. We kiss and kiss again, moving only our mouths so that we can stay on the rock.

Then who cares about getting wet? Not me, not us. We make the decision together silently, and stumble into six inches of freezing-cold water, hardly feeling a change in temperature, and we keep kissing with the sea stars overhead and the barnacles and mussels hunkered down on the walls and hermit crabs scurrying around.

It feels like we'll never stop kissing. Neither of us wants to. And maybe we wouldn't have, except for the big wave breaking through the barrier of the cave. Water surges to our knees before being sucked away again. This time we can't ignore the cold or the danger of the rising surf. We laugh and kiss again and hop around splashing each other. Brendon checks his watch. He sounds slightly drunk, and that's the way I feel, too. Drunk and shivering and happy.

"Tide is coming back in hard. We should have left five minutes ago. We need to scramble."

He leads me away by the hand. In my mind I say goodbye to the crabs, the barnacles, the urchins and anemones, and to the seal's-eye view of the Prince of the Waves.

I wonder: will I ever return to this dangerous, magical spot that exists for only a few precious moments at a time?

I can't help myself. I have no control. The next morning, as soon as I spot Alix, Stephanie, and Ambrosia—the people in the world who mean everything to me—I spill the whole story. About the boardwalk, the cave, the kissing. We're in the parking lot before school, and I rest my backpack at my feet so I can use my hands to demonstrate how we balanced together on the rock.

"Just how far did this lustfest go?" Alix asks.

"Lustfest? It was just light kissing."

The same skeptical look passes over all three faces. "Okay, okay! Tongues got involved," I admit. "And hands. But we remained perfectly vertical."

Alix wipes some crusty sleep from her eyes. "Bad taste in guys. Plan on getting it on with Gnat, too? How 'bout Rat Boy while you're at it?"

"Ew!" I screw up my face. "I'm not getting it on with Gnat or Rat Boy. That thought makes me want to puke. I'm not getting it on with anyone."

Stephanie, through a clenched jaw, accuses me of something else. "You told him, didn't you? About us. Who we are. What did you tell him?"

"Nothing!"

"You better not have."

Ambrosia comes to my defense. "Meg would never do that. That would ruin everything. Everything!"

I'm grateful that she trusts me, even though the others clearly don't. But I need their trust. And I want them—I need them—to see Brendon through my eyes. So I try explaining to Alix how he isn't one of those testosterone-fueled surfers who make her life miserable. I tell Stephanie that when Brendon talked about the ocean and the otters, there was poetry in his words.

Meanwhile a group of stoners keep inching closer to reclaim their usual before-school smoking spot by the parking-lot fence. Ambrosia, irritated by their presence, shoos them away. Studying me, she uses both of her hands to lift and twist her newly layered hair to the top of her head. She lets go of it, and for a moment the hair seems to defy gravity and balance there. Then it falls. "You better watch out."

"What do you mean?" I ask.

A quick lift of Ambrosia's right eyebrow. It holds there a second, the sharpness contrasting with the sudden warmth of her words. "Meg, Megaera, you are way too trusting. He could be playing you. In your heart, you know that's a big possibility."

"I'm not an idiot. I'm a good judge of people."

"Bullshit," Alix says.

Ambrosia quiets her with a warning finger and says to me: "If you think so, I'm sure Brendon is worthy of your trust. Not like all the other people you trusted in your life. That worked out so well. They treated you wonderfully, right?"

Her sarcasm makes its point. I feel some of my hope collapse.

"We're just looking out for you," she continues. "We care about you. We don't want Brendon to set you up and then—what's that expression?—screw you royally."

My cell phone vibrates then. It's a message from him: *U & me? Ambrosia's Halloween party?*

A part of me soars with happiness. The other part— the suspicious part—hands the phone to Ambrosia to read the text.

"See, he didn't dump me," I say.

"Could be. Or a party could be the perfect setup." Her features tighten. She's calculating something. "Leave this to me." With her sharp fingernails, she types and sends a reply: *Meet u there. I want 2 surprise u with my costume. Picked it just 4 u.*

I hit her with questions: "Why did you do that? What costume? So you don't think he's playing me? I should trust him?"

Ambrosia shifts her backpack on her shoulders. "Everything will be answered in time. I have the perfect disguise for you. Sexy but not slutty." She hands back my phone, which already has a new message: *Can't wait 2 C costume!*

"I still don't like it," Alix says.

"Neither do I," says Stephanie.

Before they walk away, Ambrosia gives me a look that's

a smile and not a smile. The whole encounter leaves me reeling. I have to hold on to the fence to settle myself.

Cue Raymond to appear when I most need him. He looks from my strained expression to the three backs walking away, and then to me again. "Whew. I need a sushi knife to cut the drama in the air. What was that all about?"

I don't hold back. "Me and Brendon."

Puzzled expression. The light goes on. "You mean, like, you and Brendon? Brendon and Meg sitting in a tree?"

I nod. "Actually, it was in a cave standing, not sitting. It's true. I think it's true. But maybe not."

"I never would have thought to put the two of you together. But that's the charming miracle of modern teen romance. I admit I have a soft spot for Brendon."

"Really?"

"If he were gay, I would be crushing, too. His brooding is so becoming on him. I always suspected that he just fell in with the wrong crowd. So many of our youth do, you know."

"Exactly! You get it! Brendon doesn't belong with that bunch anymore—if he ever did."

"Obviously a deep, meaningful conversation with the lad has won the lady's heart."

"You don't think Brendon might be playing me? He's so . . . and I'm not so . . ."

"Meg, you're a goddess walking on Earth! What more could a straight guy want? Tell me you have a date lined up."

"Sort of," I say. I show him the recent messages on my phone.

"So romantic! Costumes and everything." That really lightens the mood. I can always count on him to make me feel better. I playfully slap at his arm. "So what's this about Ambrosia having a Halloween party?"

"She put invitations in lockers."

An exaggerated hurt look blooms on his face. "Guess I didn't make the A-list."

"We're all A-list. She invited everyone. I bet the invitation fell to the bottom of your locker."

"She must not like me." A couple of fake sniffs.

"Such delicate nerve endings, Raymond. Don't be a fragile flower. I'm sure it was an oversight."

"It wasn't."

"Why do you think that?"

"Ambrosia and I have different worldviews."

"Come anyway. It's a party. Rumors are flying about the delights she has planned."

He gives me a goofy slug on the shoulder. "Delights! Oh, I will be there. Don't worry. Nothing could keep me away."

All the party rumors are true.

No parents will be here tonight. There's going to be a real band, not some high school kids who took a few guitar lessons. And alcohol. The invitation said that nobody has to bring a thing. Ambrosia will provide everything that anyone could possibly want, plus stuff that we don't even *know* that we want. She told Alix, Stephanie, and me to come in the late afternoon without costumes. She has everything we need.

So here we are at her house. Things start out a little tense because of the whole Brendon episode. I assure them again that I'd never betray their trust by revealing our secret. At Ambrosia's prompting, Stephanie gives me a quick, tentative hug and Alix mutters a sentence with the word *sorry* in it. I'm relieved that Ambrosia, too, has come around.

When we enter the living room, Alix lets out a long whistle of appreciation. This is not only about the decorations, which we all agree are beyond fantastic. There are cobwebs that look and feel real and life-sized mummies and gravestones that also seem real. Alix takes Stephanie by the hand, dragging her from table to table, a kid in a candy store, only instead of Sour Patch Kids and Hershey's Kisses there's real champagne from France in buckets of ice, premium vodka sold only in Russia, sake from Japan, tequila from Mexico.

"Plants are not the only thing that my family collects in its travels," Ambrosia explains. "I want my guests to be happy."

Alix removes the cap of a bottle of something called *rakia*. "From Albania," she reads from the label. "Where is Albania again?" She sticks her nose into the opening, but not for long. When she comes up for air, her eyes are watering. "Your guests are going to be *very* happy."

Stephanie holds a small bottle of clear liquid up to the light.

"Don't shake that!" Ambrosia warns.

Stephanie puts it down carefully. "Someone's definitely going to call the police."

Ambrosia scoffs, flicks her wrist like she's shooing away a pesky bug. "Oh, the law. As usual, it is completely useless and ineffectual. The police have been taken care of. Not to worry."

"No popo! Might as well get started, then." Alix tilts back her head, takes a sip of the rakia. "It's awful. But addictive." She offers the bottle to Stephanie, who says, "Why not?"

"So intemperate," Ambrosia says. "I like that."

I have a one-track mind. "My costume?" I ask eagerly.

I don't think Ambrosia hears me, because she's pointing with disapproval to a section of cobweb. "Does that look right to you?" She pushes up her sleeves past her elbows and thrusts her bare arms into the mass, stretching it so that the netting thins and expands. It's like she's weaving it herself, and when she's done she steps back to admire her work.

Then a spin to me. "So impatient and self-absorbed! I like that part of you. We don't get to see it enough. Costumes will come. First some preliminaries."

We follow her through the corridors and up the stairs, every inch of the house decked out with spiders, lifelike dead rats hanging by their tails, and pumpkins with sinister grins. Even if there weren't a single decoration, the red walls, dim lighting, and old furniture would be eerie enough. When we enter her bedroom, even with the window closed, I'm hit by the faint odor of rotting meat from that red plant that sits in the center of the all-white garden. It's still blooming, seems to be getting even bigger. Everything in the room is about the same as on our last visit—the wicker chair and vase of roses, the jack-in-the-box with the broken neck, and yes, the strange snow globe on the bookcase. My eyes go right for it and my feet follow. I pick it up, feeling the heft in both hands.

"You remember my little trinket. I thought you might," Ambrosia says with obvious pleasure. "Like it any better now?"

I turn it upside down and back again, but this time feel nothing as the ash falls around figures that are posed in exaggerated states of grief and horror. "Sure, it's interesting." But my mind is elsewhere. I want to see my costume. "You said something about preliminaries?"

Ambrosia takes a chest-expanding inhale, turns her palms up and raises her arms until they clasp overhead. Then she bends at the waist, keeping her back straight, until her hands are flat on the ground. She pops back up, claps her hands once. "All warmed up now. Ready to go." She steps to her vanity table and pulls out a drawer that is surprisingly long, like an artist's drawer. Instead of paints, though, it contains a treasure trove of lipstick, eye makeup, pots of rouge and face powder, plus dozens of metal gadgets designed to pluck, squeeze, snip, shave, twist, and curl.

"No, no, no!" Alix snarls.

Stephanie backs herself into a corner, plants her feet. "No way. I'm not a tool of the cosmetic industry—even for Halloween."

Ambrosia makes a calming motion like she's patting down the air. "You two, relax. Save your outrage for a better purpose."

She swings to me.

"Yes, please," I say. "The works."

Ambrosia guides me by both shoulders into a swivel chair with a thick cushion of white brocade. I don't like what I see in the mirror. I never do. I know that when Brendon was kissing me, I felt beautiful. I want to feel that way again. My eyes make a quick scan of everything that's wrong: eyes too small, pores too big, lips too thin, nose too thick, cheekbones . . . what cheekbones? Brendon said he doesn't want a hot girlfriend, but come on! I think of all the girls he's dated and know that I don't measure up. Ambrosia removes the stretchy band tying back my hair, the worst part of me. As she undoes the braid, each section springs into its usual frizzy, wild mass. I can't help but compare my hair to Ambrosia's hair, which shines like satin. She's wearing it in two silly buns like Princess Leia, and still manages to look gorgeous and sophisticated. She flicks on the circle of lights that surrounds the mirror.

"It's hopeless," I say.

Lights off. She moves aside the mirror so that I can no longer see myself. "Off limits until I'm done. Your lack of self-esteem causes wrinkles, you know. All that frowning and worrying—it's as damaging as cigarettes. Beauty is about the right confident attitude. And of course, using the right products."

She rummages through her drawer of cosmetic goodies until she comes up with the bottle she wants. The glass is deep sapphire-colored and there's no label on it, so I assume it's a homemade concoction. She shakes it hard, pours a quarter-sized spot of clear gel into one hand, and rubs her palms together. When she smooths it on my hair, my scalp tingles.

"What *is* that?" I try to grab the bottle, but she whisks it out of reach.

"Old formula dating way back. I swear by it. In fact, I was named after it."

She pours a dab onto her finger, only this time it comes out thicker and gold-colored. Instead of putting it on my hair, she licks it off her finger with a moan of pleasure. "It's anything you want it to be, whatever you happen to need at the moment."

The sample she puts on my finger tastes like honey, orange blossoms, and ginger. If Ambrosia with her perfect skin and hair swears by it, that's good enough for me. I hope this truly is a miracle cosmetic, because a miracle is what I need.

I sit back and let her go to work, following her nonstop string of orders. Widen my eyes, close my eyes, relax my mouth, puff out my cheeks, arch an eyebrow, and pucker my lips. Sometimes the miracle cream is gold and flaky to be dabbed on my eyelids; a minute later, it comes out of the bottle rich and white and she spreads it down my neck as a thick moisturizer.

Out of my line of vision, Alix and Stephanie are also busy. I hear them moving around and fiddling with things that crunch and ping. Ambrosia checks over her shoulder and orders, "Tisiphone, more flowers and vines. Weave them into those dreadlocks."

Then Ambrosia is leaning over me again, her hands moving with her usual skillfulness as she curls, sprays, pats, and smudges. When she's done, she spins my chair around and takes a critical look at her canvas. I notice that there's an actual bead of sweat on her forehead. That's how hard she had to work on me. Ambrosia never, ever sweats.

"The verdict?" I ask.

She pronounces me "magnificent."

"I want to see!"

"Not yet. We're almost there."

She disappears into her closet and emerges with three large shopping bags hooked around her elbows. Alix, her face, arms, all of her skin glimmering with a silvery powder, receives the first bag and we watch enthusiastically as she pulls out a two-piece outfit. There's a pair of very short shorts, bronze in color, with a matching midriff halter that laces up the front. This is clearly not the fabulous outfit that Alix had in mind. Can't say I blame her. It reminds me of a jogging suit—if, say, Robin Hood were running a half-marathon.

Alix's mouth twists. "I'm not the halter type."

Ambrosia ignores the complaint. "You are going to love the accessories. They totally make the outfit."

Next she hands Stephanie a bag that's twice the size of the other two. It takes some manipulating to get her costume out in one piece.

"That's more like it!" Alix says with envy.

Wings! A full set of them. Not the small, fluffy, frilly white wings that some girls wear with their underwear as part of a Hot Angel costume. These are solid, big, black, and veiny. What fabric is that? Nothing I've ever seen before. The wings look dangerous, like if you turn too fast in them you can poke out someone's eye.

Stephanie is deliriously happy with her costume, jumping up and down and clapping her hands. "Bat wings! Most people hate bats, but they're my favorite animal. Bats are totally misunderstood." She lifts the wings in front of her and spins them like a dance partner.

My turn. I plunge right into my bag and rummage around. But my enthusiasm withers quickly. It doesn't look very thrilling in there, just a couple of pieces of fabric of different sizes and shapes. I try to stay positive. Ambrosia does want me to look great. I remind myself that she wouldn't have gone to all this trouble if she didn't. The material *is* soft and silky, the color of a caramel chew, almost exactly my skin tone. I pull out a piece that looks like an extra-long scarf, and hold it at one end so it dangles limp in front of me. "Um, excuse me, but I don't have a clue what to do with this."

Ambrosia grabs it from my hand, but I can tell her annoyance is only put on. "You are helpless without me," she teases. To Alix and Stephanie: "You two team up to get ready. Tisiphone, give Alecto a hand with her hair. We need to get it all up. Don't be stingy with the gel."

Ambrosia hustles me into her giant walk-in closet, where she orders me to strip. I get down to my underwear, but she insists: "No prudishness. All of it." Good thing I've lived in so many group homes, where you quickly get over modesty in front of other girls. I stand in front of Ambrosia naked, goose bumps erupting everywhere. I feel her eyes running over me, and I realize how desperately I want her approval. She has gone to so much trouble just for me. She cares about me and wants me to look incredible. In the confined space of her closet, the perfume on her body and lingering on the dozens of hanging outfits closes in on me, makes it a little hard for me to breathe normally.

She trades my white cotton underpants for the pair of skimpy flesh-colored ones at the bottom of my costume bag. She doubles and twists the scarf-like material and wraps it where my bra used to be. Next she takes out some fabric that's been folded into a rectangle, holds it at one end, and gives it a hard shake. It's bigger than I thought, the size of a bedsheet, and it floats like a parachute before settling slowly back to earth.

I think, *She's going to burrito-wrap me in a bedspread. That's my costume?*

She counters my obvious disappointment with "Have I ever steered you wrong?"

I shake my head.

"Trust me?"

There's no reason not to.

Ambrosia begins by draping the fabric across one of my shoulders, then wraps it around my midriff, tucking it here and there, arranging and rearranging the cloth so that it swoops down to my ankles and then back up in a loop, finishing in a U-shape that dips to the small of my back. She does this without using even a single safety pin. I never understand this fashion magic, how some girls can take hand-me-downs, like an old scarf or an outgrown skirt, and turn it into something new and flattering. My costume—it's a dress, sort of a tunic-toga—fully covers one leg, but the other leg peeks out from a slit when I walk. It's bare all the way up to the hip, which makes my legs look super long and thin. The fabric makes a *whoosh* when I move.

Ambrosia snaps two fingers. "Elegant, classy, irresistible."

"Are you sure?"

"Hmmm, it's a little *too* tasteful." She pushes her elbows together. "Do like this."

I imitate the motion, which emphasizes my cleavage. In the past week, I swear that I went from an A cup to a C. I love it, but . . . panic.

"I can't wear this."

She looks surprised, even a little hurt. "Why not? You don't like the fabric?"

"That's not it. It's beautiful and comfortable. What is it, anyway? It looks and feels like another layer of skin. Only . . ." I search for the words. I think about the Meg I've been for so many years, the one with the overbite and frizzy hair and no waist, the one who hides in baggy clothes and avoids her reflection in the mirror. "This outfit is . . . not me."

"Why isn't it you?"

I point first to the bulging boobs and then to the naked thigh. "You know what I was for Halloween last year? An old man. Size 12 pants pulled to my armpits. Mustache. Pillow for a pot belly. That's me."

Ambrosia takes a big hank of my hair, which, thanks to

the miracle formula, is wavier and softer than it's ever been in my life, and drapes it over my bare shoulder. "Not anymore. This is you now. You have beauty and power. Accept it. Flaunt it. Embrace it."

"You're sure? I don't want to look pathetic and ridiculous, one of those girls who's trying to be someone she's not."

"I know exactly who you are. I worked too hard for too long on this project to have any doubts. Go ask the others their opinion."

I turn toward the closet door, but she orders me to stop. "One more thing." She leans in with a pair of tweezers, plucks a wild hair sprouting from a small mole on my back.

"Ouch!"

She extends her arm with the dagger index finger pointing. "Toughen up. Pain and sacrifice are necessary. Go!"

Barefoot, glistening with oil, half naked except for the two pounds of makeup on my face, I step out of the closet and suddenly I don't need any more reassurance. My arms, which were crossed on my chest in uncertainty, drop to my sides.

All the proof I need stares back at me. I know I look amazing because Alix and Stephanie look amazing. I know I am magnificent because *they* are magnificent. We are our costumes and our costumes are us, inseparable, spitting images of who we are inside, three different versions of the Furies, our powers no longer hidden but turned into fabric and flesh, buttons and zippers, for everyone to see.

Alix, Alecto, her skin a metallic shimmer. She has the complexion of an ancient statue. Her hair is slicked back to resemble a warrior's helmet, tufts of it gelled to stand up like a thick row of feathers curving from her forehead to the nape of her neck. The short shorts of her costume emphasize every bulge in her legs; the outlines of her quadriceps are like something you see in an anatomy book, nothing wasted, nothing extra. She pulls the halter lace tight, calling attention to the ripple of tendons in her arms. You can count every muscle in her stomach. You could serve dinner on the broad, straight plane of her back.

"These shoes rock!" she says. There's no foot, no sole or heel, only circles of brown leather from her instep to knee. It takes her several minutes to latch the dozen or so metal buckles, and when she's done, Ambrosia tells her to stand very still for one final accessory.

She brings out a long strand of seaweed that smells of the ocean and ties it around Alix's bare middle.

"Show us who you are, Alecto, and what you can withstand."

Alix flinches and sweat breaks out on her forehead. This is not ordinary kelp plucked straight from the sea. It comes from Ambrosia's collection of mysteries and it is hot, branding-iron hot. I smell flesh burning. I want to help Alix. I reach out to rip off the seaweed, but Ambrosia blocks my way. She puts a finger to her lips, a warning and encouragement.

Pain and sacrifice are necessary.

If Ambroisa has faith that Alix can withstand this test, she can. I know she can! Her eyes squeeze closed and her jaw clenches with the enormous effort needed not to yell out in pain.

Then finally the sizzling sound stops. Alix's features

immediately relax. The test is over and she has passed. When Ambrosia removes the seaweed, Stephanie and I examine the wound. There is no jagged scar or oozing open sore. Alix, amazed, runs her fingers around her midriff. Here is the perfect finishing touch to her costume, a tattooed impression of kelp, fish scales, and the tentacles of an octopus. She is part warrior, part mermaid—a furious Warrior Mermaid—and she glows with pride.

Stephanie, Tisiphone, is up next. She's the perfect manifestation of the Earth she loves so much. You can't see any hair on her head, only petals, vines, blossoms, and leaves. Her cheeks radiate pink like she's part sun. Paired with a black satin unitard, the bat wings no longer seem like a costume that she slipped on. They spring from the curves of her shoulder blades like a natural growth. I can see the pulse of—is that blood?—flowing through them. She models the wings, experimenting with the different ways they beat.

Ambrosia places a dab of liquid behind each of Stephanie's ears. That, too, must be boiling hot, but she understands what she must do. Stephanie goes deep inside of herself to hold firm against the pain. She merges with it. When the perfume finally cools, her eyes open and she smiles with an otherworldly blissfulness. The room fills with the scent of a freshly planted garden: basil, oregano, thyme, mint. The odor is so thick that as soon as I think of an herb, I taste it on my tongue.

And finally there's me, Megaera, not some shy, awkward girl anymore, but—what adjectives did Ambrosia use?— elegant, classy, irresistible. Sexy, too. Very sexy.

"You look wow." Alix lets out a whistle of admiration.

"When did you get that long neck?" Stephanie asks. I lift my hair to show off a neck that has turned lean and graceful.

To get better looks at ourselves, we hurry to the huge hallway mirror. I take it all in, the way my hair mimics the shine and intricate waves of the metal filigree. My eyes are slanted in black and the lids glisten with gold flakes. I run my hands along the curves of my torso and hips, then peer over my shoulder to check out my bottom, which sits high and round, two ripe cantaloupes. Even my toes look fabulous. I wiggle them. Sexy, purple jewels.

Ambrosia comes up behind me, leans closer, and I feel the flutter of her breath as she speaks into my ear. "You'll need privacy tonight. My room. It'll be vacant, off limits to everyone but you and him."

"You trust him, then?"

"Go party with your prince. Indulge your desires. Don't hold back on your fun. Why would you? But deep down"—she reaches around and places her palms flat on my belly; they rise and fall with my breath—"deep down, be prepared. Maybe you're right about him and he'll pass the test. Just don't lose your heart. Remember who has the power."

I shiver, and it's not only because of the skimpy costume. How would it feel not to hold back? I want to experience that, to indulge my desires. Ambrosia runs a nail the length of my arms, and the sensation causes even more goose bumps to spring to the surface.

From a fancy leather case she takes out a necklace designed to resemble a coiling serpent. "Stay awake," she reminds me. When she drapes the jewelry around my neck I flinch, expecting it to be burning hot, my trial of pain and sacrifice. But there's only the slight chill of metal, which quickly warms to my body temperature. I know by the weight and texture that the necklace must be real gold. The front clasp is a three-headed cobra with ruby, sapphire, and emerald eyes. When I tilt my head to my chest to admire it, there's a hiss and three darting tongues. It's over so fast that I wonder if it really happened.

Ambrosia disappears into her room and returns with a tray that holds four shot glasses filled to the brim with a clear liquid. We follow her lead and each raise a glass to toast. The drink has an unusual and strong odor—definitely alcohol, but also hints of cinnamon, cloves, and other spices that make me think of pumpkin pie.

"Opa! Party!" Ambrosia shouts. "This drink will turn a colorless world very vibrant."

I imitate the others and chug it down, only I'm the one who chokes because I'm not used to drinking. Alix pounds me on the back. After the burn in my throat fades, I decide that I like it. It's so cold and sweet that it makes my teeth tingle, and it tastes like licorice.

From our position at the top of the stairs, we hear the band warming up in the living room. There's feedback from the speakers, a jarring, painful electronic screech. The doorbell rings. The front door opens. Voices. Laughs. Squeals of recognition. A guitar plays a familiar nine-note riff. A boy's voice yells: "Hell, yeah!"

"Don't make your entrance too early," Ambrosia advises. "But not too late, either. Timing is everything."

The doorbell again. And again. Sounds merging together. We wait unseen, the three of us fussing with each other, making little costume adjustments and offering compliments.

Ambrosia nods.

It's time.

I remind myself: Every desire. Don't hold back.

We put on our masks, which are small, simple, and black, with holes for our eyes. I link arms with Alix and Stephanie. I feel their power and I know they feel mine. We walk down the stairs. Ambrosia throws an electrical switch. The entire house, inside and out, glows and pulses with thousands of orange lights.

One step and then another. We're almost into view.

All my confidence disappears. Total terror. I can't go through with this. I hate parties. Social stuff makes me break out in hives. The costume that a minute ago was elegant and irresistible feels silly. Worse than silly. I'm basically naked.

I consider fleeing back up the stairs. But Stephanie reaches over and takes my hand, presses it tight against her side. The rough, satiny fabric of her wings rubs against my bare arm, and that is the exact sensation I need right now. There's strength and comfort in it. Alix takes my other hand. We need each other. We have each other. What am I afraid of? I encourage myself with Ambrosia's instructions: Accept it. Flaunt it. Embrace it.

As one unit, the three of us override any hesitation. We are the Furies. We are powerful. Together we can deal with a teenage party. Of course we can!

Another step and another.

Alix's feet laced in leather, Stephanie's vine-covered ankles and my purple-painted toes land at the bottom of the stairs in perfect rhythm. And when they do, it's like we flipped an attention-getting switch. There's a final cymbal crash and the band goes silent. People stop talking and flirting.

At every party there's one group that all the energy orbits around. Obviously I've never been that center. I'm lucky if one nerd even talks to me one time. But now we are that center. I hear all the spoken and unspoken questions: Is that who I think it is? Where did they get such great costumes? When did she get such fantastic hair?

I never realized how starved for this kind of attention I am. I love it. But it's also freaking me out. Being noticed comes with its own pressure. Whom should I talk to? What should I do with my hands? What about Brendon? Where is he? Was the whole romantic cave scene just a fluke? I'm supposed to be irresistible tonight, but I'm sure that I am going to blurt out stupid, lame things.

There's another cymbal crash that signals the start of a new song, and the void fills at once with guitar licks, drum rolls, talking, singing, laughing, eating, dancing. I need some space to get my bearings. I look for a quiet corner to duck into. Perfect. It's a corner with a table full of alcohol. I need alcohol desperately. I find a bottle of the licorice drink and take another shot to steady my nerves. This time I'm ready for the kick, and it burns only a little going down. Warmth spreads through me. I remove my mask.

Alix, I notice, is having no such trouble handling all the attention. She's just fine. That's because, basically, she's oblivious. When there's this much free food and booze in a room, it's impossible for her to think about anything else. A wide path clears as she takes giant steps to the buffet table, humming happily as she piles a plate high with chicken wings, cheese, ribs, and desserts. All the ultra-skinny, anorexic girls are staring with envy at her appetite, wondering how her stomach remains so flat with all the food going into it. They aren't the only jealous ones. A group of buff guys from the weight-lifting and wrestling teams are openly admiring Alix's six-pack framed by her high midriff top. Their own muscles don't measure up.

Stephanie, too, seems relaxed with her drawing power. I guess it's easier for her because she's always been okay with making a spectacle of herself. She strolls the perimeter of the room, showing off her wings and telling people that their beer bottles need to be recycled and that their plastic cups should be refilled and reused. I do notice a phenomenon that Stephanie isn't aware of. Whenever she sashays past a group, something amazing happens. People in the middle of talking, joking, arguing, eating, *whatever*, stop cold. They take long inhales of her perfume. Each face gets the same expression, and the only way to describe it is to string together adjectives that don't normally go together—lost, eager, hungry, hopeful, like they're on the verge of recalling some old memory that they need urgently to remember.

I take another shot of alcohol, and this time instead of burning my eyes it opens them. I notice how lots of girls are admiring and are even jealous of my costume and makeup, and guys are checking me out in a whole different way than I've ever been checked out before. For example, hanging out by the band, there's this semi-popular senior who I know never noticed me in school. He's dressed as a farmer (cutoff overalls, straw hat) and he seems positively hypnotized by me. I test out my effect by walking across the room. Yes, I'm sure of it now. His gaze tracks me with complete devotion, like he's never seen anyone walk before. And when I smear some dip onto a cracker, he's fascinated, like cracker eating is the latest extreme sport and I'm world champ of the event.

Why am I hanging back? Why am I acting like the old, insecure Meg? Flaunt it, embrace it.

One more drink to steady my nerves, and as I head toward the semi-popular farmer I take a lesson from my costume and mimic the flow of the fabric. Elegant, classy, irresistible. And hot, definitely hot, because when I get to him I say something totally bland and random—"Good band"—which sends his whole body into happy twitches.

He shifts his weight back and forth between feet, reaches out to touch me on the shoulder but draws back as if I sent out an electric shock. Then he lets loose a torrent of compliments, as if *Good band* is the funniest, smartest, wittiest, most amazing insight that he's heard in months.

"Yeah, good band. Do I know you? You want something to drink? You have good taste. In music, I mean. Well, you have good taste in drinks, too. Hahahahaha. Really good music. Excellent taste. So, you like music? Who are you? You go to Hunter? I like music. Hahahahahaha. Wanna go hear more music with me sometime?"

And on and on and on.

I can't believe it. This is happening. I'm doing this. I'm flirting and it's working. Is it the makeup? The costume? The power of the Furies?

Is it *me*?

I don't care about the reason. I just want it to never stop. I like being the me I always wanted to be, the me I always hoped was buried inside.

I am beautiful and sexy and strong and nobody can hurt me anymore.

I can do what I want and fulfill every desire. Why stop myself?

I leave the farmer looking sad and lonely. Who cares about him?

I want Brendon.

Picture the face of every prince you ever heard of. Not the real-life hemophiliac ones, and those with genetic insanity or horsey features because of too much royal inbreeding. Picture Princes Charming, Eric, Caspian, the Beast, and the Frog (post kiss).

Now join it to the picture of another Prince. Long purple velvet jacket, white shirt with a bib of ruffles tucked into the waist of tight black pants. Lacy cuffs and a panel of silver sequins at the shoulder. Black high-heeled boots, a white guitar slung across his chest on a leopard strap.

Enter Brendon, flanked by Gnat and Bubonic, who are decked out as hyperactive drummers, and Pox in another rock star getup. Behind them, doing the Twist, the Double Ds are dressed in mini-skirts and white go-go boots, tambourine-shaking dancers from the 1960s.

" 'Purple Rain'! Let's Go Crazy!" Rat Boy, another vintage musician, shouts. "Party like it's 1999. Or 1969."

Gnat immediately starts sucking on a bottle of whiskey and Bubonic is making crude comments to some unpopular nerdy girls. I note with irritation that our Fury lesson has worn off on him. Pox, too, is acting like an ass. And the Double Ds clearly need a refresher course.

I'm also annoyed that Brendon has decided to come with his moronic friends. This isn't the way I imagined our second date to be. But Ambrosia invited everyone, so I shouldn't be surprised that they're here. Plus, I remind myself, all those guys have been surfing together since kindergarten, and loyalty to friends, even obnoxious ones, is a commendable trait.

I guess.

I position myself in an uncrowded corner where I have an unobstructed view of Brendon. He untangles himself from his group and stands off to the side. I could wave to him or go over. But I hold back. I like watching how his gaze methodically circles the room, landing on one girl after another. I especially like how he dismisses each one with clear disappointment. They don't measure up to a goddess. They aren't me.

"I see London. I see France." There's a familiar voice coming from behind me. I tell myself to ignore it, but there's no way to escape the hand that lands on my shoulder. I swing around, not at all unaware, or unhappy, that if Brendon does look in this direction he will see the flip side of me—the easy-to-undo bow and the way the flesh-colored fabric clings to my newly improved ultra-firm bottom.

It's Raymond, of course, and he's dressed in his color guard outfit of broad, royal-blue-and-white stripes. As part of the costume, he's painted his face half white and half blue in honor of the Greek flag. He greets me with a bow, his hand cascading like a Slinky from forehead to ankle.

"You walk in darkness. But honey, so much of you is showing in the light."

Suddenly I'm thrown back into the old Meg world of self-doubt. "Too much? I knew it! I look ridiculous."

"Not at all. You look spectacular! Your outside beauty now matches your inside beauty."

I wait for Raymond to turn that last statement into a joke, but he doesn't. "I need to look irresistible. Really, really irresistible. Speak truth! Do I?"

There's a full glass of alcohol in my hand. How did it get there? I don't remember picking it up. I must have poured it. Oh well. Might as well drink it. Down it goes.

Raymond takes the empty glass from me, sniffs, then pretends that the smell sends him stumbling backward. "Watch this stuff. It's lethal. Sneaks up on you slowly. By the time you feel it, you've already drunk too much."

"How do you know that, Mr. Bartender? You don't even drink!"

"Neither did you until tonight. Go easy, okay?"

"I promise." I wonder, though, if it's a little late for this particular promise, since the room makes a sudden tilt at a strange angle. I grip Raymond for support until the walls and floor steady themselves again.

"Oops! Nipple alert!" He adjusts my top and spreads my hair like a curtain over my chest. "This is Ambrosia's fashion sense, am I right?"

His question rubs me the wrong way. I fling the hair

away. "Why do you say that? You don't believe I could have come up with . . ."

What I see in my slightly drunken peripheral vision puts an end to this part of the conversation. Purple velvet approaches. I press my hand to Raymond's epaulette and plead with him. "Nothing embarrassing from you. Remember how I always support you with your crushes."

"Sadly, it's slim pickings for me here at Hunter High."

"This is important. Please?"

Before I get an answer, I pivot on my toes and come eye (mine) to collarbone (his) with Brendon. I lift my head until I'm looking deep into his pupils, which are green with little squiggly veins of gold running through them.

"I know you," he says.

"You do?"

"Great costume. You are supposed to be a . . ."

I've been practicing for this moment, going over my line, adjusting it and reworking it until I knew exactly what I wanted to say and how I would say it. But now that the opening is here, should I? Could I? Dare I? My lips separate. My mouth starts to move. I'm still at a point where I can stop it. But I don't. I let the words come up my throat and out into the air.

"A goddess. A hot goddess. For you."

"Oh brother," Raymond says.

I flash him another pleading look. He pretends to fix something on my costume, but it's an excuse to lean over and whisper into my ear: "Just remember who you are."

Then he cups his hand to his ear, looks out into the distance. "What's that I hear? The nonalcoholic punch bowl is calling out: *Raymond, drink me!* Well, well, then, I will leave you two to your romantic clichés."

With three marching steps he's out of earshot, and that's a relief. Flirting shamelessly is hard enough without seeing myself through Raymond's amused eyes. I play with my hair—*flip, flip.* I feel a flush of heat, then slightly dizzy but in a good way. Raymond is right about the alcohol. It comes on slowly, and now it's untying any knots of awkwardness or reserve left in me.

I let myself have a good time. I bounce to the music. I sing along to the band. I flip my hair. I laugh at anything anyone does. I'm having a really good time. I use the word *you* continually and touch Brendon softly every time I do.

"Are you sure you're okay?" he asks. "Did you drink a lot?"

"I am most excellent."

I am glad, though, that a slow song comes on and I can collapse into his arms. Standing upright in a wavy room has gotten challenging. He wraps his arms around my waist, pulls me close, and holds me there for the entire number. It's a very long song. I hear his breathing in my ear. I feel the velvet of his jacket on my arm. It's like being in a perfect dream, except that I'm sweating underneath his hands and worry that I might be a little stinky. I hope he doesn't notice.

When the music stops, he picks up one of my hands and kisses the back of it gallantly. My knees buckle and I grab onto a nearby table to keep from sliding to the floor. "I need another one of those scrumdelicious drinks."

"No, you don't," he says, playfully but firmly. "You've had enough. You should cool it for a while."

"Yeah," I admit. I wipe my forehead, which has a layer of sweat. "I should lie down for a minute."

He takes me by the hand, slowly steering me away from the crowd and through a set of double doors and along a corridor of precious vases and glowing pumpkins. Until we're alone at the foot of the stairs.

I mumble something.

"Huh?" he asks.

I motion with my index finger for him to come closer, and when he does I stand on the bottom step so we are nearly the same height. I press my mouth to his. He makes a sound, a cross between an intake of surprise and a moan of pleasure. His tongue darts and circles the inside of my mouth. But just as suddenly, he seems to remember something and backs away.

"I don't think we should do this," he says, his voice throaty.

"Why not?'

"Because . . ." He makes a drinking motion. "I like you. A lot. You're in no shape to know what you're doing. Ambrosia was worried about you. She told me that if you drink too much, I should take you to her room and let you sleep it off. She showed me where it is."

I recall Ambrosia's offer—the promise of privacy in her empty bedroom. Clever Ambrosia. Good Ambrosia. Dear, dear Ambrosia. "She is a very, very good friend." My words are slurred slightly. "Ambrosia watches out for me."

I let Brendon lead me up the stairs, and smile at our reflection as we pass the big hall mirror.

Meg and Brendon. Brendon and Meg.

Fulfill every desire.

We enter the bedroom. When I lock the door behind us, he starts at the click. I giggle at that. Many familiar things welcome me: the jack-in-the-box with the broken neck, the snow globe filled with tortured people, and the bed. I throw myself onto the pile of pillows and soft, all-white sheets.

"Want to tuck me in?" I ask.

When he's standing over me, when I see those eyes looking down on me, I take his hand and don't let go of it.

A questioning expression from him. Am I sure? A nod of certainty from me. I've never been so sure. A shy smile in return as he switches off the overhead light.

We cuddle, and then we kiss. One sweet, tender kiss before diving into each other like we're competitors in an old-fashioned pie-eating contest, wet and messy and tasting of berries, peaches, and licorice. His tongue is warm and his lips are a little cold.

I know I'm drunk, but I can't pretend that I don't know exactly what I'm doing. I've kissed like this before. There was a boy in my seventh-grade class and another in eighth, and after that a boy in my last foster home. But I always got scared and pushed them away. Tonight is a turning point for me. I can decide that all of this is a big, fat mistake. I can return to start, return to being familiar, safe Meg.

But I don't want to! I'm a Fury. I'm powerful. I get what I want, and what I want right now is *this*. I've been thinking about it from the first time I saw Brendon. My body—this new body—has its own mind and it knows what it wants, what everyone talks and dreams about. I want to lose control and be swept away with this intense feeling.

He's the one who's a little shy and hesitant at first. I encourage his hands to wander the length of me, rubbing the back of my neck, palms sliding down my chest, fingers dancing on my back under the bow. I roll over. His knees straddle my legs and he massages my back. "You like that?" he asks into my ear.

When I nod, he says, "Tell me what you like. What else do you want me to do? I want to make you happy."

Before I can answer he kisses my neck, a dozen nibbles. How did he know exactly what I was thinking before I even had the words for it?

I'm on my side now. We are two spoons fitting perfectly together, my breasts in the cups of his hands. The room is spinning; we are spinning.

No holding back. I point to my ear. "I want . . . your tongue. My ear."

He follows my orders and I moan. I move under him, like a sea creature that's one with the flow of the current. I stay with it. I go with it. It all feels so good—the spinning, the piney smell of him mixing with my smell, hearing myself moan aloud and not be ashamed—good like nothing else in my life has ever felt.

I begin to unknot the bow of my costume, and he reaches out to stop me but I push aside his hand. "I don't want to stop. You don't want me to stop, do you?"

In response we fall back to the mattress together. I feel a

moment's flush of shyness to be naked to the waist in front of him, even though it's so dark I know he can't see much. I squirm slightly under the pressure of his weight. In the dark I add the expressions that I want, that I hope are there on his face: longing for me, admiration, wonder, and yes, lust. And love.

He leans in and whispers: "I think . . . maybe . . . I love you."

In my mind, I hear all the warnings. *Don't trust him. Don't lose your heart.* I feel him waiting for me to respond. I try to hold back, but I don't want to. I take the leap and let go of any hesitancy, any distrust I ever had for him. "Me, too. I love you, Brendon."

That's when it happens. There's an explosion, a brutal blast of white radiation that cuts through me like a knife entering my stomach and exiting through the small of my back. And a sound that pounds my eardrums. I swear that the sudden violence of it lifts me off the bed and drops me back down, battered.

The radiation is the overhead light snapping on.

The sound is laughter. Many voices. From the closet. From under the bed. Gnat. Bubonic. Pox. Rat Boy. All the Plagues. The Double Ds. So many hateful faces from the halls of Hunter High.

"Your tongue. My ear," someone says in a falsetto.

Another fake girlish voice: "I love you, Brendon! Stick it to me, big boy. I want it all!"

My hands flail. I try to cover myself. Too late. A cell phone is aimed, a picture snapped. More laughing. More pictures.

On the side of my vision, a blur of movement, a morphing shape. Brendon.

"Way to go, bro," someone congratulates him.

Do something! I plead with him in my mind. *Hit someone! Defend me! Pay them back! Get revenge for this crime! Get even! Destroy them!*

But he only hands me a sheet to wrap myself in. He is numb, dumb, useless.

I was warned. The ones who care about me told me to keep up my guard. It was a setup. How could I have been so stupid? I scream in Brendon's face: "Liar!"

His look bounces quickly to his friends, then back at me. "No, Meg."

"Yes!"

"Meg, I didn't know."

His words lie. His coal-dense eyes lie.

Who led me up the stairs? Who took me by the hand? Who is still not defending me? Case closed.

I curl into a fetal position, and while they continue to laugh and lie, I drain myself of trust. It pours out of me. Gone! Next to leave are understanding and forgiveness. When I'm empty of all that worthless stuff, I even let go of embarrassment. Who needs it? Who wants it? It all dies in a split second. And in the hard, empty place that's left, something else is born in me.

Fury—pure, hot, and undiluted.

I uncurl from the fetal position.

I unwrap from the sheet.

I rise.

Standing on the mattress, I tilt my head to the ceiling

and, like an animal with no compassion for my prey, I unleash a roar as naked as myself. It comes from deep in my belly and my past.

"Oh shit! She's slutty *and* psycho. I'm outta here." Pox pushes Gnat out the bedroom door. Others follow, nearly falling over each other, a few snickering nervously, more looking back with genuine worry.

In the chaos, Stephanie and Alix force themselves against the human tide into the room. I don't know if they actually heard my scream or if they've come because I summoned them in a way they couldn't ignore.

It's only us and Brendon now, and he is still trying to apologize and defend himself.

Look how his lying mouth moves. Listen to the meaningless flow of consonants and vowels. I am immune to this backstabbing prince, deaf to anything that his deceitful lips can say.

He has no name.

Stephanie spreads her wings to block his exit. The jewelry around my neck opens its golden serpents' mouths. I hear the hisses and smell the venom. I see the flicker of three tongues tracking their quarry.

I move in. We sing.

Fury cannot tell *its own story. If it could, it would not be what it is. It would be something less potent: a little anger that time can heal, or a grudge that an apology could resolve. With true fury, there is no stepping outside of one's self to tell the tale; there is only stepping into more blind fury.*

It is up to me to describe the scene that follows.

I was in the room below. I wore no special costume this night—just my usual black on black, a skirt and sweater—but I was the most disguised person at the party. While I waited, I unraveled the two tightly wound coils of hair at my ears. I held them firm at the neckline, and with a sharpened pair of gardening shears I lopped them off. They fell to the carpet like two dead animals. Gone! Good riddance to anything extraneous. The hair that was left on my head, I cut and hacked at.

Finally my satisfaction came. Above me, she howled with three times three to the thirty-third power of undiluted rage.

The others were so easily manipulated and played their roles so admirably. The chorus hid where I told them to hide. My target was captured by love and lust, as I knew he would be. These young princes are so predictable.

Megaera remained my only question mark. Would she soften? Had life twisted her precious psyche enough? When it came down to it, would she have the right vengeful stuff?

But isn't this what they say about slow learners? They take their own sweet time, but when rage finally comes it is deep, profound, and unshakeable.

His perceived offense hit her smoldering pain like a splash of gasoline.

She called the others and they turned on him with the outrage of every loss in their lives.

She wanted to be swept away with feeling, and so she was. She lost control in the service of ultimate control.

They swarmed him like delirious, demented flies. He swatted. He begged for relief. He was innocent this time, but what prince doesn't have regrets? They uncovered every slip of his toxic tongue, every crime.

> What mortal man is not terrified,
> gripped in fear and horror
> To hear their sacred law.

Those girls, those Furies, did not smell the delicious stench that the hormones of their rage released from the maggot-loving plant.

They did not see the storm cloud building over the house. They did not see the ash in the snow globe falling on all the old trapped princes, plus this new one, snagged and helpless.

They opened the window and invited him to step through it.

"Jump," they sang. "Here is your reprieve. Escape our misery. Jump and find peace."

Leaping from the heights,
The hard, heavy downfall.

I walked to the window, heard that glorious rush of air, and it felt like a drug coursing through me. I saw his flailing limbs and his body hitting the clump of bushes.

I heard the screams of the so-called innocent bystanders. But nobody is innocent here, all are bound together by the guilt of everyone else.

FOURTH STASIMON, THE BOOK OF FURIOUS

What happened? What did we do?

I have no solid recollection. It was different from the other Fury times. We were *in*, but we did not seek out any particular incident, not even the memory of what just happened between Brendon and me. I was too far gone. We latched onto everything at once—a whirling mass of his regrets and guilty feelings. I saw splashes of old girlfriends hurt and lies told. Then, quickly, even those visions shut down. An intense wind of rage blew out any light in my mind, leaving me blind.

The sound of a window opening. The touch of a curtain blowing.

I remember ordering, *Jump*.

And then I am back in the whiteness of Ambrosia's bedroom. I have to shake my head to regain my vision. The world slowly comes back into view. The door is still closed. There's no Brendon. Curtains are pulled apart. I hear screams rising from beneath the window. My stomach lurches from the stench of rotting meat.

What happened?

Quickly, I wrap the remnants of my costume around me. Alix, Stephanie, and I rush down the stairs, and by the time we get outside everyone has gathered under the window. I tremble from the first blast of cold on my half-naked body. The chaos of the scene that greets me matches the chaos in my mind. There's yelling and crying, and my heart is pounding so hard I can hear the whooshing pulse in my ears. Girls dressed as mermaids and flappers hold on to each other and sob, mascara dripping down their cheeks. Devils, cowboys, and astronauts shout overlapping orders that contradict each other. "Elevate his head!" "No, don't move him!" "Raise his feet!"

My body feels disjointed, as if the parts of it—legs, arms, tongue, toes, elbows, head—are strangers to each other and have traveled a long distance to meet up here for the first time. They are awkward, uncertain of how to act naturally with each other. I check around frantically. *How bad is it? What do people know? Do they suspect me? What about Brendon? Is he . . . ?* I can't let myself think the end of that thought.

Pox is shouting at 911 through his cell phone.

The Double Ds keep repeating, "Oh my God, oh my God."

Their red-haired best friend whimpers into her phone, "Mom, pick me up. Now!"

Gnat to Bubonic: "Dude, we better get rid of any drugs."

Off in the distance, an ambulance siren illustrates the Doppler effect that Mr. H explained in class. The sound shrieks at a higher and higher pitch as it gets closer.

I want to see.

I don't want to see.

I can't see.

Then: "I *need* to see him."

Stephanie tries holding me back by grabbing on to my wrist, but I break free and inch my way through the crowd. My fingers pull at my hair as I weave between clusters of people. I push through four layers of costumes and finally stumble into the inner circle.

I can see him now. Brendon. He's all alone in the center, spotlighted by a long beam of moonlight. His face is pressed against the bush he landed in, his curly hair falling over a neck that's twisted in an unnatural position. I shudder. Only a few minutes ago I was running my fingers through that hair.

He was running his fingers through mine.

My gaze darts from detail to detail: the ruffled cuffs of his Prince shirt, the square of his muscled back, the way that back doesn't rise and fall with an inhale and exhale. I can't breathe, either. It's like all the oxygen is being sucked out of my head. A buzzing fills my skull; my vision starts shutting down like the ring of darkness at the end of an old-fashioned movie. I'm going to faint.

I reach out to the person next to me. Alix! Thank goodness it's her. I drape myself against her shoulders for support. Chunks of her silver makeup are gone; it looks like her skin is sliding off.

"Get a grip!" she orders from the corner of her mouth. "Don't freak out."

"Alix, what did we do?"

In a harsh whisper: "Exactly what he deserved."

"He did . . . he shouldn't have . . . I wanted him to—"

"Shhhh!"

"Alix! He's not moving. I can't believe we did—"

She pinches my upper arm hard. "Did? What are you talking about?" She widens her eyes dramatically, a signal that draws Stephanie through the crowd to my side. "Steph, do you know what Meg is talking about? Who did anything?"

Stephanie positions herself between me and Brendon, expanding her wings slightly to block my view of his body. The flowers have fallen out of her hair and the dreads look like thick hairballs coughed up by a prehistoric cat. I notice that two of her teeth are long and pointed. When did that happen? She could puncture a can with those fangs. Her voice comes out preachy, a vice-principal's scold. "Meg, you had too much to drink."

The explanation and reprimand are for the benefit of two guys who are eavesdropping on our argument. I see how they are looking at me. Word of what happened between Brendon and me has clearly spread. All those cell phone pictures have made the rounds. They know. I turn my head left and right and notice others glancing my way, some gawking, others whispering. Everyone must know. And not just about the sex. I don't care about that anymore. Everyone must know *everything. This!* What we did to him.

Alix, hostile, turns to the group closest to us—"What the hell are you all staring at? Meg can't hold her booze. She's talking crazy"—and everyone quickly backs away.

Alix's hair, too, has come undone, and there are

stains—oil? blood?—down the front of her costume. She takes me by both shoulders, gives them a hard shake, leans in so only I can hear. "If anybody *did* anything, there would be fingerprints. Witnesses. There would be evidence. There is no evidence."

"He jumped," Stephanie hisses. "He must have felt guilty about what he did to you. No one touched him. No one saw anything. We left the room before any of this happened. Understand?"

There's new commotion then—sirens, shouts, doors slamming—and I'm moved aside with the rest of the crowd as a team of paramedics forces us to step back and give them room to work. They hunch over Brendon's motionless form and gently lower him to the ground. A stethoscope, tubes, and wires appear from bags like a series of magic tricks. A breathing tube is hauled over, but not used. I see a monitor turned on, stared at, and turned off.

And then all activity comes to a stop. The only sound is the metallic, deep-throated caw of a mockingbird overhead. The four paramedics sit on the ground, heads bowed, shoulder to shoulder, showing us the backs of their uniforms.

Get up, I urge silently. *Tell me it isn't true. Tell me everything is going to be all right.*

A long beat of silence until the paramedics push themselves to standing, and one of them, the tallest and oldest, brushes some dry grass off his knees. "A parent?" he asks. "Is there an adult in charge here?"

Pirates, cowgirls, and bunnies look at their feet.

The paramedics exchange defeated looks, one of them

swearing, "Shit." Another shakes his head. "Of course, no parent. Perfect."

A small voice from the crowd then. "Brendon's going to be okay, right?"

The main paramedic suddenly looks tired and older, like he's grown a gray stubble on his face in only the last few minutes. "I'm afraid . . . Brendon, that's his name? . . . I have some bad . . ."

"No!" someone shouts.

"Do something else!"

"Try!"

The hysteria starts all over again. Some parents have arrived by now, and they're shouting, too, and there's so much turmoil that I might be the only one watching as two paramedics gingerly lift Brendon and a third slides a stretcher under him.

I want to look away, but I can't. What did we do? What did I do? I think I should be crying like everyone else, but I don't. Nothing about me is working. Not even my tears can move. I'm paralyzed, stuck in the horrible understanding of what we did to him. I've never been this close to a dead person before and I stare at the figure, trying to make sense of it. This is Brendon. This is *not* Brendon. Death does not look how I thought it would look, not like sleep or sickness. Death looks more like a series of *nots*—familiar things about a person that are no longer there: Brendon's not warm. Brendon's not breathing, not moving, not thinking or planning or eating or dreaming or wishing.

One of his arms, pulled by gravity, slips and dangles

over the side of the stretcher. I recall the feel of that arm around my shoulder and down the center of my back. That was . . . when? Only minutes ago. I try to shake away the memory but it doesn't budge. A paramedic lifts and tucks the arm under the torso. I see him take a deep breath as he pulls a sheet over the body, over Brendon, and tucks it tight.

I'm following every detail, which is why I should have been the first one to scream. Only I don't. I see it, but shock prevents me from reacting.

It's one of the Double Ds who lets out the first piercing cry that sounds like part firecracker, part speaker feedback. At first only a few people look her way because there's so much other noise in the garden. But then she starts doing this extreme screaming/pointing/eye-widening/hand-flapping dance and then someone else sees what she sees and joins in.

The paramedics drop their bags and their jaws and rush to the stretcher.

Brendon's hand with the hair on the knuckles that once filled me with such longing. It's come out from under his torso. It's moving. It's tearing at the sheet.

Quickly they unfurl him. "Don't move!" a paramedic insists.

But Brendon twists his head to show us his face, which is white and waxy with a line of smeared blood on his mouth, and the sight of it makes most everyone shriek. But this isn't *Halloween* the movie. Brendon's not a vampire, either. He's alive.

I smell Ambrosia's perfume an instant before I hear her whisper in my ear. "Hound him to hell. Down, down, deep in the earth. He'll never be free, protected, not even by death."

I whirl around. "What are you talking about?"

"You hate him."

"I don't."

"After what happened in the bedroom?"

"But I didn't want him to die. I'm glad he's not dead."

"Of course you are!" Ambrosia sandwiches my hands between hers, gives them a supportive squeeze. "You don't want him dead. That's why you pulled him back."

"Me?"

"You couldn't let him take the easy route. Death would be so unsatisfying. Death would let him off the hook. You don't want that."

Abruptly, I take back my hands. I reach behind my neck and undo the clasp of the snake necklace. I make Ambrosia take it. "I don't want anything to do with this anymore!"

She dangles the necklace in front of my face like a hypnotist. "Don't play coy with me."

I slap at the jeweled serpent.

The necklace disappears into her pocket. Her voice turns blunt. "When you thought he was dead, you felt guilty. I'll give you that. You were also scared that you'd be caught. You even felt sad that your romance had to end on this tragic note."

"Shut up," I insist.

"But you felt something else, too. Look deep. Admit it. You were a little disappointed that it was over so soon."

I start to protest, but she presses a finger to my lips. "Death? The peace of the void? The perpetual rest of the night? Sleeping in the winged arms of Thanatos? A quick death would be like sentencing him to eternity in a hammock. Where's the justice in that?"

She runs her hand over my face. My eyelashes tickle slightly, and in the split-second that my eyes stay closed I'm whipped back into the night's humiliation. Every second of it. My proclamation of love. His lie of love. The overhead light snapping on, the laughing, the photos. He planned it all. He must have planned it. Did he defend me? Did he hurl himself on Pox and fight for me? Did he do anything but stand there in his lame, pathetic way and claim to be innocent? He's as guilty as all those other Plagues.

Ambrosia is right. I'll never get over this. Why should he? As long as I suffer, Brendon should suffer.

Ambrosia gives me more words: "He threw you away like garbage, just like your parents did. This little two-story tumble isn't enough payback. You want more. The score isn't settled yet."

My cheeks flare hot with the recognition that she's right. She cups them with her palms, which have turned icy in the night air. "No need to be self-conscious, Megaera. Is a spider self-conscious about its desire to weave? A snake about its need to swallow its prey whole? This is your nature and it's your right. Don't overthink it."

Across the crowd I spot Raymond trying to get my attention, the features of his blue-and-white face twisting into a dozen frantic expressions. He knows exactly what happened and I know what he'll say, that we went too far and abused our power.

Ambrosia notices where I'm looking. "Whom did Brendon betray? Who gets to decide when the score is settled? Who deserves justice?" She strokes my hair, which is no longer soft and wavy but a coarse mass of strands that keeps crawling over my eyes and into my mouth.

I pretend not to see Raymond. I look away.

Alix and Stephanie make their way to us, and we are standing together as Brendon is strapped back onto the stretcher and a paramedic orders us to clear a path to the ambulance. There's a parade of ghosts, angels, wenches, and witches following him in a drunken line, joyful about their friend's amazing good luck. To fall like that and to still be alive.

Luck is deceiving.

When Brendon passes us, Ambrosia flicks four spiky nails in his direction. I see that her hair has been cut very short and spikey. It frames her face like a ring of razors. "Sleep well, Prince," she whispers. "Enjoy your dreams."

Overhead, the mockingbird mimics a squeaky gate, a train squealing around the corner, a human whistle of nine familiar notes.

27

Alone in my bedroom, looking into the mirror, I practice what I'm going to say to Raymond when he confronts me. I know he will. I make sure to keep my expression flat and certain, a shield against his arguments.

He'll say: "You almost killed him!"

I'll say: "I bet he doesn't even have a broken bone."

Raymond: "You went too far!"

Me: "We haven't gone far enough."

Only Raymond doesn't phone that night, not even a text. I'm puzzled but relieved. Why should I have to convince him of anything? Ambrosia got it right. This is my business. Brendon didn't humiliate Raymond. Raymond wasn't half-naked with half the school laughing in his face. I'm the one who gets to decide when justice has been served. I'm the one who deserves to pay him back.

Who cares what Raymond thinks?

It's 2:00 a.m. by the time I get into bed. Lying in the dark with He-Cat at my head, I burrow into the sheets, imagining Brendon in the hospital and how he must be moaning fitfully in his sleep—if he *can* sleep—and I get a sense of satisfaction. If I can't sleep, neither should he.

And then it's 2:30 a.m. and all I can think about now is how Brendon will eventually get over it. The doctors will stitch up his lip and he'll be released from the hospital. His family will rally around him. His friends will offer sympathy and support. He'll surf again and sleep well and have girlfriends, and gradually the memory of that fall through the window will fade. He's a prince. Life is like that for the princes of this world. All the shame and guilt we put into him will disappear. This Halloween night will too quickly become a small, vague memory in his long, happy, entitled life.

He will forget about what he did. He will forget me.

Unless . . .

I do something to keep the memory and the guilt alive.

I check the clock. It's 2:45 a.m., and now all I can think about is the refrigerator. I head into the kitchen and begin my raid. There's a big slab of leftover lasagna that I don't even bother to pop into the microwave. I down it cold right out of the casserole dish. I fill a bowl with ice cream and top it with a large dollop of Cool Whip. I eat a half jar of garlic pickles. I would eat more, but that's all that's left.

He-Cat, excited by all this middle-of-night action, rubs against my legs, but I'm in no mood to give him or anyone any affection. I nudge him out of my way.

I must be fed.

I think of the Leech asleep in the next room. Why does she get to sleep so soundly when I can't? Why did I settle for just a new bedroom when she owes me so much more? She should be racked with shame and guilt for the way she treated me. I want both of them, Brendon and her, to beg me for forgiveness. I want their sleep to be plagued by nightmares until they pay for what they did to me.

This hunger gnaws, like I'm feeding some creature that's all appetite. I grab a pen and a piece of paper and draw: a hungry ghost with a huge maw of a mouth, a neck so long and thin that everything eaten burns and hurts as it travels down to a bloated, bottomless pit of a stomach.

That hungry ghost is inside of me. It is me.

A word, coming from that hunger, springs into my thoughts. I text to Alix and Stephanie—*Hunt*—and right when I hit Send, two messages come in simultaneously.

Hunt, says Alix.

Hunt, says Stephanie.

We can't stop. We must be fed.

Over the next few days the police talk to a lot of kids who were at the party, and my name comes up in every interview. In an empty classroom a policewoman gently guides me through every detail of the night. Was Brendon depressed? Did he ever talk about hurting himself? Did anyone ever threaten him? When did I last see him?

I stick to my rehearsed story. He was drunk. I was drunk. There was the ugly, ugly scene in the bedroom, and I was mad and hurt. Who wouldn't be? But when I left the bedroom, he was still standing. The window was shut. Yes, he did seem upset and remorseful about what he did to me. Alix and Stephanie back me up on that point.

Brendon doesn't remember much, so the police come to the conclusion that I lead them to: A distraught, drunken kid lucked out by not killing himself. The real victim is the poor, sensitive girl whose heart he broke.

At the end of my interview, the soft-spoken policewoman asks if she can give me a hug. I let myself be folded into her arms. "Honey, he treated you wrong. None of this is your fault," she says. "But don't be surprised if the episode continues to haunt you for a while."

I know it will.

The hospital keeps Brendon under observation until midweek. The doctors can't get over how all his vital signs disappeared and yet he came out of it with no serious injuries. They draw blood and do an MRI, but they don't see anything abnormal.

At school, of course, everyone's talking about Brendon's miraculous escape from death. I overhear Mr. and Mrs. H in the cafeteria arguing about what happened.

"Pure luck," Mr. H says. "He must have hit at the exact angle to dissipate the impact. It's all a matter of vectors."

"You and your vectors!" Mrs. H says. "Why can't you admit that there are some things we'll never understand?"

I smirk, knowing how wrong they both are. I pulled him back. I am not done with him.

That's why I don't care about the rude comments and snickering that follow me as I walk through the halls. That's why it doesn't matter to me that the photos of naked me have been e-mailed around. The Plagues spread a rumor that I did something terrible to Brendon. They don't know what and they don't know how, but they blame me.

Let the rumors fly. Let everyone shun me. Let them laugh.

Let them think that this is over and they have won.

Later that week, Brendon walks into Western Civ and is welcomed with applause and a gush of admiration that usually greets war heroes or someone who scored a fake ID. I notice how he doesn't look in my direction, but lets himself be smothered in boobs by all the girls who insist on hugging him.

"Dude!" Pox offers up a fist to bump. "Lookin' good."

Rat Boy, always the master of the obvious, says, "You're alive."

The Brendon lovefest ends only because Ms. Pallas, not looking her usual cool and calm self, enters the room and flicks the lights a couple of times. A few minutes after the late bell sounds, Raymond, equally frazzled, slides into his seat next to me. We haven't talked since Halloween night. He hasn't been in school. I didn't call to find out why, and he didn't call to tell me why.

I do know one thing, though. He and Ms. Pallas didn't both just happen to come in late. They don't fool me. Nobody will ever fool me again. They were obviously having a private summit meeting, and it wasn't about his grades. Ms. Pallas was no doubt filling his head with her so-called civilized ideas about justice. And Raymond was taking it all in with complete devotion. I catch him checking me out with a set of disapproving wrinkles etched on his forehead. I give him a mocking, tight-lipped smile that dares: *What are you going to do about it?*

Today it's our group's turn to give an updated report on our final project, but when Raymond takes out the papers he prepared, I lean over and slap a wide-open palm on them. My first words in days to him are: "We don't need your contribution anymore."

I motion for Alix, Stephanie, and Ambrosia to follow me to the front of the room. "Our report." I drop the papers on Ms. Pallas's desk. "It's a script. You said we could be creative, so we wrote and memorized a scene, based on the works of Aeschylus."

One of the Double Ds takes out her cell phone, holds it in my direction, and snaps a picture, a reminder that it will be a long time before Halloween night is forgotten. Half the class laughs; the other half looks away embarrassed.

"Dawn, put that away now," Ms. Pallas orders.

I don't care. I strike a pose, hand on hip, chest thrust forward. Take all the pictures you want. I'm about to show them whom they are dealing with. Let's see how much they laugh then. I face the class.

"The princess," I announce.

Ambrosia takes three steps forward and holds her arms out to the sides, palms up and head back in prayer to the gods. She recites, "I have been wronged and I have called up the Furies to punish the ones who harmed me."

Ambrosia then gestures—"My Furies"—and I link arms with Alix and Stephanie and the three of us say, "Hunt," so that the *H* emerges in a rasp from the back of our throats and the *T* is hard and final, like a trapdoor slamming closed.

Ambrosia: "My contempt will stab your liver, a spurt of bile to prick the conscience. Give him a blast of your reeking, bloody breath, send it into his waking hours, ignite the fuel of his endless nightmares."

"Hunt," we say. "Hunt."

"Burn him in your stomach's acid fire. Track him down!"

"Hunt, hunt, hunt."

"He will not escape."

Speeding up. "Hunt, hunt, hunt."

"He can run to the ends of the earth."

Speeding up more, a race. "Hunt, hunt, hunt."

"But he'll never be free."

"Enough," Ms. Pallas tries to break in.

I feel the powerful tug of her but draw on my own power, our combined power of three. We don't need to listen to her. We have no one to obey but ourselves. "Hunt, hunt, hunt, hunt, hunt, hunt, hunt."

Let them try to escape me. Let them—

This time there are two voices—Ms. Pallas and Raymond shouting in unison "Enough!"—and I stop. But not because of them, only because *I* decide to. I want to savor all the expressions of shock, fear, and confusion. I stare at Brendon. His lips part and he mouths a string of words in my direction—*Meg, please stop! We need to talk! I can*—but I shut him down with a cold glare. Hope slides off his face. Good! He feels the rush of the misery that's coming his way.

On the outside, only a small scrape on Brendon's mouth and a purple bruise on his elbow are visible. But inside, my enemy is now hemorrhaging. It's not blood and not anything that would register on an X-ray or that a doctor could stitch up. It's his sanity, and we will make it bleed right out of him.

The next day Brendon's eyes look sunken into his skull. He seems to have shrunk an inch overnight. By the next week his lips are cracked and he wanders the school hallways like he's lost in a nightmare.

The rumors grow thicker and darker. I am doing this to him and I won't ever stop. Me and Alix and Stephanie. No one dares accuse me out loud. No one laughs, either, or points a cell phone camera in my face anymore. Even the Plagues step aside as we pass.

Brendon soon stops coming to school. I hear things. The Double Ds say that he stopped eating, not a bite. One of his cousins reports that he's not sleeping at all; no amount of medication can knock him out. His skin is breaking out in pustules. He complains of migraines and arthritis in his toes. His medical doctor recommends a psychiatrist and the psychiatrist recommends a neurologist, but nobody can bring him any relief.

For days he flails at invisible enemies, and then for a solid night he cries deep, animal sobs. His pleas for forgiveness turn into loud, wordless moans, which dissolve into near-silent whines of pain.

Then, not a sound from him. I hear that he huddles in a corner of his room.

"Like some dude trapped under glass," Pox tells a group of surfers.

"No!" Gnat disagrees. "Like he's being held underwater."

Exactly, I think. Under glass, underwater, like the figures in Ambrosia's snow globe. It is not a piece of art. It is a prison. Brendon's essence is there, with all the other princes. Trapped with sharp, black shards of guilt falling all over them.

Curtain down. Exodos *in the Greek theatrical tradition. All the players, major and minor, having served their purpose, exit the scene. The princess avenged. The Prince doomed. My enemy Pallas defeated.*

So why when I shake my snow globe do I not taste the soul-tingling relief I so long for? I need a calculator to add up all my princely pounds of flesh cooked into a stew and served up for supper in my House of Revenge.

Yet I am still not released from this appetite as I wander the dank netherworld and the locker-lined halls of Hunter High.

What gives?

Warning: anti-drug message coming at you.

Revenge is like any of those other gateway drugs that you have been warned against. Your first experience? It's what it's cracked up to be: an all-encompassing, headlong rush of endorphins into sheer transcendence.

The second time? Well, that was pretty good, but it lacked something, a certain zesty zing. As the Hunter High bathroom *stoners always complain:* You should have been here for that *other* shit.

Ambrosia's Law: The most recent act of revenge is never as satisfying as the one before it.

It's all about recapturing the first time, a desperate chase to relive and reclaim your moment of the undiluted bliss of vengeance. You always want more.

Chase. Chase. Chase.

That's why I have to double the dose. Triple it. Hunt it down and ingest it straight.

Keep hunting, I order.

Hunt. Hunt. Hunt.

FIFTH STASIMON, THE BOOK OF FURIOUS

Definition of satisfaction: knowing that you got back at someone who stabbed you in the back. Brendon will never forget
what he did to me. Justice has been done. I feel at peace.

But then, I don't.

The peaceful feeling turns into an irritating itch, and the
itch works on me until I'm half crazy with frustration. My
mind won't rest. I can't sleep or eat. I can't stop thinking
about all the others.

"Why should they get away with it?" I demand of Alix
and Stephanie. "The Double Ds laughed at me. The surfers
hid in the closet. All those people who did nothing to stop
it. What about *them*?"

Stephanie loops her arm around my waist. "Ambrosia
said that there's nothing to fear from the Furies if you don't
get in their way. She warned them. They *are* in your way."

Alix smacks a fist into her palm. "Eye for an eye. They
shouldn't get away with it. They should feel what you felt."

"Suffer what I suffered."

Here is an undeniable truth of human nature that we Furies take advantage of: everyone has a point of entry. We are like mice that can always find a way into the foundation of the most fortified building. We mutate our shapes and squeeze into the tiniest crack in a person's thick wall of defense.

Our experience with Brendon taught us how to go deeper, to burrow down to the very core of shame that exists in everyone. We find the thing that you can't ever truly apologize for, that you can't deny or rationalize.

Like the first hurtful lie you told before you learned to justify your lies.

Like the first heart you broke before you figured out how to harden your own heart.

Everyone has a memory that sits at the cusp, dividing life into before and after.

Before: You fumble your words when you lie. You feel the sting of your own mean actions. You experience the hurt of others like it's your own hurt.

After: You don't give a shit. You want what you want, and you take it.

That's the long-buried memory that we dust off and stick in each of their faces.

In the late afternoon, we stand on the cliff and home in on Gnat in the surfer lineup. He's straddling his board while waiting for a wave. Into this serene scene we unleash his personal vision:

He was seven, stole five dollars from his mother's purse

and lied about it, claimed his little brother took the money, and his parents believed him.

In the middle of the ocean, he tries to blink away the memory. We show him his mother's face and the disbelief in his brother's deceived eyes, the monumental bond of trust that he broke and never got back.

This was the start, we remind him. *After this lie, your whole life became a string of lying to others and lying to yourself.*

Gnat stares directly into the sun. A wave slams him on the head. He doesn't even try to paddle. Two surfers—we'll deal with them next—haul him in to shore.

At midnight we position ourselves outside of Pox's house. While standing under a streetlamp, we sing into his sleep to play and replay his moment of truth lost:

He was six, and in a snit he walked up to his sweet, trusting dog and kicked her, just because he could. Pox jolts awake and turns on a light, but he can't stop living in the nightmare of his dog's betrayed eyes.

On the bus, we sit behind the Double Ds and take them back to age eight, when they made every kid in their class stop talking to a girl who thought she was their best friend. They announced all of her secrets. We force them to experience the full brunt of their treachery. They feel that girl's shock and loneliness. By the time we get to school, they are curled up in their seats and unable to move, paralyzed by regret.

And when the pleasure of that payback leaves us longing for more, we usher in others. The friends of our enemies are guilty by association. Soon they move like sleepwalkers in an endless nightmare of sadness, fear, and regret. They twitch and stutter. Their minds wreck their bodies with weight loss and hives, immune systems sent into complete disarray. We multiply their pain past the point of unbearable.

It's fantastic. Who doesn't deserve it?

We want even more.

The principal convenes a special parent-teacher conference to enact emergency health precautions. Everyone washes their hands so much they get dry and raw, even bleed. Mr. and Mrs. H start a trend by wearing surgical masks to school. Students stay home even when they feel perfectly fine. PE classes are cancelled. E-mails swirl. There must be something toxic in the air ducts. A ventilation specialist comes in. There's nothing in the air ducts.

We keep bringing them down.

The show-off lead in this year's production of *The Sound of Music*.

Our class treasurer who gave Stephanie only $100 for her anti-littering campaign.

The Eagle Scout who keeps bragging about getting early admission to Stanford.

The girl whom we just find to be irritating. She chews too loud.

The local TV station does a special report on the mysterious illness at Hunter High. A parent blogger lists the names and symptoms of the fallen.

An expert from the Centers for Disease Control flies out from Washington, DC, to investigate the possibility of a terrible new viral strain that invades the cells of healthy high school students. She looks down throats, draws blood, and orders X-rays. I wonder if Raymond is going to denounce us, but what can he say that anyone would believe? There are three girls who have the power of the Furies? He's way too smart to try explaining the truth. The doctor leaves town with lots of notes, but no diagnosis.

It remains a mystery, except to a few of us.

"Meg, a moment of your precious, valuable time."

A familiar voice with a sardonic, elevated tone equals Raymond equals a lecture that I don't want to hear. With my back to him, I finish hanging up my jacket in my locker and fuss with some other stuff—as if killing a little time will make him give up. But he's not leaving. I swing around. It's not only Raymond, but sneaky Ms. Pallas beside him, both of them with their color guard batons propped in front of their chests.

"Pray tell, what's this?" I can be sardonic and elevated, too. "An intervention? You're here to say that you love me deeply but are concerned about my anger-management problem. Oh goody. How thoughtful."

They exchange looks and have an entire conversation with their eyes that I can't interpret, other than the fact that it ends with Ms. Pallas giving Raymond an encouraging pat on the back. Aren't they the perfect pair? He doesn't say anything until she and her swishing silver outfit are down the hall. Good riddance.

Then a thump of his baton. "Meg, what the hell are you doing?"

Innocent me with a singsong in my voice. "What do you mean? I'm not doing anything."

"Stop that! I need you to tell me the—what's that thing called again?—oh right, the truth. No, wait, I already know. You're not fooling anyone else, either. The whole school knows that it's you behind the Hunter High epidemic. They don't know exactly what you're doing or how or why, but they know it's you."

"Really?" I put on a distressed expression to match the concerned tone in my voice.

"Really! Look at how everyone is looking at you."

Two juniors in surgical masks happen to be passing, so I whip around with a loud "Booga-booga!" They jump back, their eyes circles of horror, and scurry away. I laugh, rubbing my hands together like a movie mad scientist.

"You know what people are saying? That Brendon was innocent, that he didn't know what Pox and the others were up to."

"People don't know what they're talking about. Brendon took me by the hand into that room."

"Because Ambrosia told him to. Have you thought about that? What about her role in all this?"

I order myself not to listen to him. No! I will not listen. These are just tricks designed to make me question what I already know. I was there that night. Brendon took me into that room. He let it happen. He didn't do a thing to stand up for me. There's no defense for that. And Raymond has no right to drag down Ambrosia. She rescued me from my old life and showed me who I can be. She's on my side.

"Brendon got what was coming to him. They're all getting what they deserve. If people are smart, they'll stay out of our way."

"Is that what you want for real? For everyone to be terrified of you?"

"Let me think about that." I press a finger to my temple, remove it immediately. "Thinking is over. Terror is working. Why mess with proven success? I know what I'm doing!"

"Explain it to me then, because all I see is misery!"

"Do I really have to spell it out for you, Raymond? Look around. Because of us and what we're doing, the Leech will never mistreat another foster kid. Alix says that it's been totally chill out in the ocean with all the Plagues on indefinite bed rest. And around school? No bullying. No practical jokes. Our warning has been heard. We're doing what needs to be done."

He mimes pointing a gun in my face and pulls the thumb trigger. "By any means necessary?"

"If we don't do it, who will?"

Raymond's features collapse into his deep-thinking pose. He strokes the part of his chin where a beard would grow if he were far enough into puberty to grow one. I get impatient waiting because I know what he's going to say. Here come all of his old, tired arguments. We've gone too far. We're abusing our sacred power. There's a justice system designed to punish the guilty. Or the karmic chain of the universe will eventually get around to sorting things out and making life fair. The righteous will be rewarded and the guilty punished.

But I don't see evidence to support any of those arguments. I never have and never will.

The animation returns to Raymond's face. At least he doesn't insult me with clichés: "Meg, I honestly don't know who will punish them. Or if they'll get punished at all. Or if they deserve punishment. I can't say that life will even things out or that it's fair. Because I don't know."

"Wow! The Raymond oracle admits that he doesn't know something."

"Want to know what I *do* know?" He pauses. I don't bite. "Well, don't you want to know? The old Meg would be dying of curiosity."

The new Meg shrugs with a complete lack of enthusiasm. I even fake a yawn. "Sure. Knock me out with your wisdom."

He ignores my snarkiness. "I know that *this*—what you're doing—isn't right. You claim to be on the side of justice, but you're as mean as the people you're punishing. Frankly, you're more vicious."

"If we back off, it will be chaos again. People will do whatever they want 'cause they know they'll get away with it. Hunter High needs our law and order."

"It's all black and white with you. People are people and they make mistakes. You don't give anyone a break. You're . . ."

"I'm what?"

"You're a colossal, monomaniacal tool. You're power crazy."

"I'm just using my power!"

He gives a double thump of his baton. That's how I know I've gotten to him. "Meg, your power is using you. And so is someone else—Ambrosia. She's manipulating you."

"You never did like her, Raymond. You're jealous. You just want me to be your harmless, patient, forgiving little friend again. You think I should reenlist in the Good Girl Brigade."

"Did I say that? No! I like having a sassy straight friend. You do have things to be angry about. So does Stephanie and so does Alix. I'm not arguing with you about that."

"What's your problem, then?"

"You think you're in control, but Ambrosia is twisting your anger for her own purpose. That's what Ms. Pallas told me. Ms. Pallas knows that you won't listen to her, but you might listen to me. You *need* to listen to me. This is serious. You are up against something very powerful and dangerous. I want to help. I'm on your side. But I can only do so much. Ms. Pallas—"

I break in mockingly, spit out the words. "Ms. Pallas. When did you become completely devoted to her? What a suck-up! You sound exactly like her."

"You want to talk about swallowing someone's entire way of thinking? You sound like Ambrosia!"

"What if I do?"

"Ambrosia is not who she says she is."

"And who is Ms. Pallas? Not some first-year teacher! What's she up to?"

Instead of answering, he waves his hand in front of his

nose. "Whew. Your breath. Have you been eating your young? Take a look at yourself." He spins me around so I get a close-up of my face in the small locker mirror.

"What? What am I supposed to see?"

"You're that blind? Let's do a vision test." He stands behind me, points to my eyes: "Healthy or bloodshot?" To my lips: "Kissable or cracked and raw?" To my skin: "Caramel-colored or puke green?" To my stomach: "Flat or bloated? And what's with the enlarged pores? Honey, your complexion is like the surface of the moon. You're unraveling fast, a total mess. You look as bad as your victims. Everyone but you can see it."

I have to admit that I do look like Grade C dog doo. I let him fuss with my hair a little and push back some brittle strands, but others spring up to take their place. "I'm a little tired, that's all. Maintaining law and order is a full-time job."

"A little tired? What about Stephanie and her new fangs? Alix looks like the Incredible Hulk. Ms. Pallas says—"

Poof. Raymond's moment of being tolerated is over. I don't want to know what Ms. Pallas—whoever she is—has to say. I push away his hand. "Let's do *your* vision test now. How many fingers am I holding up?" I flash him the middle one.

Raymond swallows hard. "I hardly recognize you, inside or out. All this hostility and anger, 24-7. Meg, when you make others live in misery, you wind up living in it, too."

"There's a certain someone," Ambrosia says. "A meddling type. She and I go way, way back. Sometimes she calls herself Athena, sometimes Minerva, sometimes she fancies herself up as *Pallas* Athena."

I start to say *I knew it*, but Ambrosia tells us to listen. "She demands complete obedience, but I'm having none of that. She's jealous of you three—your youth, your power, your unwillingness to compromise. She thinks that minor goddesses should kowtow to someone of her elevated stature."

"Who's she calling minor?" Alix readies her fists for a fight.

Stephanie's jaw tenses. "No authority tells me what to do or not to do anymore."

Ambrosia makes a tent with her hands, taps the fingers. "She's stopped me before with her meddling. And now she's brought in a compatriot and together they plan to dilute your power. This compatriot pretends to be your friend. He offers comfort and understanding, the family you never had. That's how he sucks you in."

I fold my arms over my chest and press my belly against the ocean railing. I'm barefoot and the cliff is cold against my feet. Out in the water, a pod of dolphins breaks the surface. Waves pound the rocks. Overhead, thick fog blocks out any hope of a sunny day.

"Your true enemy is doubt," Ambrosia goes on. "They try to instill it in you. The slightest hint of doubt holds you back, keeps you from fulfilling your natural potential as jury and judge. You know why they do it? You know what they want?"

"To strip us of power," Alix says, flexing her biceps.

"To tame us." Stephanie runs her tongue over her fangs.

"Exactly! Athena wants to take the glorious, relentless Furies and dress you in nice, comfy aprons of bland femininity. She's done it before. She's trying again."

Ambrosia opens her copy of Aeschylus, and in a sappy, mimicking voice she reads a section near the end of the play. "We sing of the gifts we will give: No storm-winds will strike at your trees, no searing heat will ever burn scorching the earth, blistering your buds."

With the book raised overhead, she shouts, "Not this time, Pallas!" and hurls it into the ocean. "Do you know what the original Furies got in return for giving up their rage?"

I do know. I finished reading the play. The Furies are appeased and settle for minor-goddess status. They get a nice altar in a nice city. Some citizens honor them by giving them a new name: the Kindly Ones.

"Kindly!" Ambrosia points her sharp fingernail at the book floating in the ocean, and it springs back into her hand just so she can have the pleasure of heaving it back into the water again. "The original Furies—the OFs—had it all! Weak, pathetic humanity trembled in fear before them and begged them for their justice and protection. But they traded it all for . . ."

Her mouth bunches like she bit into something sour, bitter, and hot. She spits out the words in disgust. "For popularity."

A wave picks up the collected works of Aeschylus and pounds it against the rocks. The current sucks it back out a little, but then it washes in again for another pounding. And another. And another. The pages are saturated and the plays sink.

Ambrosia's face is so close to mine that it blocks out everything but her. "So what's it going to be, Megaera? Your justice for the entire human realm? Or a nice friend to eat lunch with?"

"The OFs took a rotten deal," I say. "I don't want to be minor anything ever again."

With her fingernail she draws an invisible star on my forehead. "Give yourself an A-plus for that answer. But it means certain things must be taken care of."

I forgot to mention the football team.

Despite the fact that half the cars in the school parking lot have a waxed surfboard buckled onto the roof, Hunter High is not a beach-town freak in the world of high school sports. The glass display case at the front entrance has football trophies right next to the surfing ones, dozens of bronze-colored, muscle-popping masculine figures clutching footballs and frozen in mid-run. Like everywhere else, autumn means football, and we are smack in the middle of the traditional season. If this were any other year, there would be scrimmages and pep rallies, everything leading up to the all-important homecoming game.

Oh well. Traditions are made to be broken. People need to get used to that. This year just about the whole team is out with the mysterious wasting disease, and the rest of the student body is bummed about it. The cheerleaders, poor things, are shadows of their former bouncy selves. They're all on some combination of Prozac, Ritalin, and antibiotics in hopes that a miracle of modern medicine will revive their perkiness. Plus, none of the coaches, players, parents, or band members from the other schools will set foot on the Hunter High campus. It's too scary.

That's why I'm flabbergasted when, during Western Civ, the *ding, dong, ding* of the classroom speaker comes on and, instead of Mr. and Mrs. H, Raymond's voice blasts out a cheery:

"Don't be square. Be there! Today's big homecoming event!"

There's a surprised, happy buzz among the few students still left in class. How irritating! I exchange grumpy looks with Alix and Stephanie. When did Raymond become pumped up on school spirit? All this cheeriness gives me a pounding headache. I lay my head on the desk, cupped in the circle of my crisscrossed arms. I get a concentrated sniff of something not good. What's that funky smell? There's something familiar about it. Oh yeah, the stink of the plant at Ambrosia's house—and yeah, I guess it's coming from me now, my rank breath coupled with my eau de armpits.

Raymond's voice goes on with its optimistic chirp: "Who needs big bruisers in shoulder pads slamming each other to smithereens? Homecoming is about the music and the marching. The band and color guard—what's left of it!—are all rehearsed and ready to wow you with their precision stepping and flag-twirling."

Somebody in the room actually applauds, and I have to look up to believe it. It's one of the band geeks whom we let slide—so far. How disrespectful. And then the Danish foreign exchange student shakes his fist in the air in triumph, and a girl known for her buckteeth makes a choking sound that turns out to be tears of joy. Joy!

For the first time since the Fall of Brendon, I feel a serious lack of anxiety among my fellow students. I actually sense the room growing lighter. All because of a public performance by the mercilessly mocked color guard? What's this about?

Raymond again: "Today! Right after school in the football stadium. Music! Marching! Instant satisfaction guaranteed!"

I don't like it.

Neither does Ambrosia. She stands, and the way her hands knot at her sides I think she's going to take a flying leap at the loudspeaker, superhero-style, and destroy it with one perfectly placed blow of her fist. But she stays earthbound and stomps one of her designer pumps. She finally manages to mutter, "Not this time!" before storming out of the room.

Ms. Pallas looks pleased. Very pleased. To the already-closed door: "Permission to leave granted, Ambrosia."

From the loudspeaker comes a triumphant blast of recorded Hunter High band music. At first I think it's what Raymond refers to as a John Phillip Snooza tune. It sets my teeth on edge, makes me grind them with each flare of the trumpet. But something about its awfulness sounds familiar. I know this tune. I hum a few notes ahead and wait for the music to catch up. What is it? Where have I heard it before?

My mind adds the sound of a violin, and I recognize the source. It's the song Raymond was writing—part pop, part show tune—the one that he said came out of nowhere and got stuck in his head. I guess he finished composing it. I cover my ears with my palms, and notice that Alix and Stephanie have done the same. It's excruciating. But strangely, nobody else seems to mind. The jarring trumpet and the snappy beat of the snare drums are actually perking up everyone's mood. Disgusting. Ms. Pallas is snapping her fingers and doing some kind of folk dance. Goddesses her age should never shimmy their shoulders like that in public. A few kids are chair-dancing, bump-bumping their bottoms and hand-jiving, like the music is filling them with inspiration. I can't stand it. All this positive energy is intruding on my negative brain.

I zero in on the worst culprit. The super-blond Danish kid is wiggling his fingers and vibrating his lips, the whole sickening air-saxophone routine. He thinks he's on fire with the music. I'm the one on fire. Death is too good for air musicians. I invite the other Furies to join me in a special impromptu session. I tune up my internal pitch pipe and we hum with perfect rhythm and harmony.

We swarm. We enter. But something's wrong, terribly wrong. We manage to dip only one tiny toe into that boy's mind before the door is slammed in our faces. We try again, but it's a no-go. We're met with static and electronic jamming signals, then driven away by the saxophone part of Raymond's corny song blasted back at us.

Panic on Alix's face, uncertainty on Stephanie's. Both those reactions take turns in me. My forehead creases, my bottom teeth make a hard pull on my upper lip.

That's when I see a flicker of approval on the corners of Ms. Pallas's mouth. She snaps her fingers faster and happier. Her smile is as bright as her voice: "Our own battle of the bands."

I now understand what's at stake, why Ambrosia flew out of the room in anger. This is a full frontal assault on us. This is not *any* piece of music. It came from someplace deep and true inside of Raymond, and it reflects everything that he is, everything that he believes and values. It was composed from his trusting nature, a musical by-product of his loving mom and his damn happy home. The homecoming performance is a planned strike, them against us, a terrorist attack to drown out the righteous fury of our sacred music.

They mean business. They've been practicing. But so have we.

On our side, we have human nature with its inexhaustible taste for rage, hatred, and revenge.

Their big gun? My gawky, good-natured former best friend parading around in a lame-o high school band uniform.

We cut our next class and don't bother getting excuse notes. Who would dare try to give us detention? We meet in the parking lot and sit on the hood of Alix's Volvo.

"I know we need to take action. It's just that I . . ." I feel my mouth twisting, fumbling for words. "I want to at least consider another way."

Stephanie rests her big head of hair on my shoulder. She smells about the same as I do. "I hear ya. It's one of those *dear old friend* things. That makes it hard. Wanna talk about it?"

"We could . . . we should have . . . if he would . . ."

Alix peers at me over her sunglasses, blows off all my objections with an irritated "Coulda, shoulda, woulda."

Stephanie gives me a funny little smile. "It's your doubt speaking, Meg. That's what they want. Ambrosia warned us about doubt, remember?"

Alix jumps off the hood, brushes her palms against her pant legs. Dust explodes from them. "Steph, don't coddle her with that touchy-feely stuff! She's a big girl. She knows what she signed up for." To me: "Grow up!"

"I'm just saying—"

"You have a better idea? You don't have a better idea."

They're right, of course. This is not something that I want to do, but there's only one choice and it's as clear as the big black crow that's hopping across the parking lot and gobbling up every stale, moldy, rotten thing it can find. Stephanie is already warming up her voice. She's committed to improving the harmony part of our song, making us sound a little like one of those girl groups from the 1960s. Diana Ross and the Supremely Powerful. I hug my knees against my chest. "I'm in."

Alix hits me with a high five.

"We're going to go easy, right? Nothing permanent. He's not like the others. We only need a diversion. The plan is to shut down the rally. That's all."

"No major badass stuff," Alix confirms.

The three of us are in agreement.

First we're going to eat an entire box of powdered doughnuts for energy.

Then we're going to kidnap Raymond.

31

Right after school, I stake out the boys' locker room in the stadium. When Raymond emerges in his full-regalia blue-and-white uniform with a shiny whistle around his neck, I follow as he heads to the band staging area outside the football field. I've never been known for my grace and agility, but I'm doing a decent job of sneaking around. It helps that Raymond seems hyper-focused on his upcoming musical extravaganza. For an absolutely brilliant human being, he can be completely oblivious to what's going on around him. He doesn't seem to notice the skulking figure with the *Go Hunters* cap pulled low on her forehead to hide her mass of dry, split-ended hair.

He turns the corner and I turn the corner, landing in the middle of enemy territory. It stops me. Under a sky that's so bright it hurts my skin, there's a whole army decked out in matching blue uniforms with white, tasseled marching boots. Everyone's warming up their instruments, humming the same notes and moving to the same rhythm. I hear the trill of trumpets, the running scales of clarinets and flutes, and the four-four-time beat of the drums, and it makes me dizzy.

Under the cacophony I make out Raymond's song like a thread sewing together instruments and players, twirlers and marchers. That's the power of certain music. Even when it's a style of music you don't usually like, a song can get inside of you. That's what's happening here. This is Raymond's song, and it's everything that he is—enthusiastic, honest, optimistic, trusting, forgiving, fair. Everyone is tapping into it. The song is contagious.

Damn it.

As Raymond passes through the crowd, people reach out to touch him. They rub his epaulettes like they are a combination rabbit's foot and genie's lamp. Hope is written all over their faces. This is what they've been waiting and practicing for. They need him and his song. They're nothing without Raymond and his golden whistle at the helm. It's what I suspected, and it scares me.

I peek through the gate leading into the stadium. I squint into the sunlight—no rain or fog to keep people home today—and I pick out individual faces in the stands. Mr. and Mrs. H with all the other teachers. Every kid untouched by us is there. I want to kick myself for being such a softy and not taking care of them when we could.

Behind me, the horns come alive. In front of me, I see other things that make me not happy. Not happy at all! So many moms and dads in the stands, including Alix's father and Stephanie's mother. The Leech! What is she doing here? In the second row of the home-team side, waving weakly, sit the Double Ds. And I'm not happy that right behind them is

Pox, eating something. A fat, greasy corn dog. He's definitely on the mend. And next to him, Gnat, Bubonic, and Rat Boy. In that section alone, I count at least ten other people whom we dispatched to a lifetime of misery and regret. Ten people recovering and getting a second chance.

I want to blink it away. I want to redo what's being undone because right there, front-row center, is the ultimate slap in my face. This has got to be one of the worst sights of my life. Worse than my social worker's annoyed look when I complain about a foster home. Worse than the eyes that looked back at me in the mirror when I was powerless.

Brendon. The sight of him makes my stomach muscles tense. He's got a blanket wrapped around him and he looks like Grade-D crapola, but I can make out his eye crinkles because he's smiling slightly. He has no right to be smiling. Things are moving fast in the wrong direction.

Damn the sunlight. Damn the flutes. Damn the color guard and its leader.

Why am I sneaking around? Who cares who sees me here? I'm the one with the muscle.

I charge through the clarinet section and walk right up to Raymond, who's having an intimate conversation with a majorette in a short, twirly skirt. She's happily humming the dreaded tune slightly off-key. I know he knows I'm there because he's going overboard with his gay hairdresser routine. "Wear your hair up!" he tells the majorette. "Show off your lovely swan neck." I tap him on the shoulder, and when he holds up a *wait a sec* finger I say, "I need to talk to you."

"Later, Meg. *After* the rally. By the way, nice disguise. Oh so tricky."

I rip off the cap, let my hair fly loose and set my jaw. "It's important we talk."

To irritate me further, he takes his time pinning up the girl's hair and pulling out tendrils around her temples. "Don't you stress over those fire batons. You're going to be incendiary!"

"Now!" I insist.

The majorette flashes me a dirty look. Me! I can't believe she has the guts to do that. I'll deal with her and her disrespect another time. Her eyes question Raymond: *Do we have a situation here, or what?* His eyes assure her: *I can handle this.* We both watch her walk away and then Raymond turns to confront me. He has his whistle in the corner of his mouth, so he has to talk out of one side of it and it's making a little toot with each breath. He's doing this on purpose. Being passively-aggressively annoying is one of his best argument techniques.

"You want to talk, Meg? Talk." *Toot.*

I steady my mind. Don't let him get to you. No doubts. I have to use extraordinary means here. I need to pull out all the friendship stops and hit him with every bit of warm and fuzzy that I can. I drop my gaze to show that I'm all humbleness. "It's . . . it's . . ."

The whistle shifts to the other side of his mouth. "It's . . . what?" *Woot.*

"Private. It's a private conversation."

He removes the whistle, waves it at me like a weapon. "No secrets here. Everyone is up front. You can say what you need to say." His gaze is steely. He turns his head slightly, shows me his profile in that ridiculous feathered helmet.

I put a quiver into my voice and the start of tears into my eyes, regret for my insensitive actions, hints of good times past. I need them all. "Please, Raymond. I need to talk to you. Like old times. Remember them? I only need a minute."

I motion for him to follow me to the big live-oak tree that stands at the edge of the parking lot. Branches jut out in every direction. I don't give him a chance to turn me down or ask too many questions. I walk away at a steady clip. I sense his hesitation, but I keep moving. When I glance back over my shoulder, he's tilting his head toward the sky like he's heard something up there, and that's when I think: *I blew it! He's going to run off in the other direction. We're done.*

But he tosses off whatever stopped him, an actual shake of his head like a golden retriever shaking off water. He takes a couple of steps before breaking into a run to catch up. He's got a real goofy run, feet splaying out, whistle bouncing on his jacket. His right hand keeps his helmet from flying off as he makes straight for me. I lean against the tree, but he stands back a good three feet, suspiciously checking right and left. The ground is spongy with decaying leaves. A leaf falls from the tree. I step closer and he flinches when I brush it off of his head.

"Alone at last." He says this flatly, cuttingly. He takes out his cell phone and sets the timer. "You asked for one minute. Talk!"

"Is that necessary?"

"You're down to fifty-five seconds."

"Jeez! I just want to say I'm sorry."

He arches an eyebrow. "Let me get this straight: you're apologizing?"

He doesn't believe me. More extraordinary measures must be taken. I look wounded and thrust out my pinkie.

"Pinkie promise? You're offering me our Holy Sacred Vow of Pinkie Trust? Meg, you know that you're jinxed forever if you're lying. You know that, right?"

"I know all about eternal damnation. The Furies practically invented it!" For good measure, I give him an extra-sincere puppy-dog look. "I went out of control. We all did. I know that now. "

I see his brain conducting a lie-detector test, scanning back and forth to size me up. I guess I pass with flying colors, because he presses his hand to his chest, taps it, and addresses his heart. "Be still, baby. Everything is going to be okay now. Our Meg has come back home to us."

To me: "I'm so relieved. Ms. Pallas wanted to do something even worse. Something permanent. She wanted to . . ." His voice drifts away for a second, comes back stronger. "That's all over and done with. I persuaded her to try the homecoming rally first. I knew you weren't lost. I knew you'd come to your senses. I knew—"

I break in. "It's like you said. People are people. Everyone's human. I have to forgive them sometime."

He motions for me to rub the powdered-sugar mustache off my upper lip. "Doughnut," I explain. "Besides, we Furies are too weak to fight against you and her. She's a major goddess, after all."

"So you know then about Ms. Pallas! Athena walks among us. Crazy, right?"

"The whole *thing* is crazy. Us, her, you. "

A shyness comes over him. "So we're good then, you

and me? All is right in the wonderful world of Raymond and Meg?"

I answer him with a hugging motion. He steps in with arms spread wide.

From her hiding place up in the tree, Stephanie drops a sheet over him, and Alix springs out from behind a bush to tackle him in a bear hug before he can get his whistle to his mouth. Raymond's a good screamer, but the horns and drums drown him out.

We rush him into the back seat of Alix's car, held down by me and Stephanie. Engine on. We tear out of the parking lot.

The blue sky directly over the stadium opens up and spits down hail the size of eyeballs.

"You lied, Meg! You broke our holy pinkie pact!"

"I *am* sorry! That's the truth. I'm sorry for *this*!" I pound the cracked leather seat between us.

"Sorry for the foam padding that's popping out?"

"I'm *sorry* we had to kidnap you, but you left us no other choice. That's why it's technically not a lie."

Raymond shakes his head sadly. "Meg, you are paddling hard and breaking a sweat to keep afloat on that famous river in Egypt. Da Nile. Denial."

"I get it, Raymond."

Alix clicks on the radio, blasting KSRF, all surf music all the time, *where reverb is king.* She shouts over it: "You two shut the hell up. You're driving me crazy."

"Your BO is driving *me* crazy. All of you," Raymond complains. "Can't we open the window a crack? If I'm going to die a lonely, miserable death, I want my last inhale on earth to be fresh air, not this stench."

"Nobody is going to die," I insist.

"No, you're just going to make me carsick and then banish me into a life of eternal agony."

"We're not. We're just taking you on a little detour."

Alix points the Volvo out of town along the straight, flat coast road. On a day like this—one that started sunny and warm but has suddenly given way to blustery wind and hail—there's hardly any traffic along this stretch. I pop a stick of gum into my mouth. All we need to do is keep Raymond away from that rally. Without him, the band and color guard will give their normal, mediocre performance, and everyone in the stands will go home without hope. Our justice will prevail again.

On the radio, Dick Dale segues into Los Straitjackets, but that doesn't keep Raymond quiet. "Denial," he goes on. "An unconscious psychological mechanism that keeps a person from acknowledging painful realities, thoughts, and feelings. Meg, you've got it bad. You used to hate bullies. Who's the bully now? All of you!"

Alix yells back over her shoulder. "Hey, Sergeant Pepper! For someone who's completely under our mercy, you have a big mouth. I'm sick of hearing that yapping. Steph?"

Stephanie's response is to take the blue sash from Raymond's uniform. He catches on quickly to her plan and in desperation starts to hum his song. This only makes her look sad. "That's all you got? Against us? No backup singers? No harmony? No brass section?"

She moves the ribbon toward his mouth. He manages to get in one more verbal jab—"What about your dreams, Stephanie? To make the world a better place? For whom?

Ambrosia?"—but it's no use. There's a final whine of protest before the sash covers his mouth.

"Not too tight," I urge her. Then to him: "It's your fault, you know. You can't blame us for this. You always need to get in the last word."

That's all anyone says for a while. Ambrosia has given Alix a map to a spot up the coast where she says we can hold Raymond in secret for the rest of the day. The plan is to meet her there. We pass the nine-mile marker. Through the fog I see the faint outline of the big ball of sun starting its plunge into the ocean. When we pass the fifteen-mile point out of town, the Volvo slows. On the left I notice a small turnoff, the sign of a parking lot for a hidden beach.

But instead of making a left toward the ocean, Alix makes a sharp right. We skid a little, then pull onto a narrow, unmarked, unpaved road.

"This is it." Alix reaches under her seat, comes up with a flask, and takes a mouthful before handing it to me. "A present from Ambrosia to get us through a cold, long night."

I drink. The thick, licorice flavor immediately sends warmth through my body.

Raymond flashes me a look. Is that terror in his eyes? Pleading? A warning? He looks down at his tied, useless hands. He shivers from the cold and from everything else. I take another drink and pass the flask to Stephanie.

The car climbs, bumping and weaving through thickening brush and dark lines of trees. We're heading into the coastal mountain range that runs down California like a twisted spine, east where the sun has already set. We pass nothing, not a house, not a ranch, no telephone or electricity poles. It looks like a long, tree-lined driveway that would lead to the edge of outer space. I smell the change of our direction, the clear, fresh salt of the ocean giving way to the scent of redwoods. It's so thick it lands on my tongue and tastes like spicy rain.

Alix turns on the headlights and wipers. She squints through the windshield, making sure she doesn't lose the path under the tires. Dancing ghosts of fog usher us forward.

Raymond mumbles, and I know him well enough to translate. "He says he's getting carsick. How much longer 'til we're there—wherever *there* is?"

Alix squints through the fog and dark into the distance. "About ten."

"Ten miles?" I ask. Raymond groans, and I feel the same way.

"No, ten seconds."

She guides the car slightly to the right, and there must be a clearing that I can't see because we don't go tumbling down the face of a sheer cliff. When Alix cuts the engine, it rumbles in relief from the hard climb. The driver's door opens. Alix's voice is bright and eager. "Ambrosia said we'd need to hike from here."

We all get out, and a light explodes, blinding me. When I blink through it, I see that Alix is wearing a headlamp. The light makes an arc as she scans the landscape and illuminates a forest path that's narrow and hard to pick out. It looks like it was made by squirrels for squirrels.

"This way." She takes the lead, followed by Stephanie, then Raymond, and me at the rear. For a long time we walk in silence, except for the snap and crunch of branches and leaves underfoot, and soon we start a steep climb. I sense the altitude in the pull on my quadriceps. We must be on the east side of the mountain range now, the drier part, almost desert, that's walled off from the ocean and rain. The few trees at the top are blackened from a fire—leafless, twisted needles.

Stars blink in the cloudless sky. The fog hasn't made its way here. We round another bend. The few spindly trees part like a curtain, and the moon—full and white—greets us.

Alix's arms spread wide. She spins. "Check it out."

Where we've landed, the top of the mountain, the whole expanse as far as I can see looks like close-up photos of the moon. Bare, rocky ridges and cliffs are stacked like giant Legos. Monolithic crags like sentries with misshapen spines stand guard over this weird place. Moonlight bounces off of them, and they glow like they're lit from inside.

On nearly every rock and boulder, someone has left a sign that they've been here. There's the usual stupid bathroom-type graffiti—*So-and-so loves So-and-so*—but there are also mysterious carvings and etchings, sculptures popping up like islands in this sea of stone.

I remove Raymond's gag and free his hands. Where is he going to run? Whom can he yell for?

I hear a familiar voice then but can't make out the words. It's Ambrosia. She must have gotten here before us, even though there was no other car at the trailhead. At first her voice seems to be coming from behind me. Now from my left. Or is it below us? Raymond, too, is looking for the source. He points, and I track the line of his finger into the near distance.

The moon has been rising fast, but it jolts to a stop and trembles, suspended as if its beam is purposely set to spotlight the tallest sandstone monolith. Lounging comfortably in its top curve, there's a silhouette sheathed in black, her legs crossed at the thighs, a shoe with a very spiky high heel dangling off of one foot. In the night air I smell Ambrosia's perfume. Her head is completely shaved. She's all angles and bone, a living skull. Her eyes, without lashes, don't blink. The snake jewelry around her neck slithers and flicks its prey-seeking tongues. Her mouth is a twisted slash of red. She blows a kiss and it lands hard and wet on my lips.

That kiss, bitter like venom, does something terrible to Raymond. He collapses to one knee and holds his stomach like he's been punched.

"Don't!" I yell. "You said he wouldn't be hurt. I promised him." I extend a hand to help Raymond, but I'm stopped by a voice that I feel in my marrow.

"Awake, Megaera! Awake! I didn't come this far to be defeated by some silly sentimentality like friendship."

My hand goes numb. My heart goes hard.

Another voice coming from everywhere.

On another formation stands a figure in a helmet that sits low on her forehead. The wind plays with her long, blue gown, makes it billow and wave and then stand out straight as a sail.

Ms. Pallas, Hunter High's toughest grader, the all-powerful color guard faculty sponsor, Pallas Athena, Minerva, goddess of civilization, wisdom, justice—and, when necessary, goddess of war.

"Why wasn't I invited to this little party, Ambrosia?" she asks.

Pallas points her baton and nudges the moon forward so that the beam now slants across her face, catching a hint of the fire in the cold marble blue of her eyes. She aims the baton again. Below her, a scraggly piece of sagebrush bursts into flame.

"Fire?" The word erupts from Ambrosia's mouth as a cruel laugh. "That's all you've got? The burning-bush routine? Hasn't that been done to death? I'm shivering."

A spit from Pallas Athena and the fire goes out. A trail of smoke snakes into the air.

"What's next up your sleeve?" Ambrosia mocks. "Threaten them with a failing grade?"

Despite their positions on the high crags, I can make out every expression as in a close-up: the taunting smirk on Ambrosia's lips, the antagonism etched on Athena's features. Their battle is playing out before me like a movie, but a movie where there's no popcorn and I'm tied to the seat and the screen is huge and my eyelids are propped open and the sound is blasted high.

Ambrosia arches her back. "Of course I didn't forget to invite you. I knew you'd follow if we dangled your little teacher's pet. You need your devotees. I picked this setting especially and lured you here. A mountaintop should be familiar to you, give you a little advantage, even. Isn't that considerate of me? But enough dilly-dallying. Enough of your getting in my way. It's time to end this forever. Here, now."

"No more calling them awake," Athena orders.

"No more putting them to sleep."

"You know it isn't up to us anymore. We've picked our weapons in the human realm. They must battle it out." Athena points her baton at Raymond, and from a heap on the ground he floats several inches into the air before being set upright on his feet.

Ambrosia in a snide huff: "Ah yes, Pallas's little kiss-up. All devotion. The living, breathing representative of all that's good and merciful in mankind."

"I'm not—" Raymond tries to protest, but Athena silences him with a smack of her baton against the rock. It thunders. "But you are. You must be all that! I say it is so."

"I won't!"

"You will! Finish the job!"

Ambrosia turns her attention to us, her voice, in contrast, steady and cool. "Girls, are you taking it all in? I sense a rift between our enemies." She wags her finger, a miniature windshield wiper in the air. "No falling asleep on the job, right?"

"Question!" I shout. "This weapon you're talking about? If he's all that's good in mankind, we must be—"

Athena sets another bush on fire, just for the light show. "You are all that's bad!"

I feel both confused and hurt. "But aren't we the good ones? Righting wrongs? Punishing the guilty?"

Ambrosia laughs again, tinkling like shattering glass,

the moonlight shining off of her eerie, hairless face. "I understand your confusion, Megaera. I despise this good-bad distinction. It misses the whole point and the subtlety of the situation. I prefer to think of you Furies as the living, breathing, wailing, reprimanding embodiment of all that's natural in mankind. Tisiphone, for instance. What do you do best?"

Stephanie extends her right leg in front, dips forward in a dancer's curtsy. "I punish the guilty. Especially if they hurt Mother. Mother Earth."

"Exactly! And you never stop punishing! You must be right all the time. You never let anyone off the hook. Isn't that the essence of human desire? To be judge, jury, and executioner of anyone who disagrees and gets in your way?"

"Off with their heads," Stephanie says in a strangely mechanical way.

"How about you, my invincible Alecto?"

Alix is hanging off the side of a crag with only two fingers in a hole. She bends her elbow and, as if she weighs nothing, her entire body moves straight up like she's in an elevator. "Anyone hurts a family member, I pay them back. You can count on it." She jumps down, stands by Stephanie, and performs a deep formal bow. "At your service."

"My precious powder keg of vengeance," Ambrosia says with admiration. "History is made up of revenge. It's the stuff of world wars, ethnic cleansing, neighborhood spats, and fights between former best friends. If it's so commonplace, how can it be wrong or bad? It's what *is*. This is mankind au naturel."

Her attention turns to me. "And Megaera. So damaged and distrusting—"

"You're not!" Raymond shouts.

"So bitter about your past and envious of what you have been denied."

"Don't listen to her!"

But I hear myself say simply, with acceptance, "I am all that." One of my legs slides behind the other. My fingertips hold out the edges of a nonexistent skirt and my knees bend in a curtsy.

"No!" Raymond shouts again.

I feel pressure in the small of my back, like a firm hand of wind that moves me away from him and ushers me to where I belong. With them. With the Furies. With my true self. With my others. If Stephanie is unforgiving, it's because people are unforgiving. If Alix is cruel, it's because human nature is cruel. If I am bitter and envious, so be it! Who made me that way?

The three of us hook arms, lean in, and clink together at our foreheads like magnetic kissing dolls. Our powers come together as one.

"The world is corrupt and evil," Ambrosia reminds us. "You three speak its language of greed, hate, and delusion."

"Don't be her puppet!" Raymond shouts.

Athena's voice now, like the rumble of a hundred trucks on a freeway exit ramp: "Let Raymond's pure goodness take them on. Destroy the Furies permanently! Banish them for all eternity. Let it begin."

He turns on Athena, defiant. "I'm not your puppet, either. I'm not your weapon. I'm not pure anything! I'm just me."

Here, in their argument, we find our opening. Alix, Stephanie, and I come apart only long enough to close in on him. There's nowhere for Raymond to go, no place to run in this empty terrain. He's on his own.

He speaks again, but the words sound weak and clouded. "Meg, your power! It's up to *you* how you use it!"

Then no more words. We are beyond that kind of communication. To protect himself, Raymond hums his melody. He gives it a good shot. But alone on a mountaintop, his simple song is porous, a cloth of notes that's full of holes.

We sing ourselves in. We come into his light.

So much light. Too much light. SPF 25,000 sunscreen bright. His thoughts are filled with it; his brain sparks with it. His memories glow under the polish.

This is unlike any of our other Fury experiences, and we flail around. We're used to landing in people's shadows, seeking out gullies, gloomy corners, and deep coves of depression. We are unwelcome visitors who never leave.

Raymond's light, though, blinds us in a way that darkness doesn't. I struggle to stay close to the others, but we keep losing our connection. We break apart, come together, break apart again. I find myself hunting alone in this space of endlessly reflecting mirrors and refracting lenses, and understand what Raymond meant when he said that he isn't perfect. He's *not* all goodness. I see his mistakes, the ways that he hurt others and caused pain.

But here's what's different. Raymond hasn't buried his memories and mistakes like other people do. They haven't shaped him into something mean and ugly. Eagerly I head into what looks like a warped road of defensiveness, only to find a straight pathway leading to an open door of apology. An old embarrassment explodes in a bright moment of insight. Everywhere I search, there's forgiveness requested and forgiveness given. Instead of blame, he has accepted others and accepted himself.

Still, I am not fooled. I remind myself that we got in, and I know what this means. A jar of jam with a tiny crack isn't sealed. It's as vulnerable to bacteria as a jar left wide open on the kitchen counter in the heat. Somewhere there is a chink in Raymond—a lie, a moment of guilt and self-doubt. All I have to do is find it.

I catch a glimpse of something then. A blink and it's gone. Another blink and it's back in sight. What is it? A lie never confessed. With a tinge of shame and a hint of regret.

That's all I need. With it I can summon the others and we can bring him down. And once he is down, nothing will stop us. Athena will be powerless, and we can give the whole world our kind of law and order. We can bring it to its knees.

Sing!

I hear the command from Ambrosia. She orders me forward with every bit of rage and hate from our combined pasts. Her will comes over me through deafening shrieks and rank smell and putrid taste, all of that, but nothing like that, not anything I have ever experienced with any of my senses before.

Call the others! Join together. Sing and destroy!

It's up to me. We'll swarm over him, pumping all of our darkness until we transform that tiny pinprick of a lie into his personal black hole.

Do it! Now!

I lift the edge of the dark corner where Raymond's trembling little lie waits in terror of discovery. Thrilled, I move closer to it. It quakes and shivers at my approach. It can't hide from me anymore. I watch in fascination as his lie—our weapon against him, the means of Raymond's destruction—replays itself, as if in real time.

Raymond and Ms. Pallas alone in her classroom. She shakes her head, her expression one of firm resolve. "Meg has to go. I must eliminate her."

Raymond's head down, accepting. "What will you do? What will happen?"

"They must never rise again. Meg is the third in the trio, the key, and I will banish her from both realms. She'll be neither human nor goddess, orphaned into eternity, separated from family and friends, belonging nowhere and to no one."

I let any hesitation in me fall apart like a sand sculpture under the chop of the ocean. Orphan me? Toss me away again? Never! I open my furious mouth. I fill my furious lungs to prepare for our song.

I will take her down. I will take him down.

But in the nanosecond before the vibration of that first note can work its way up my throat, Raymond speaks: *"I swear!"*

This stops me. I close my mouth.

"Meg said she's only playing along with Ambrosia."

I listen. I see.

Ms. Pallas holds Raymond in her threatening gaze. "We have only a small window before their power solidifies. If we don't stop them forever when we have this chance, it will be too late. Too late for you, Raymond. For me. For the whole world."

"I promise. You don't know Meg like I do. She would never go too far. She's just fooling Ambrosia. She told me so."

There it is, a bald-faced lie to a goddess, with guilt and uncertainty pressing in on him. A lie that puts everything, the present and the future, the whole world, at risk.

Raymond told it for me. To protect me and save me.

Remember, Meg! Remember!

He defied Athena because he believes in me. Because he knows the deepest part of who I am. Because he loves me and trusts me and would never let anyone throw me away.

I press my palms over my ears, trying to ignore Ambrosia's bellowing order to sing. I need to think. I must understand what's happening more clearly.

Ambrosia won't stop clamoring, though. She must keep my fury burning, and to do that she lashes me to memories of my own humiliation and abuse. I'm forced to relive it all, my whole history of cruel foster parents and promises broken and the parents who threw me away. I see and hear it like each episode is happening for the first time. My body spasms and my mind thrashes feverishly with the loneliness and loss.

I hear Athena, too, issuing orders to Raymond. "She's weak now, and vulnerable. Shut her down! Do it!"

But underneath my pain and exhaustion, through it and despite it, I start experiencing other things: a whisper, then a whiff, a tingling, and the thinnest sensation of Raymond's touch on my hair. He's here. For me and with me. He won't let go. He's steady and loyal. I sink into the comfort and strength of his love.

Together we repeat his words like a mantra: "This power. It's mine. It's up to me how I use it."

"No!" Ambrosia and Athena roar in unison.

Their anger makes us more determined to defy them. I hum a chorus of Raymond's song with him, and the notes fill me with another kind of power. It makes my mind bright and clear. Ambrosia tries to pull me back. I feel the deep sting of her nails as they claw at my flesh. But I push through the agony and follow Raymond's melody out and back to the mountaintop. I have escaped from a dark and terrible place.

We keep singing, and Alix, adding her own harmony, comes to us. We are three in the night air, individual voices but together. We sing Stephanie out of Ambrosia's grasp and reel her safely to our side.

A scream then, high-pitched and animal-like. In outrage, Ambrosia jumps to the ground and stamps her foot, stamps it again and again with a deep, dull thud that makes the ground quake.

Athena, too, lands with a crash that echoes along the mountaintop. The goddess of war, justice, and strength raises her right arm. She points her scepter at the horizon.

A rumble of thunder.

That's what I think it is at first, because there's also what looks to be a storm building, a solid bank of gray-white cloud, iridescent in the dark, moving toward us. I squint to bring it into focus, and that's when I make out moving shadows in the cloud, and as they get closer the shadows become individuals—people large and small, old and young, naked and in uniforms and tattered clothing, people of every race, eye shape, and hair color. People crying and moaning. They are all blind. Animals, too, hoofed, feathered, and clawed. I fall to my knees and cover my head as these sightless figures swarm us.

Who are these hideous corpses marching in blind unison, an endless stream of bloody soldiers in ripped military gear of every nation that ever existed throughout time and space? Who are these moaning, skeletal women lugging the torn and limbless bodies of unseeing children? Who are these sightless ghost horses pierced with arrows, riddled with bullets, and split open by knives?

I feel a bone-chilling wind as they move through me.

This is Athena's army, the wailing, writhing, aching victims of senseless wars, blood feuds, family vendettas, and unrestrained revenge. These are the embodiment of eye for an eye.

I huddle with Raymond, Alix, and Stephanie. Through the chaos we see another cloud gathering force on the horizon and watch in awe the approach of what can only be Ambrosia's army: the unavenged, the unjustly accused and punished, the unmourned, all of them silenced and unable to rest.

They, too, pass over and through us—millions of abandoned children with gags around their mouths, speechless slaves who built the pyramids and died in the fields, political prisoners rotting in chains, the raped, the tortured, genocide victims dumped into mass graves. They, too, are all skin colors. They once spoke in every language. Animals make up this army, too: songless birds, sea creatures struggling to breathe, and huge horned mammals, all the senselessly slaughtered creatures that have gone nameless and unappreciated to their extinction.

They all meet on the mountaintop, a thick crowd of suffering. I smell their stench of fear and death. Athena rips off the golden serpent from Ambrosia's neck and replaces it with the circle of her hands. Ambrosia's fingers hold tight to a clump of Athena's golden hair.

And then victim grabs on to victim, and I can't tell which side is which anymore. They are so alike. I wonder if they have grabbed each other not out of hatred but out of recognition, the need to touch and hold on to something as tortured and forgotten as themselves.

It's a whirlwind then, above, below, all around us, a swirl of arms and legs, feathers and claws, tears and blood, a spitting, sweating, vibrating mass. They spin so fast that they create their own weather system, all weathers fighting at once for domination, wind giving way to snow to rain to blinding sunshine to lightning to hail to hurricane.

Through it all, we keep singing. We sing of these unsung victims. Of the earth, the ocean, and the whole scarred world. We sing of ourselves. Of our living, our breathing, our hopes, our right to be good *and* bad, angry *and* forgiving, not pure anything, not anyone's puppet. Of our right to be full and human.

Our voices echo off the cliffs.

Locked on to each other, Athena, Ambrosia, and their armies drag each other into the vortex of the past, or maybe of the future.

It all goes black.

We are spit out into the darkness of ordinary night.

Solid ground.

The world returned.

The hold on me smashed. The hold on all of us undone.

Hours must have passed. I know this because the moon

sits much lower on the horizon, making it hard to see in the dark. The wind has died down. It's that slack time of night, the chilly, peaceful period right before a new day begins. I study the crags where Ambrosia and Pallas Athena tried to use us as weapons for their ancient feud. They are gone, but I feel their presence like the last sliver of something bitter slowly dissolving on my tongue.

The four of us who remain, our small group of exhausted and disheveled high school students, huddle close, shivering with sweat and chills. We are dazed, hungry, very thirsty, but near giddy with relief that what could have happened didn't happen.

We are alone, except for so many names and designs carved deep into the mysterious rock. We stand and stretch. It's time to begin a long, silent hike back to the car. Our shoes scramble over proclamations of love, hate, hope, and existence. Just as the sun rises, I pause and use a sharp rock to carve one more thing into the sandstone: THE FURIES WERE HERE.

If you are expecting *an explanation of what transpired, figure things out for yourself. You have all the information you need. I'm too furious to write about it.*

I have bags to pack, plans to make.

A certain goddess to avoid.

But only until that rare alignment of sun and stars and flesh and injustice and greed and suffering shows its face to me again.

As it will.

As it always does.

Until then, I have time to kill.

FINAL STASIMON, **THE BOOK OF FURIOUS**

Exit the mysterious illness at Hunter High, which disappears as suddenly as it struck.

Exit the guilt-ridden insomnia and paralyzing regrets. Each day, the memory of them softens, the way the flu never seems so bad after it's all over.

Exit our control over Alix's dad, Stephanie's mom, and the Leech. They are back to being pretty much the way they were before we got involved.

Exit Ms. Pallas, who e-mailed the principal to say that she won't be teaching anymore. No explanation why. No apology for leaving mid-year. A rumor goes around—who knows how these things get started?—that Ms. Pallas had been living a secret double life.

According to the Double Ds, who hold forth in the girls' bathroom: "You only had to look at her fabulous clothes to know that she comes from money, big money," says one. "She was totally slumming for the hell of it," says the other.

I overhear a conversation between Mr. and Mrs. H, who

agree that they were suspicious of their fellow teacher all along.

"She had this certain aura," Mrs. H says.

Mr. H tries to dissect the mystery with a list of questions: "Why didn't she ever hang out in the teachers' lounge? Why did she act like she was so much better than everyone else?"

A permanent sub—a nervous middle-aged man who seems as clueless about the ancient past as he does about modern teenagers—takes over Western Civ class. Our group, minus Ambrosia, of course, volunteers to go first with final reports. Standing in front of the room, I explain classical theater structure, how the *exodos* "is the singing exit, the section of the play after the final stasimon. In the Aeschylus trilogy, the Furies renounce violence and are renamed the *Eumenides*, or 'Kindly Ones' because of their new personalities. To honor them, the citizens of Athens welcome them in a parade."

I motion to my right. "Take it away, Raymond."

On his violin he plays a light but haunting melody that he composed especially for this occasion. Alix, Stephanie, and I line up behind him as he leads us in a solemn procession up and down rows and in between desks. It's not easy to take this seriously with all the snickering and snide remarks, but this is important to us. We want to do it right. As we pass Pox, he says loud enough for everyone to hear, "The Furies were hags, right? Good casting."

Exit any hope that Hunter High is a newly enlightened Athens.

When we return to the front of the room, Raymond

plays a final note, the vibration hanging long in the air. A few kids applaud, and I announce: "Exodos. The play ends."

We wind up getting only a B for our report because when the sub quizzes us—"So when it comes down to it: these Furies, are they a good thing or a bad thing?"—none of us can give him a definite answer.

The B grade disappoints us, but Raymond agrees not to make a big deal out of it. A C would have been a different story.

Exit the fearful looks as we walk through the halls.

Exit Raymond as leader of the color guard.

Raymond's mom goes through a pile of paperwork to qualify as a foster parent so I can move in with them. Exit the Leech from my life. I even get to take He-Cat with me since—on his own, with no interference from the Furies—the cat despises her.

"Good riddance to both of you," she says.

I'm standing on the sidewalk with Raymond and everything I own in a suitcase. He-Cat is in my arms. When the Leech slams the door on us, I get a shudder of anger, that familiar feeling boiling up in me.

Raymond puts a hand on my shoulder to calm me. "She wasn't born a leech, you know."

"Meaning?"

"She came into this world waiting to be written upon," he says. "What she lacked in inbred guilelessness she made up for as a sweet, adorable, tiny, innocent babe in arms who—"

"Raymond?" I interrupt.

"Over the top?" he asks.

"Way over."

He laughs. "You get my point, though."

I do. Now that the Leech no longer has any control over me, I can almost see into her past, how she, too, was probably hurt and unloved, and how it turned her ugly and cruel. Instead of despising her, I suddenly feel sad and sorry for her.

That's a beginning. Because if I can feel that for the Leech, maybe someday I can begin to forgive others in my life. Even the nameless, faceless parents who have always been so hateful to me. I guess they weren't born that way, either.

"I'm ready," I say.

Raymond picks up my suitcase, and together we begin walking into my new life.

Exit my jealousy for the family that others have.

Exit the gossip about Brendon and me on Halloween night. That was *so* last month.

It's taking Brendon longer to recover than all the others. He's still pale and thin. I see him in class, in the cafeteria, and on the bus, but we both pretend that the other doesn't exist. Of course, I notice things. He's not hanging out with the same friends so much anymore; he doesn't hang out with any particular group. I'm almost sure he doesn't have a girlfriend, either. He's back surfing, and I'm happy about that. I feel relieved when I spot him paddling hard into a wave. He's definitely quieter—not unhappy, I think, just more thoughtful.

One afternoon after fifth period, I round a hallway corner and we practically bump into each other.

"Oh!" he says. I recognize the surprise, but *not* surprise, in his voice. We both knew that this was inevitable. Hunter

High is too small a world to avoid someone forever. I wonder if, like me, he both dreaded this meeting and wanted it to happen.

With my head tucked, I step aside quickly but he steps in the same direction and then back again. Trapped. Neither of us is going to make that lame "care for a dance?" joke.

"Hey," I say, hesitant.

His eyes lift, and I meet them with mine. The curtain rises for just a second, long enough for me to see so much in them. Hurt and confusion, sorrow and, yes, definitely some anger. I can't blame him for that. I don't think he remembers all the details, but what we did to him—what *I* did—cut deep and terribly, and he won't be free of it for a long time.

"See ya," he says quickly and takes off down the hall.

Brendon and I are not going to fall into each other's arms anytime soon. We both remember too much. There are too many questions left unanswered, too much broken trust.

But I can't help wondering: Does Brendon ever think about that afternoon in the cave? And that other time, the amazing way that our bodies spooned together right before the light snapped on?

Maybe one day in the future we'll talk about everything. He'll tell me again what I now know to be true—that he had no part in the plot and that when he whispered about love, he meant it. Who knows? We might even *have* a future. But before that can happen, I must say things to him that I'm not yet ready to say. Things like "I'm so, so sorry for what I did to you. I was wrong. Can you forgive me?"

Exit any hope of an easy reconciliation between us.

Exit Ambrosia. Word goes around that her wealthy and

politically connected family decided to move to Greece, where Ambrosia is practically royalty. A couple of her former minions claim that she e-mailed them all the details, but I know better. What a pack of social-climbing liars.

One afternoon the four of us drive to her house, and we're all expecting to see an ultra-dramatic 180-degree turn-around of the place. I imagine everything reverted to the old haunted-house days with peeling paint and broken windows. I picture gardens that have shriveled and turned brown overnight, the Secret Garden before the floral makeover.

But as soon as we pull into the long driveway, it's clear that things are more or less the same. There are still flowers blossoming in the shape of tiny, silvery fairy bells, and a line of cactuses as big as men. The all-white garden is still stunning with its tulips, roses, and albino cabbage plants.

The only difference is the sharp, silvery spear from the strange red plant. It's wilted, dying. But that's to be expected, isn't it? Things bloom and then go dormant. Who knows when this plant will blossom again. Two years? Two hundred years?

Inside the house everything's the same, and we walk on the antique red carpets through rooms with rouge-red walls. We don't spend much time downstairs because we have a destination in mind. It's our mission.

When we get to the top of the stairs, I notice each of our reflections passing by the filigreed hall mirror.

Exit the tattoo of kelp that Ambrosia burned around Alix's midriff.

Exit Stephanie's fangs.

Exit Raymond's strained expression when he was so worried about me.

My complexion is still a little sallow. But exit the sunken eyes and cracked lips. I'll never have the shiny, stick-straight hair that I've always admired, but what's wrong with thick, wild waves? I'm more like me, not anywhere near perfect, but I notice I've kept some of my Fury curves.

In Ambrosia's bedroom there are only two things missing: *The Book of Furious* and the object that we specifically came to claim. We're not surprised. The snow globe with its tortured figures—all those captured princes from the past, the prison where Brendon was almost lost—is gone from its place on the bookshelf. That sends a chill through us. There's a ring of dust where it once sat.

Next, Alix picks up Simon and drives us all to the ocean. After being in that house, we want fresh air and the sun on our backs. With the Prince of the Waves statue behind us and Simon running happy circles around it, we look out to the sea. It's a classic surf day with waves rolling in strong and steady. I can tell the others feel as grateful, hopeful, and alive as I do.

Exit Stephanie's passion for protecting Mother Earth?

Exit Alix's determination to defend her brother and herself?

Exit my ability to finally stand up for myself after a lifetime of being powerless?

Exit memories of Athena and Ambrosia and all the suffering souls?

Exit our anger, our outrage, our fury? Exit our ambition and confidence?

Enter a sweet, passive trio eager to please? Enter the Kindly Ones?

No! Never!

"There's a line somewhere," Raymond says. "I don't know where it is yet. Neither do you. You have to find it."

Alix, Stephanie, and I rest our bellies on the iron railing and, holding on, we bend forward until our feet leave the ground. We tilt gradually until we're balanced on our hip bones, our legs and bodies parallel to the treacherous rocks below. Any farther and we'd tip over.

That's when I hear music coming from nowhere and everywhere. Alix and Stephanie hear it, too. They tilt their heads to try to tune it in. It's a faint sound. We can't even hum along yet.

But still. A tune is a tune, and we recognize that it comes from us and belongs to us.

Carefully, we let go of the railing and join hands. We feel so light, almost as if we're levitating.

Simon claps at our trick. Raymond snaps a photo with his cell phone.

Our feet settle back onto the earth.

That picture, it's a keeper, evidence of one moment of perfect balance.

EXODOS